WHAT NETGALLEY ARC REVIEWERS SAY ABOUT ALEXANDRA SLATER'S BOOKS

"This was fantastic, just what I have come to expect from this author and look forward to carrying in my bookstore."

—Baylee I, Bookseller

"Ooo, this was delicious. A little contemporary romance for CoHo & Hildebrand fans. A little Alice Hoffman-style *Practical Magic* (sans the magic perhaps). A little mystery/thriller a la *Lost Summers of Newport*. And a writing style reminiscent of Backman's *Anxious People* and Ng's *Little Fires Everywhere*."

—LeeAnn, Reviewer

"Slater's prose is breezy and elegant, her pacing pitch perfect. *Big Little Lies* meets *The Summer I Turned Pretty*—but for grown-ups who like their beach reads with a little scandal, a lot of heart, and a setting that feels like vacation in a book. This was unputdownable. I laughed, I winced, I rooted for each woman, and when I turned the final page, I immediately wanted more. Perfect for fans of: complex female friendships, love triangles, second chances, and coastal fiction with depth."

—Reviewer1054526

"This felt like watching a reality tv show play out in real time! I was captivated by the story line, and this was the perfect transition to summer read. The characters were relatable, I found myself nodding along to their thought processes and laughing out loud with them throughout the story. I loved the depth of women's experiences from all of the ladies and the integration of the older generation toward the end. Overall - LOVED this read. Eager to read more from the author! Thank you to NetGalley and the publisher for providing me with an ARC in exchange for my honest review."

—Isabelle E., Reviewer

"Thank you to Green Leaf books and NetGalley for an ARC of this book in exchange for my honest opinion. It's been a while since I completely devoured a book like this. I simply couldn't put it down. It was like an episode of Desperate Housewives! A tale of friendship, the secrets of affairs, sex, violence, and crumbling marriages, this book had it all! Reading it was like spending a day out on the beach and sun on the Cape! And I feel like this will be the hottest read this summer!"

—Reviewer 892273

"Friends with Boats by Alexandra Slater was a very fun and entertaining read. Three friends—challenged with marriage, work, children, and self-doubt—all fall for the same man. Ummmm, what's not to love? This book has it all.... Sex, fun. It was the most entertaining, fun, and intriguing story. The writing drew me with in with its fantastic characters and awesome writing. I will definitely read more of Slaters books in the future."

—Rubee C., Reviewer

THE MESSY YEARS

ALEXANDRA SLATER

HUDSON HOUSE PRESS

This book is a work of fiction. Names, characters, businesses, organizations, places, events, and incidents are either a product of the author's imagination or are used fictitiously. Any resemblance to actual persons, living or dead, events, or locales is entirely coincidental.

Published by Hudson House Press

Cover and book design by Brian Phillips

Print ISBN: 979-8-9997922-0-4

eBook ISBN: 979-8-9997922-1-1

First Edition

For LT, my husband,
who appreciates messy.

messy years

adjective/noun

/'mes.i/years

The "messy years" generally refer to a period of life, often encountered in one's twenties and thirties, characterized by significant life changes, increased responsibilities, and a lack of clear direction or stability. It's a time of transition where individuals are navigating career choices, relationships, financial independence, and personal growth, often with a feeling of being overwhelmed or uncertain.

Part One

JUNE

Chapter 1

MAEVE

Maeve doesn't cry when she loses the promotion. She's grown accustomed to life's disappointments and adds it to the mounting list of things she's never let herself feel.

"Guys, I want to introduce you to our latest hire," CEO Rick Watts says. "This is Pope Morris, our new senior publicist. He'll be heading up the restaurant division, alongside Maeve."

Maeve folds her arms across her chest, her hazel eyes narrowing, as Pope swaggers into the conference room. He's tall, with wavy, sable hair and cornflower-blue eyes. She imagines strangling him by the copy machine, his Nantucket-red bow tie falling to the floor next to his seersucker suit.

"Pope comes to us with an impressive resume, most recently working for State Street," Rick says.

Pope nods and flashes a very expensive smile.

Judging from his tan, Maeve guesses he spends more time on the beach than on his "impressive resume." And he is wearing a bow tie, which, in her book, makes him a tool. *He probably owns a sailboat and loves to play golf.* She pictures him at a Vanderbilt football game, red Solo cup in one hand, some Delta Gamma's tight ass in the other.

"Great to meet you, Maeve," Pope says, extending his hand. "Looking forward to learning the ropes from one of the best."

Maeve gives a thumbs up that reads more *f-you* than *go team.* "Teamwork makes the dreamwork!" Wow, she's in a foul mood. He's giving her privileged vibes.

Maeve did not grow up privileged, though she was surrounded by it in the town of Hingham, twenty miles south of Boston. She was raised by her grandparents in a modest, cedar-shingled, Cape home, with chipped paint and a slouching front porch on Crow Point, where she now resides alone with her golden retriever.

When the meeting is over, Maeve returns to her corner office to text her best friends the news.

MAEVE: *You won't believe it.*

HADLEY: *Uh oh. What's up?*

MAEVE: *I didn't get the promotion.*

LIZZIE: *WTF! That sux. Who got it?*

MAEVE: *Some preppy finance guy in a seersucker suit. (barf emoji)*

HADLEY: *OFC. (angry emoji)*

LIZZIE: *Sweetie, maybe it's for the best. You kind of hate it there?*

MAEVE: *I'm starting to drink on the ferry home while plotting my resignation. (middle finger emoji, martini glass) MEH!*

Maeve had believed she would be promoted to senior publicist, not just sharing the role with Pope. *Maybe I should give my notice,* she thinks. And if she's going to, she should do it before summer gets rolling. That way, she can go to the beach, read books, and finally finish building her bird feeder. Cardinals remind her of Sam.

Pope knocks twice on the side of her office door. "Hey there."

Maeve glances up from her phone. "What's up?"

"Oh, um, I just wanted to say hello, you know, now that we will be working together."

Maeve blinks twice, a nervous habit. "Hi."

He laughs. "So, um, how long have you been working here?"

Maeve tucks a chocolate-brown curl behind her ear and considers lying. Having worked at Watts for nearly five years, she should not be sharing the senior publicist position. She can handle it on her own, thanks. Just like she handles everything else in her life—alone.

Maeve smirks. "Long enough to get this corner office." She recalls the book, *Nice Girls Don't Get the Corner Office.*

"Great view of the Common," Pope says, still lingering, his head nearly touching the door's archway. He stares at her with eyes that match the color of the small blue boats on his tie. Pope points to the framed silver photo on her desk. "Is that your dog?"

"Yes." She softens. "His name's Brutus."

Pope ruffles his brow.

"I was a Classics Major."

He nods.

"Do you have a dog?"

"No, a cat. Her name is Sylvia."

Of course he has a cat. Cat people and dog people are opposites, she thinks.

"Well, if you don't mind, I'm super behind on this press release, so can we chat more later?" She forces a flat grin.

"Oh, yeah. Sure, no problem... Sorry to bother."

"No bother, just busy." Maeve begins to type furiously on her laptop, like Jack Nicholson in *The Shining. All work and no play makes Maeve a dull girl.*

When he leaves, Maeve stops typing. She looks out her window longingly at the Boston Common. The magnolia trees are bursting with pink spring flowers, like puffs of cotton candy, and she spots three girls lying out in bikinis, something she would never now do in a public park. She remembers when she, Lizzie, and Hadley would lay out and tan in the college quad, back when she was carefree and didn't have sixty-hour work weeks.

Maeve returns to her computer and the painful reality that she is sharing the job she wanted with Pope. To prove that she deserved it, herself, she begins an exhaustive Google search of all the press she's gotten for her accounts. *Forty-five mentions in one month.* She prints these out and documents them on a spreadsheet. Surely, Rick will see this and recant his decision. *This is ridiculous,* she thinks. What was the point of all that work when some *random guy* from State Street is given the same consideration for her job?

Unable to concentrate, Maeve shuffles to the kitchen to grab her bento box lunch, filled with last night's sushi from Salt Society. She spies a twelve-pack of diet coke with a yellow sticky note attached that reads: *To whoever's diet coke I stole when I was dying of thirst, here's a payback.* She closes the fridge and heads back to her office, first passing by Pope. Rick is seated across from him, relaxed with hands behind his head, elbows out. He's regaling Pope with a story about his recent golf trip to Pebble Beach. Maeve rolls her eyes and thinks how amazing it would feel to hit Rick with his golf club, right in the nuts.

. . .

The next day, Maeve catches the 7:28 a.m. Greenbush Line from West Hingham and arrives at Boston's South Station at 8:09 a.m. She orders a dark roast coffee with almond milk from Starbucks and hustles through the littered streets of Downtown Crossing to Park Street, where she purchases *The Boston Globe* and the *Herald*. The smell of weed permeates as she weaves between commuters and passes several homeless men sleeping on park benches. She crosses the park to her office and runs into Rick when the elevator opens.

"Morning, Maeve," he says, holding a cup of coffee in a ceramic mug that reads *Because I Said So*. His salt-and-pepper hair is slicked back with gel, like a *Mad Men* executive, and he's wearing a Tommy Bahama Hawaiian shirt, because it's a casual summer Friday. Read: No one comes to work.

"Exciting plans for the weekend?" Rick asks.

"Oh, probably not as exciting as yours."

Maeve's a master at deflection. Her grandparents taught her early on to play her cards close to the vest. As New England Irish Catholics, flashing money and sharing your problems are a definite "no." She recalls what they always said: When people ask how business is, you always say "great!"

"See you in a bit," Rick says, leaving a pungent trail of musky cologne in his wake. Maeve hates the way he walks on his tippy toes, upright, like he's holding a potato chip between his butt cheeks.

As she turns the corner, she overhears Pope on a call. Yet, there is no way *not* to hear him, because the call is blasting from his speaker phone. Pope's voice is charged, and he's using a lot of office jargon, like "circle back," "ping me," and "out of pocket." He acknowledges her by raising his square jaw when she passes by his door. It's unfortunately next to hers.

She sits in her chair and lays out the newspaper on her desk, her morning routine. But this morning, she can't concentrate with Pope's obnoxious volume. First, he was talking about business, but now he's yapping about the Red Sox.

Her computer dings with a Slack message.

POPE: *Where can I find the office supplies?*

MAEVE: *Down the hall in the closet next to the copy room.*

Ding! Another Slack.

POPE: *Know where I can locate the Crabapple's account? Is it on the shared drive?*

MAEVE: *It's on the E:/ drive.*

Ding! Another Slack

POPE: *Do you have documentation on the press strategy for O'Reilly's?*

MAEVE: *Yes, I'll find it.*

Another Slack... *Ding!*

"Jeeeeeezus," Maeve mutters. *Can he get off my jock?* She mutes her computer.

Pope ducks his head into her office. "Hi, want to get a head start on the Sammy's account? I could use an update on where we stand with that. Figured it's easier to talk than Slack."

She takes a deep breath and shifts in her skirt, the back of her thighs sticking to the chair. "Yes, sure."

"You good?" Pope asks. "I mean are *we* good?"

Maeve raises an eyebrow. Of course they are not good. "Yes, why?"

"I don't know. You're giving me *Mean Girl* vibes."

She finds it hard to believe he watched that. "Are you saying I'm Regina George?" she scoffs, testing him.

"Well maybe not as bad as Regina."

She is intrigued. "So should I call you Katy?"

"Well, I wouldn't say I resemble Lindsay Lohan, but I *am* technically the new guy."

"Yes, and now my partner," she tuts. Maeve's skin itches, like she's getting a rash. Maybe he has cat hair on his pants.

"Okay, I just need to grab my laptop, and I'll be right back."

Maeve glances at the photo of her late husband Sam on her desk. Their wedding seems like yesterday, even though he's been dead for four years.

Pope returns. "So where shall we start?"

"How about we go in alphabetical order, starting with A?" As she scrolls through files on her desktop, she notices him staring at Sam's photo.

"Is this your husband?" he asks.

"Yep," she says, still scrolling.

"Looks like a nice guy."

"He is."

Or was, she means. But Pope doesn't need to know that. It's Maeve's personal business, and she wishes he'd stop peppering her with personal small talk. They are not going to be friends, so he should just stay in his lane. She doesn't need more friends, anyway. Hadley and Lizzie are enough.

. . .

The next morning, Maeve feeds the betta fish, refills Brutus's dog bowl, makes her bed, and grabs her dress bag for Hadley's wedding on Cape Cod. She lays the lavender bridesmaid dress out carefully, so she won't have to iron it, and scans through her closet to find an outfit for the rehearsal dinner. Maeve slides the hangers across the rail, partially pulling each dress out, like she's shopping. She can't decide if she should wear the green, spaghetti-strapped, short dress from Chel Bella, or the more ethereal, flowy sundress from Kloth, so she packs both. The green is a more flattering shade against her fair, freckled skin, but it may be too short and tug in the wrong places. A size eight, Maeve is neither too thin nor chubby, but she never quite feels comfortable in her body. She prefers a one-piece swimsuit to a bikini, and she wouldn't dare wear a midriff.

She hides a house key under the grill cover for the dog sitter and drives up Main Street to make a pit stop at The Barrel for a chicken salad and soda. When she gets out of her car, Ray, the toffee-colored rabbit, peers at her from his pink wooden cage. A slew of elementary-aged kids pass her on bicycles, and teens gather around the red picnic tables and take selfies for Snapchat. Maeve opens the heavy wooden door, and the bells chime as she gets a strong whiff of bacon from the prepared breakfast sandwiches. She beelines to the salads, where she spots Cassidy Lewis stocking up on White Claws in the back.

"Don't mind me loading up on booze at 11:00 a.m." Cassidy chuckles.

"No judgement here," Maeve says, checking expiration dates on the salads.

"You look cute. Where you off to?"

"My friend's wedding on the Cape. Hoping to get out of here before the traffic hits."

Cassidy shuts the fridge, her gold bangles clanging, and approaches Maeve. "Oh, is this the same wedding Lizzie's in? Is it Hadley's?"

"Yep. Should be fun. What are you guys doing this weekend?"

Cassidy giggles in her stiff, trucker, baseball cap that reads *No Wake*. "It's more like what are we *not* doing? Teddy has a lax game, Crosby starts his caddying job at Cohasset, and Matt and I are hosting a party with our neighborhood crew."

Maeve wonders if Cassidy knows it's not fun to hear about parties you haven't been invited to. But she wouldn't fit in anyway with the "crew," a group of four families who vacation together, play sports together, party together, and possibly even sleep together. Rumors about underground swinging in Hingham, (a.k.a. "Swingham") exist for a reason, she thinks. Maeve slides a bottle of prosecco from the wine shelf under her armpit. "Yikes, sounds busy."

"Well, you know how it is. This is a crazy time of year, but we *must* get together. I know we always say that, but I *mean it*," Cassidy coos. "Oh, and there are a couple newbies on the market. Seems like divorce is in the water around here."

"Oh, really? That's too bad," she says. She doesn't ask who.

Cassidy checks behind her to ensure no one is listening. "Darby and Jack Thompson, and Lauren and Craig Rider," she whispers. "I could really see you hitting it off with Craig." She winks.

"Seems a bit soon," Maeve says. "But yeah, I'll think on that."

Or I will not.

Cassidy places her hand on Maeve's shoulder and leans in close. Maeve can smell her lilac bodywash. "Aw, sweetie, I know it must feel like yesterday, but I wouldn't say it's too soon for you to be out there."

"Oh, um, I meant 'too soon,' because they're just getting divorced?"

Maeve wonders how it became Cassidy's place to decide when she's ready to date. She's not.

Cassidy blushes. "Oh, I am such an ID-I-OT," Cassidy says. "I thought you meant..."

"No worries. Listen, I have to head out."

"Okay, well reach out after the wedding! Promise?"

"Will do."

"You better!"

Since Sam died, Maeve's noticed how uncomfortable people feel around her. Either they want to put a band aid on her pain, like setting her up with someone new, or they just avoid her altogether. Sometimes she thinks it's better to just stay home.

Two hours and a bottleneck of Sagamore bridge traffic later, Meave pulls up to the Piping Plover Inn. She can't wait to chill out, have a cocktail, and see her best friends. She will leave her phone and laptop in her room. She heads directly to the bar to meet Hadley for rehearsal instructions—these instructions are apparently *"very"* different from the other fifteen sets of instructions Hadley texted her that morning. She saddles up on a bar stool and lays her clutch down. The bartender slides a plastic cocktail tent in front of her, and she orders a Bourbon Smash. Maeve's skin warms in the salty ocean breeze, fragrant with beach plums as Jimmy Buffet songs play in the background. For the first time in weeks, Maeve is at peace.

But then it ends.

Within earshot, there's a familiar voice. It's loud. The raspy laugh is also familiar.

No, it can't be, she thinks. *It better not be!* She hesitates, afraid of what lurks behind her, and sure enough, it's Pope Morris. *But how are you here? And more importantly, why?*

Chapter 2

LIZZIE

Lizzie circles around her bedroom, opening and closing drawers as she tosses clothes, shoes, makeup, and hair products into her suitcase. She's on her way to the Cape for Hadley's wedding. She doesn't enjoy weddings, since she blames herself for her divorce, but she's hopeful she might get lucky enough to find a single man.

As Lizzie ties her long blond hair back into a ponytail, her phone rings.

"What's up?" she asks, sweeping the bangs off her face.

Grace, another bridesmaid, is on the other end of the line, breathless. "When do you get here?" she asks.

"Not soon enough."

"Well, you may want to hurry, because Hadley's starting to have a meltdown that you won't make it on time for the rehearsal. Bridezilla is rearing her ugly head."

Lizzie huffs and swallows two Advil. She's done with Hadley's wedding and all the fuss: the engagement party, the bridesmaid's trip to Nantucket, the Miami bachelorette party, even Hadley's pity-party! Why does it have to be such a production? If Lizzie *ever* gets remarried, it will be a town hall quickie or elopement. She shivers thinking about the $150,000 down the tubes from her wedding to Hank. That would have been better spent on her mortgage or funding the boys' lacrosse camps.

"Tell her to take a freaking chill pill. I'm on my way."

"Okay, but there's one more thing—" Grace utters.

"What?"

"Are you ready for it?"

Lizzie's stomach twists. "Seriously, Grace? Spit it out. I need to go," Lizzie says, wheeling her luggage down the plush carpeted hallway to the spiral staircase. She's in no mood for Grace to pile on the drama.

"Wade is coming to the wedding."

Lizzie stops dead in her tracks. Wade, the man she loved before her trainwreck marriage, is coming to the wedding. "How do you know that?" *This can't be true.*

"He's Macy's date." Macy is Hadley's first cousin, who lives in Boston. *She's totally vanilla and too young for him,* Lizzie thinks.

"Does Hadley know this?"

"Hadley's the one who told me. She's afraid to tell you, so she asked me to let you know so you aren't surprised."

Lizzie's blood pressure rises. She likes surprises, but not this kind. How could Hadley not share this information with her?

"I guess Macy has been, like, *seeing* Wade? For a few months or so? He's her plus-one."

A few months or so? Lizzie leaves the house, slamming the door behind her, and tosses her luggage into her Range Rover. She presses her hand with ballet-pink nails on the yacht club sticker to ensure it's closed and glances at her reflection in the window. *Bring it, Macy.* "Whatever, I don't care." Lizzie sighs. "I'll see you at the dinner."

But she does care. She cares *a lot.*

Wade was her first real love. Their breakup left an irreparable emotional scar. It took her one full year to get her appetite back, two years to stop dreaming about him, three years to throw out his cards and letters and to fall in love again. That is when Lizzie met Hank. Hank was her rebound. She never loved him like she loved Wade; he was more of a place card: right time/right place.

But Lizzie is not about to let Wade Wilson and Macy O'Brien threaten her happiness. She thinks of her mantra, repeating it over and over in her head as she drives down Route 3, crossing the bridge to the Cape.

I am not a follower; I'm a leader. I'm the number one realtor on the South Shore, winner of the country club's women's member/member golf tournament, and President of the Hingham Newcomers Club.

She exhales, reassured of her worth, and sings along to her Happy Vibes playlist.

When she arrives at the Piping Plover Inn, she discovers a blue Tiffany's gift bag on the dresser. There's a welcome letter, a map of Cape Cod, a bottle of water, a small bag of almonds, saltwater taffy, and a bar of lavender-scented soap with *Hadley and Jack* engraved on it. She opens the water, then moves to the mini bar for something stronger. There is a chilled bottle of Domaine Ott rosé, and she pours herself a glass. The pink wine slides down her throat, leaving a pleasant floral taste on the tip of her tongue. She carries it onto a small balcony with two chairs and a table overlooking the ocean—well sort of overlooking —it's a bit off to the left. *Hmmm,* she thinks. *This is what you get for "ocean view" prices.*

Even with wine and an ocean-adjacent view, Lizzie is spiraling about seeing Wade. Although it's been a long time since their breakup, it still stings. She loses herself in the memory of when he'd told her he couldn't trust her with his heart, that he was moving on. She'd hurt him too many times with the on-and-off breakups. Her fickle temperament and persistent belief that the grass is greener elsewhere crushed his confidence. *I pushed away the greatest guy ever because I was too stupid to see it.* Lizzie shakes her head as if to wake herself up. She will not make a scene with tears and apologies, and she will remember all the reasons she dumped Wade in the first place. *There were so many*, she thinks. *Like... well...* She can't recall even one of them now. *I'm hosed.*

Chapter 3

HADLEY

Hadley twirls in front of the mirror in an ivory Monique Lhuillier wedding gown, shifting side to side, fanning out the fifteen-foot train. She's slim, with fair coloring, hazel eyes, and strawberry blond hair. Her mother, Constance, gushes from an armchair in the corner and clasps her hands together in front of her chest.

"Oh, Hadley, darlin.' You look simply marvelous. And your hair—it's just like a Nantucket basket, the way they wove it in and out into such a perfectly braided sculpture. It's positively scrumptious. Reminds me of a Cinnabon!"

Hadley notices Lizzie on the floral ottoman, sipping a champagne flute of Veuve Clicquot. She clutches a pillow over her stomach like it's a support animal.

"Do you need me to pin your train?" Lizzie asks.

Way to show up last minute, Hadley thinks. Lizzie's hardly taken her bridesmaid role seriously. She didn't calligraphy the name cards for the place settings, she forgot to keep track of who gave what at the bridal shower, and—the icing on the cake—she left the rehearsal dinner early in a huff. *It's not about her. Today is my day, and Lizzie will not steal the show in her typical fashion.*

Thus far, this is the biggest day in Hadley's life, something she has always dreamed of. Growing up a Southern Belle, Hadley was raised with Friday Night Football, church, grits, and etiquette. And since reuniting with Jack after twelve unsuccessful years of dating post-college, she's had the goal of being *Mrs. Jack Forrester*. She's envisioned "HF" monogrammed beach totes ever since their first kiss.

There is a knock on the door, and Constance scurries over in her kitten heels. The best man hands Constance a box with a large blue satin bow atop. "This is from Jack."

"Oh, delightful," Constance says. She closes the door and hands the box to Hadley. "I think this is your bridal present."

Hadley clutches the box and carries it to the bed. She removes the top, rests it on the pink duvet cover, and pulls out a large scrapbook. Inscribed on the first page is a note from Jack:

To Hadley, my wife (!):

Here are the mementos I've saved since the first day we met. I always knew you'd be my forever. I cherish you and all these memories...

Eternally,
Your husband Jack

Hadley's eyes pool as she flips the pages. There's a coaster from the Anchor Inn on Nantucket, a crumpled napkin from The Cliff House in Maine, two ticket stubs from the Eric Church concert at Gillette Stadium, a cork from a bottle of Dom opened at The Chatham Bars Inn on Valentine's Day, and a sticky note that Hadley left by his bedside table after their first sleepover. "I can't believe he kept all of these," she gushes.

Constance sniffles. "Lucky girl. What a thoughtful idea. I wish your father had one tenth of the sensitivity that Jack seems to possess. Pretty sure he's tossed everything I ever gave him, including his wedding band."

"Mom, can you please *not* on my wedding day? Give Dad a pass, just this once?"

"Fine. I'm just saying he—"

"*Mom*, enough!"

Constance makes the A-okay gesture with her hands.

"That is really super sweet, Had," Lizzie says. "Need me to get you anything?"

"Actually, can you hold my dress while I pee?" She laughs. "Like, up in the air over my head?"

"That's what I'm here for!"

Lizzie and Hadley shuffle into the bathroom and close the door. It reminds Hadley of the many times over the years that Lizzie has rescued her in the bathroom stall: holding her hair back while she threw up Jägermeister shots on her twenty-first birthday celebration at Dick's Last Resort; consoling her when she and Jack had a blow-up argument at the U2 concert; and hugging her when she learned her grandmother passed.

"My mom is killing me today," Hadley whispers.

Lizzie grips and gathers the white tulle and lace of the gown, hoisting it up carefully while Hadley squats. "I hear you. I think she's just trying to help, but yes," Lizzie says. "And by the way, I forgive you for not telling me about Wade and Macy." She groans, narrowing her eyes.

Hadley leans forward to wipe. "Oh, yeah... sorry about that." She sighs. "But today is about *me*, remember?"

"I know. Forgive me. I will be better. I promise."

When they exit the bathroom, Maeve appears. "Okay, it's almost time! The music has started!"

Lizzie claps. "So exciting! "You good?"

"Yes. Ready." Hadley nods.

She *is* ready. Marriage has been her ultimate end-goal since she was a child, dancing her Barbies down the imaginary aisle. Jack is her *perfect* man, and they will have the *perfect* life as husband and wife. She just knows it.

Lizzie squeezes her hand tightly. "I'm thrilled for you, Had. Honestly."

"Me, too," Maeve says.

Hadley makes the sign of the cross, inhales, and walks toward the aisle in her white satin heels lined with pearls. "Let's do this."

Chapter 4

LIZZIE

Lizzie fans her clammy brow with the wedding program and peers out from behind the curtain as the other bridesmaids make their way down the aisle. The afternoon sun blazes above, and the ocean waves roll onto the shore of the Piping Plover Inn's private beach. The inn has been transformed into a dazzling wedding venue with bouquets of pink peonies, white hydrangeas, and roses. Hadley's Pinterest boards have been realized, complete with an ivy photo wall decorated with dangling champagne flutes and table assignments painted on the flip side of oyster shells.

Lizzie sniffs her armpits and readjusts her Spanx. She juts her head out to get a better view of the guests. Hadley is behind her, embracing her father. The string quartet begins to play a rendition of the Verve's "Bitter Sweet Symphony." And as the guests turn to face them, Constance makes her way down the aisle, waving in white gloves. She's dressed in a tasteful, lavender, Vera Wang, mother-of-the-bride gown, so as not to upstage the bride. Jack stands, beaming, in a gray, fitted suit, under a floral archway of vibrant blue hydrangeas.

Next, Maeve goes down the aisle. She makes a false start. Lizzie nudges her and locks arms with Jack's best man. They count to two between steps down the aisle. *One, two, pause. One, two, pause.* When she arrives at the front, the harpist begins to strum Pachelbel's *Canon in D.* This is Hadley's cue.

Like a ray of sunshine, she emerges from the double doors, and Lizzie gulps, holding back tears. She isn't sure if she's crying with joy for her best friend or with sadness that her own marriage ended in divorce. She envies Hadley and Jack. Why couldn't she have married her person? What was she even thinking accepting Hank's proposal?

She hadn't been thinking. She'd just been desperate to keep up. She should have taken it more seriously. But why does she always get the shit-stick? *Life is unfair.*

Hadley floats down the aisle, smiling at various guests, her spectacular hazel eyes accented by a creamy white shadow and false lashes. The ceremony begins.

Blah, blah, blah.

Corinthians.

Love is kind... blah... and in the end, there is love.

Is there really love in the end, Lizzie wonders? She scans the wedding guests until she lands on Wade. Her stomach drops. Yes, there is real love—*and there he is. Wade.* She can't believe it. He looks the same. Even better. Shit. Macy's head is on his shoulder! This royally sucks. *I hate my life.*

Lizzie shifts focus to her cuticles and chips away at her manicure. *Repeat the mantra,* she thinks. *I am not a follower; I'm a leader. I'm the number one realtor on the South Shore, winner of the country club's women's member/member golf tournament, and President of the Hingham Newcomers Club.* I WILL GET WADE WILSON BACK!

. . .

Twenty-five minutes later, (thank god it was a short service), Lizzie spies Macy and Wade mingling near the bar. She looks Macy up and down, sizing her up. *Is she pretty? Is she prettier than I am?* She reaches into her purse and extracts a small tube of lip gloss to maximize her naturally voluminous lips.

Okay. I can say hello now. Be brave. Be cool, she thinks.

Lizzie taps Wade on the shoulder. "Well, hello there," she says. *Wait, was that too perky and weird? His after-shave smells delicious. F*ck.*

He turns to face her and smiles. "Lizzie! So good to see you."

Wade is dressed in an off-white linen suit with a pink, Hermès pocket scarf. His long Roman nose, sable hair, and trustworthy brown eyes give him an air of royalty. He looks so hot. *Try to remember why you ended it,* she thinks. Her mind goes blank.

"Hi, I'm Lizzie Mixon. You're... Macy, right?"

Macy grins. "Yes! Hadley's cousin. How'd you know?"

"Well, Hadley has, of course, mentioned you, and I recall inviting you to the bachelorette party."

Macy makes a pouty face. "Oh, yes. Sorry I couldn't make it. I had a work thing."

A work thing. That seems kind of sus. She was probably gallivanting on vacation with Wade somewhere on Martha's Vineyard. Lizzie reaches for a champagne flute and takes a sip.

"So how do you two know each other?" Macy asks. She sweeps a strand of glossy hair behind her right shoulder.

Lizzie spots a dainty black heart tattoo on her wrist. *Is she even twenty-five?*

Wade and Lizzie exchange glances. "It's complicated," they say in unison.

Wade reaches for Macy's hand. "Well, not that complicated. We used to date, but we've been friends longer than that. Old friends," he reassures her.

Macy furrows her angled brows.

"Yes," Lizzie says. "Friends."

What in the actual eff? Wade was her best friend and partner for years. *Talk about a demotion or stretching of the truth.* Lizzie watches Wade as he looks at Macy. She wonders what kind of narrative he will spin for damage control. *Don't fall for it, silly Macy. Shoo shoo, away now!*

"So, are you still living in Hingham?" Wade asks.

"Yep," Lizzie replies. "New house, though. The kids and I outgrew the old one. I'm still doing real estate, keeping myself busy. The usual. How about you? Still in Boston?" She takes another, bigger sip of champagne, squirming.

"Yes, South End, near the Pru."

Macy interjects. "Well, not for long! He'll soon be moving to Beacon Hill—with me." She kisses him on the cheek.

Her exuberance is off-putting. How can he like someone so chirpy?

"Well, we'll see," Wade says.

Macy's mouth turns downward. "Honey, I hate when you say that," she whines.

"No, sweetheart, I just mean... I don't know... Let's talk about this later."

"Arms hurt from all that backstroking?" Lizzie jokes. "You walked into that one, Wade. Don't take it personally, Macy. He's said far worse to me."

Macy purses her lips and puts on her Gucci sunglasses.

"Always fun to see you, Lizzie," Wade says.

This is not good, she thinks. At thirty-five, she should either be married or in a committed relationship, not a divorced single mother with no prospects in sight. *I'm giving loser vibes. I can't let Wade see me like this.*

Trying to appear busy, she takes her phone out of her clutch. She has two missed calls from her kids, twenty-nine work texts from panicked homebuyers, and three messages from summer friends on the Cape.

Suddenly, it occurs to her. What if she finds a last-minute date? Maybe one of her summer pals, Cal or Mike, could jet over and meet her. It's only twenty minutes away. Yes, what a brilliant idea!

But then, instead, as if the universe gifted her, Lizzie spies someone jaw-dropping and dashing walking toward the bar. Someone *right here at the wedding*, much closer than Cal and Mike. She checks herself to make sure she doesn't have any boogers or eye crust and beelines to said man. It's time to turn on her club champion charm.

"Hi! I'm Lizzie Mixon," she says. "A.K.A., Hadley's bridesmaid."

"Hi, Lizzie. I'm Pope Morris," he replies. "And don't call yourself a maid. Housekeeper is a bit more PC."

Lizzie cackles, too loud. "Well, I'm glad to know there are some PC folks around here. I was beginning to wonder... And Pope? That's an interesting name. Are you, like, super religious?"

He laughs. "No, it's just a silly nickname I got in college."

"Oh, boy, now here's a story. I need to hear this one."

Pope takes a sip of his drink. "Well, I wish it were more interesting... But it's because when I was rushing my fraternity, I had to give a speech, and as a history major, I brought up the tragedy in Pompei, the Vatican... and well..."

Lizzie yawns.

"Have I lost you? Sorry... but yeah, it's a reference to the actual pope. My brothers were basically making fun of me. And now I sound like a complete nerd."

"Yeah, that's kinda lame." Lizzie laughs. "But I like nerds."

"I'll take that as a compliment, I guess."

Lizzie licks her gleaming lips before posing her big question. "So, where's Mrs. Pope?"

He cocks his head to the side.

"Your plus-one? Where is she?" she asks.

"Oh, I don't have a date."

"Shut up. *You?* Don't have a date. What *happened?*"

"She bailed last minute."

Lizzie slaps him on the arm. "See? I knew it. You were *supposed* to have a date."

"Well, we broke up just a few months ago actually, after two years together."

Lizzie grimaces. "Oh, I'm sorry. Too soon." *But just in the nick of time.*

"Thanks. It was amicable. I think?"

"That means she's pissed. You devastated her, didn't you?"

"Ultimatum. she gave me one, and... I don't know. I passed. It's the best for both of us, in the end." He finishes his drink and places it on the high-top table. "So, tell me more about you."

"Listen, nerd," Lizzie says. "I know this sounds crazy, but could you do me a favor? Even though we just met?"

"Intriguing. Should I say yes?"

Lizzie stands on her tippy toes and whispers into his ear. "Pretend you're my date."

Pope erupts with laughter. "Wait, what? Are you serious?"

"Deadly."

He gulps. "Huh. Okay, let me take this in for a moment."

"What's to take in? Want me to turn around in a circle so you can check me out? I'm usually met with approval—just saying."

"No, I mean... you're gorgeous, obviously."

"So be my plus-one! *Seriously*, I really need this favor. My ex is here, the one who broke my heart into a million pieces. I feel like a complete loser. Even worse, he's dating Hadley's cousin, who is young, pretty, and stylish. Do this old maid a solid, Pope. Do it for *Pompei*."

Pope chuckles. "Well, when you put it that way... You had me at Pompei."

"I will be good," Lizzie says, linking her arm in Pope's. "No funny business, just work."

"But what if you start to actually like me? Still no funny business?"

He's a charmer, Lizzie thinks. *Potentially dangerous.* But no, anyone with a name like Pope must be a saint, right?

"Well, that's another story..." She winks.

The game is on.

Chapter 5

MAEVE

From Table 4, Maeve watches Hadley shimmy her way around a big clapping circle on the dance floor to the sound of "Play That Funky Music White Boy." She moves her tongue about her mouth, trying to free the shred of lobster stuck between her teeth.

"Is this seat taken?" asks a familiar voice. Maeve knows this voice. It's the same irksome voice she overhears at work all day.

"Yes," Maeve answers quickly. "You didn't get a seat assignment?"

Pope laughs. "Funny seeing you here. I had no clue you knew Jack and Hadley."

"Yeah, I'm just as surprised to see you. How do you know Jack?" *This is terrible. I hope he didn't see me avoid him at the bar yesterday. I don't want to be reminded of work.*

"Grad school," Pope answers. You?"

"College. Hadley was my roommate. We've been unlikely friends ever since." She immediately regrets using the word *unlikely*, as it sounds cold and judgmental. But truth be told, they are opposites. Hadley is all fuss; Maeve is no fuss. Hadley arranges her dresses by color in her closet; Maeve hates even wearing dresses. Hadley enjoys jogging every day; Maeve only runs when she's chased. The list goes on.

"Right, I knew she went to BC," Pope says. "I guess I never put it together."

"Well, you're not exactly *sharp*."

"Zing," Pope says, shooting an imaginary arrow. "I can take it. Keep going. What else do you think of me? Now that we are out of the office, you can say whatever you please." He pulls the chair out and sits.

Maeve raises an eyebrow. "What happens on Cape Cod stays on Cape Cod?"

Pope nods and sips an Aperol Spritz. It's Jack and Hadley's signature cocktail for their "love of Italy" and honeymoon plans.

"Well, I *would* enjoy roasting you, but I will refrain from doing so. Besides, not sure you have skin thick enough to take it."

"What makes you say that?" Pope asks, shifting in his seat.

"Let's just say I've overheard some of your personal calls."

Pope's mouth drops open. "You're eavesdropping?"

"I hardly call it eavesdropping when they're on speaker phone."

"You sure do have that New England acerbic... is it wit? Or just bitterness?" He twists his red cocktail straw into a knot.

Maeve laughs. "Okay, Mr. Buckeye, from the great state of Ohio. Why is it that you Midwesterners think you're so affable? I've met many a douchebag from Cleveland."

"So, I'm not the first?"

But before Maeve can reply, Lizzie appears. She nearly stumbles trying to pull her stiletto heel out of the grass. "Here's my date," she announces, zigzagging in some sort of dance move toward them. She plops down next to Pope and grabs his hand.

Maeve gasps. "Your date? Pope is your *date?*"

"Wait, you know Popie?" Lizzie coos, petting Pope on the head like he's her pet chihuahua.

"Popie? Never heard him called that before," Maeve says.

"Lizzie and Popie! Kinda has a ring to it, doesn't it?"

"We work together," Pope clarifies. "At Watts. I think I told you that over breakfast one morning?"

"Shut up!" Lizzie shouts. "I can't believe that! Small world!"

"I'm sorry—how do you two know each other?" Maeve asks.

"Oh, we don't," Lizzie says, grabbing Pope's drink and taking a big sip.

"So the jig is already up?" Pope asks.

Lizzie makes her way onto his lap. "Shhh, no." She winks and whispers, "But Maeve is my bestie, so she can be in on the secret."

Maeve grabs Lizzie's arm, squeezing it tightly.

"Ow," Lizzie cries.

"Lizzie, Pope is *the one* who screwed up my promotion," Maeve says, widening her eyes like saucers. "*Remember?*"

Lizzie's stares blankly.

"We *work together?*" Maeve continues.

Lizzie tilts her head. "Ohhhhhh..." she registers. "Wait, shoot! This is the seersucker douchebag?"

Pope recoils. "Seersucker douchebag?"

"Sorry," Maeve says. "I was upset."

Lizzie stands, steadying herself in her heels. "Wait, okay, this is weird. Pope, how do you know Jack?"

Pope runs his fingers through his hair, now curled with humidity. "Grad school. I feel like I just had this conversation."

Lizzie stops a server and grabs a chicken skewer. "Thank you." She smiles and turns back to face Pope. It seems she's forgotten that she asked him a question. She opens her glossed lips wide and pulls the chicken down the stick with her teeth, like a sea bass swallowing a minnow. "Wait, that's in-*sane*," she says.

"Hey, Lizzie? Do you want to go over our speech one more time?" Maeve says.

Lizzie finishes chewing, covering her mouth. "Yes, oh, right. The speech. We should practice."

Maeve stands and grabs her drink. "Excuse us, Pope."

She heads inside the inn, searching for a private room. Lizzie hobbles after her. There is a library down the hall to the right, and Maeve turns to Lizzie, gesturing her to follow.

Maeve lets out a huge sigh as she sits in a floral, wingback chair. She takes off her heels to air out her feet and hides them under an ottoman in case anyone sees. Her toes are swollen from the heat. "This is too much," she says.

"Hey, girl," Lizzie says, taking a seat next to her. "Oh my god, my skin is on fire." Lizzie also removes her heels and puts her feet on top of the coffee table next to a book titled *Old Cape Cod*.

"Yes, but listen to me," Maeve says, leaning in. "You need to find another pretend date."

"But he's so cute," Lizzie whines. "And you don't like him anyway."

"That's not the point. He stole my promotion! Plus, he's annoying. You wouldn't want to date him anyway. He never shuts up."

"I don't care if he's annoying. All I care about is making Wade jealous."

"You're doing this because of Wade?"

"Duh, yes. I don't want to look like a loser while he's parading around with Miss Perky over there."

"She's perky?"

Lizzie shrugs. "She says they are *moving in* together."

"Let me ask you this: Why do you care? You have tried dating him—many times—and it didn't work. You were bored! Do I need to remind you of his nickname, Turtle Time, because he was complacent and had no fire under his ass?"

Lizzie shakes her head.

"How about that he was so routine and vanilla. Turkey Tuesdays and Fish Fridays? You couldn't stand that."

Lizzie frowns. "But we also had a lot of great years!"

"Yes, you did... *but!* You kept ending it, because you knew it wasn't right. And then when *he* finally ended it, you forgot why you didn't like him in the first place and pulled a Lizzy on yourself! Trust your gut."

"I can't. My picker is off."

"Well, this is a conversation for another day. But for now, find someone else."

"There is no one else! I am like the last single person at this wedding! Please, Maeve, pweeeese?" Lizzie says, like a baby, making a pouty face. She nuzzles up close.

Maeve throws up her hands. "Fine, whatever. Just don't tell him anything about me."

Lizzie raises an eyebrow. "Anything else, you mean?"

Maeve shoots her a death look.

"Joking! I won't tell him a thing."

"Okay. Well, go pretend then."

Lizzie grabs her heels and shoves her feet back into them. "You coming with?"

"I'll meet you outside."

Maeve clenches her fists and closes her eyes. *I miss Sam*, she thinks. *I want to go home.*

But Sam won't be at home. His side of the bed is cold. Four years ago seems like yesterday. Well, some days it does. Other days, it feels like an eternity since he died, and she panics that she will forget the way he smells. This is when she reaches into her closet for his pajamas, sealed tightly in a plastic bag to retain his scent. She presses her nose firmly to them, remembering.

Chapter 6

HADLEY

The new Mr. and Mrs. Forrester arrive in Rome at 7:20 a.m., jetlagged after a sleepless flight on *Delta One*. They swiftly make their way through customs and hail a taxi. A short ride later, they arrive at Hotel de La Ville, situated grandly atop the Spanish Steps. A tall man with a navy-blue button-down coat and hat retrieves their luggage from the trunk.

"Welcome to Hotel de La Ville," he says with a thick Italian accent. The air is humid and hot at 105 degrees.

Hadley wipes her sweaty brow. *"Grazi!"* she says, proud to use the Italian she learned from the Ciao! download she's been practicing for months. She gasps as they enter the hotel's grand foyer with its black marble floors. "This is marvelous!" She gazes at the impressive crystal chandelier and absorbs the scent of gardenia emanating from the gift shop, which is stocked with designer perfumes and soaps.

"We made it!" she squeals, fanning her arms out at 180 degrees, like she's Leonardo DiCaprio on the bow of the *Titanic*. She leans in and gives Jack a kiss on the cheek. "This is *beyond*," she says. "My *husband* really knows how to put a plan together."

"Thank you, sweetie," Jack says, making his way to the reservation desk. "Only the best for you."

Hadley's body softens after a year of anticipation. The wedding went off without a hitch! Their first dance, a waltz they had practiced ad nauseum with an instructor, was flawless. Oh, and the cake! Four tiers shaped like presents, layered with white chocolate seashells, was devoured. And Lizzie managed to make Hadley cry during her speech, like she wanted, so her bad behavior was forgiven.

Hadley ogles the winding staircase and glass elevator to the right of the concierge. She watches as guests ride up and down while Jack checks in.

"Ready?" Jack asks. "They'll bring our bags up."

They land on the second floor and walk down a red, plush, carpeted hallway. The walls are lined with Roman art in gold frames, and at each turn, there is a bust of an emperor. They arrive at room 203, and upon entering, Hadley spies a note next to an ice bucket with champagne and two crystal champagne flutes. It reads: *Welcome, Mr. and Mrs. Forrester. Please enjoy this complimentary bottle of champagne on us!*

"Jack, did you see this?" Hadley exclaims. She turns the wire around the neck of the champagne bottle and unwraps the gold foil. Using her thumb, she dislodges the cork, and it shoots up to the ceiling. She ducks and giggles as the bubbles cascade down the side of her hand.

Jack emerges from the bathroom. "This room in insane. You have to see the heated towel rack and freestanding tub."

But Hadley is already outside on the narrow balcony overlooking a garden with lemon trees in the hotel's courtyard down below. An older couple is playing cards at a wire top table with a bright yellow-and-white striped umbrella.

"How glorious!" she exclaims, as Jack grabs her from behind and wraps his hands around her waist. "We can finally relax," she says, turning to face him. They kiss.

"I never want to think about table numbers again," he says.

"Or flowers. I can't believe how expensive they are."

"I warned you."

"Well, I couldn't exactly not get them. My mother was all over me about the centerpieces."

"Do you think she had fun?" Jack asks.

"Oh, my god, yes. She texted me about six times just this morning, gushing over our first dance—and, of course, the flowers."

"What about your dad? I feel like I didn't see him much."

"He may have hemorrhaged after getting the bill from the inn. Did you see how many bottles of wine we went through?"

Jack laughs. "Well, my groomsmen alone drank about two hundred Bud Lights."

Hadley walks back into the hotel suite. She sinks into a comfy couch facing a fireplace and TV. She sips her champagne and starts to plot how she can get pregnant, stat. *Maybe I should put on that lacy negligee*, she thinks. *Yes, we will have champagne, and then I'll seduce him.* Jack joins her on the couch. She faces him, proud that he's now her husband, her forever, and grabs a chocolate-covered strawberry plated on a chilled silver tray. He's wearing the hotel's soft, white robe and slippers. *Slippers don't read sexy, but who am I to be picky? I want sperm*, she thinks.

Jack reaches for his champagne flute. "Dude, this is amazing. Cheers!" he says. "You have slippers, too, you know, next to your bed."

"I think the white ones on your feet are mine. Yours are the gray. Look how small they are!" She giggles as the bubbles rise to her head. "They definitely belie the large package underneath that robe." She winks, toying with his sash. "Let's consummate this marriage," she whispers. Lust glitters in her eyes.

Jack chortles, pushing her hands away. "Sweetheart, we will. No need to rush… can we just, like, chill for a minute and catch our breaths?"

Shame washes over Hadley, followed by the embarrassment of unrequited attention, then anger. *This is our honeymoon, for god's sake. Shouldn't we be tearing each other's clothes off, naked in bed, having sex for days on end?* What if this means he's already over it? Hadley's heard other women talk about how they basically never have sex with their husbands. Maybe that's already started. She's inclined to get up and walk out, to punish him for rejecting her. But instead, she puts on a happy face. The last thing she wants to do is foil her chances of having sex later. She wants to have a child in ten months. Thirty-five is nearing what doctors call "advanced maternal age," and she can't risk infertility. Unfortunately, a couple glasses of champagne later, Jack's fast asleep, snoring, his mouth agape. Hadley will have to wait till later to have her way with him, if all goes according to her plan.

Chapter 7

LIZZIE

When Lizzie arrives at Coldwell Banker the Monday after Hadley's wedding, she finds a large bouquet of red roses on her desk. She assumes they're from the Pattersons, who are now in escrow on their house in Baker Hill. *Score! One more sale in the books for the year,* she thinks. The satisfaction Lizzie gets from winning a sale is what drives her to succeed. She thrives in competition, which is what she never understood about Wade. He shied away from it, the ultimate turnoff. Lizzie turns over the card on the bouquet to read it.

For my wedding date,
Want to go on an actual date?
Thinking of you.
Pope

"Holy shit!" Lizzie exclaims, running around her office like a schoolgirl. *Pope likes me!*

To be fair, Lizzie is not completely surprised to hear from Pope again. After all, they did have a blast at Hadley's wedding, pretend-date or not, and she was on her best behavior. Once she got Maeve's blessing, Lizzie leaned into fun.

"What are you chuckling about over there?" Brandon asks. Brandon has been Lizzie's assistant for two years. He's her go-to for all things client related *and* all things personal. He's more than an assistant; he's her busy-body, extra, outlandish close friend.

"Nice roses," Brandon sings, reading the card without permission. "Oooooh, Pope? Sounds hot! Who is this cat? And what is this about him being your wedding date? Is there something here I should know? Spill the tea."

Lizzie giggles and rips the card from Brandon's manicured hand.

"Is that a new neon gel they have at Glossy?" Lizzie deflects, running down the hall with the card, like a dog begging to play chase.

"Gimme the tea!" Brandon shouts.

"In my office."

Brandon shuffles down the hallway and closes the door behind him. He plops down into the plush, pink, floral armchair and leans in for the scoop. "Spill it. Tell all. Smoking hot?"

"Very."

"Tall?"

"Six-three."

"Impressive," Brandon coos. "And so, how did it happen? Did you Lizzie him?"

Lizzying someone means winning them over by coercion. Brandon coined this phrase to describe how Lizzie is a shark in the real estate market and manages to get her clients to do mostly anything she wants by subtle force.

"Pretty much." Lizzie shrugs. "But hey! It worked! Check out these rosebuds!" She caresses the flowers like she's snuggling a baby.

"And did you show Pope your rosebud?"

Lizzie cackles. "Wouldn't you like to know!"

"I would!"

"I'm not a ho! I am a proud mother of two boys, and I have a reputation to protect in this small town. Word gets around, as you know. So, no. The answer is no."

"Well, you must have done something right," Brandon says, leaving her office. "I'm happy for you, sweetie."

There is a small, rectangular window carved in the wall between Brandon and Lizzie's adjacent offices, so they can talk freely, like having walkie-talkies or a can and string back in the day.

Lizzie grabs her phone and starts to text Pope a thank you, but she instead reaches out to Maeve. She snaps an image of the roses and hits *SEND*.

LIZZIE: *Dying. (coffin)*

MAEVE: *Pope? (cringe)*

LIZZIE: *(thumbs up)*

MAEVE: *He's slurping coffee and talking on decibel 100. My ears hurt.*

LIZZIE: *Aw, so cute.*

MAEVE: *Not cute.*

LIZZIE: *Did he say anything about me?*

MAEVE: *I didn't ask.*

LIZZIE: *Can you?*

(just bubbles, like she's writing something)

LIZZIE: *Hullo???*

MAEVE: *I guess.*

LIZZIE: *What are you going to say???*

MAEVE: *I'll figure it out. I'll get a temperature.*

LIZZIE: *Omg. K. Text me IMMEDIATELY after.*

MAEVE: *You realize he's super annoying, right?*

LIZZIE: *Don't talk about my boyfriend like that! (LOLing)*

MAEVE: *(eye rolling) TTYL.*

LIZZIE: *Love you!!*

Lizzie drops the phone and shouts to Brandon. "She's asking him how he feels about me! What do I do?"

"Send a thank you text. And *wait*," Brandon says. "Now, can we talk about 33 Main Street? We have an open house at noon. Are you joining? Or should I just bring your roses as decoration?"

Lizzie ignores him and walks to the kitchen. She checks the refrigerator for fresh creamer and crinkles her nose at the smell of leftover sushi. Next, she circles around the office, chatting with her coworkers. Then, she goes to the bathroom to brush her teeth and put on lipstick. She returns to her desk, scrolls through emails, and repeatedly checks her phone. Finally, she gets around to texting Pope.

LIZZIE: *I thought you'd never ask. And thanks for these! (pic of roses) They are beautiful.*

POPE: *So are you.*

LIZZIE: *(chagrined emoji with flushed cheeks) Aw.*

POPE: *Thursday after work? I can come to you.*

LIZZIE: *Perf.*

POPE: *Okay, gtg. Text soon.*

LIZZIE: *K. Bye!*

Lizzie is grateful for the distraction from thoughts of Wade and Macy moving in together. She can't let this happen. Seeing him again after all this time just confirmed what she already feared: that she had lost her one true love. *Maybe he felt the same*, she wonders?

Chapter 8

MAEVE

Maeve picks the onions out of her chopped salad and tosses them, one-by-one, into her trash can. But then she can't stand the smell of her trash, so she extracts them and places them in a plastic bag that she ties tightly by her feet. She's always been a neat freak, which is why Hadley and Lizzie referred to her dorm room in college as "the clinic." It was sterile.

"Maybe next time order the salad without onion? Unless you like dumpster diving," Pope says, grinning.

Maeve glares at him.

"Just trying to help" he says, holding his hands up in the air like he's under arrest.

Maeve flips through the latest *Ad Week* while shoveling salad into her mouth. She's starving, having tried intermittent fasting. She made it twelve hours.

"So did you have fun at the wedding?" Maeve asks.

"It was a blast. Your friend Lizzie is something else."

"Yes, that's a good way to describe her," Maeve mutters. "Did you guys exchange digits?"

"Maybe yes, maybe no, maybe *wouldn't you like to know...*" He tosses a paper airplane onto her desk.

Maeve catches the plane and crumples it up in her hand. "Are you five? I think there's a Gymboree downstairs. I'm sure your mommy can drop you off for the afternoon."

"But then I'd miss our meeting, my favorite time of day," he says.

"Whatever. I don't even care. I was just asking."

"For a friend? Namely... Lizzie?"

"No, I haven't even talked to her. I was just curious."

"Well, if you want to know, yes, I asked her out on a real date. She's pretty great."

Maeve's face flushes. She wishes someone would call her pretty great, but with her trust issues, coupled with never wanting to go out, that's not likely to happen soon.

"I think she had a good time, too," Maeve says. "You two make a nice fake couple."

Pope laughs. "What about you? I didn't see you dancing much."

Maeve covers her mouth with her hand to finish chewing a giant wad of lettuce. "I enjoyed the cake. Want to meet after you finish lunch?"

"Ready whenever you are."

. . .

Pope leans over Maeve's shoulder while she reviews the account information with him on her spreadsheet. She feels the warmth of his body behind her, like when Brutus snuggles up while watching TV. Pope's taking notes, and he smells of baby powder and Coppertone, a blend of bath time meets vacation. She is wearing her favorite scent, Chloe. She wonders if he can smell it; maybe it's too much. A text message from Lizzie pops up on her computer.

"Ah, my pretend girlfriend Lizzie," Pope utters. "What does she have to say?"

Maeve is reticent to open the message in case it's about him. "Focus," she says. "I'm almost done."

"You don't want to know what she says? Maybe it's an emergency."

"I seriously doubt it," Maeve replies. "She's too bold and dramatic to send a text if she's in trouble. We'd hear helicopters and her screams by now, even in Boston."

"All right, all right. So, what about you?"

"What about me?" Her chest tightens. Grief is not just emotional, it's physical. Sudden tears, fogginess and exhaustion are just some of the side effects she often feels.

Pope shuts his notebook, sits down, and rolls back his chair, ready for a conversation. "I don't know. Tell me something, anything. You keep it very close to the vest. Inquiring minds want to know."

Maeve pretends to read her spreadsheet. "You tell me about you."

"*See?* This is what you do. You deflect. Don't think I haven't noticed. I'm on to you."

Maeve turns to face him. "Okay, well? What do you want to know?"

"Hm. Let's start with where you're from."

"I grew up in Hingham, and I live in my grandparents' home now, a small house on Crow Point."

"So, what, 6,000 feet?"

"More like 1,200."

"I'm sure it's charming."

"Where did you grow up?" Maeve asks.

"Cleveland," Pope says.

She scrunches up her nose. "Sorry."

"Ah, we have a little New England snobbery here! No need to be sorry; Cleveland's awesome. It's underrated."

"I'm not a snob. It's just—I don't know. Sounds grim."

"I know you're not, Maeve," he says. "I'm just busting your chops. So, now let's get down to it... You're married? Divorced? Madly in love with someone?"

She blinks. "Yes, my golden retriever."

"It's so fun getting to know you."

She holds up her palms, heat staining her cheeks. "Okay, fine. Yes, I was married. My husband Sam passed away when he was thirty-one. He had a heart attack."

The color drains from Pope's face. He is speechless. He inches forward and places his hand on Maeve's forearm. It's warm against her blouse. "I'm so sorry, Maeve. I had no idea."

"Thanks," she says. "Yeah, it hasn't been easy."

. . .

The summer Sam died, he and Maeve were driving to visit Sam's parents at their lake house in Maine. They owned a summer cottage on Moosehead Lake, and the drive was about eight hours door-to-door. Sam woke up that morning feeling nauseous, but nothing completely out of the norm.

They'd had a few drinks the night before with friends, so Maeve assumed it was a hangover.

Sam drove, as Maeve was anxious and defensive behind the wheel. It would take them an extra two hours were she to drive. But about three hours in, Sam began to complain that the nausea had gotten worse.

"I just feel off," he said, tugging at his seatbelt. "And I'm kind of dizzy."

"Want to stop, and I can drive?"

"Yeah, sorry, baby," Sam said. "Maybe I can sleep it off."

They pulled over at the next service exit, and Maeve bought Sam Pepto Bismol and a Gatorade. She then took over driving while he closed his eyes in the passenger seat.

"Just get some rest, sweetie," she said, patting him on the leg. "Drink your Gatorade, too. You're probably just dehydrated." She turned up the air conditioning and adjusted the fans so they'd face him.

Maeve turned her audio book on low, occasionally checking on Sam to see if he was sleeping. She clutched the wheel, her hands at ten and two. When they reached Kittery, Maine, on I-95, Maeve began to relax. But nearly two exits later, Sam suddenly gasped loudly, a sound she'd never forget, and he jerked his head back hard on the head rest of his seat.

"Sam!" Maeve shrieked. She turned to him, and his mouth was agape, his eyes open wide.

Maeve screamed his name. "Sam!!! Wake up!" she cried, pulling over the car and immediately pounding on his chest.

"Sam! Sam! Wake up, Sam!"

Maeve called 911, then stood roadside, waving down strangers to help. Two vehicles stopped and dragged Sam out of the car onto the grass next to the breakdown lane. One happened to be a doctor, and he performed CPR before the paramedics arrived, to no avail. Maeve deserted their car by the side of the road, and the ambulance sped them to nearest hospital emergency room.

But there was nothing they could do to save him.

Sam was pronounced dead on arrival. He died of an acute myocardial infarction, or heart attack, resulting from an unknown underlying congenital heart condition. They presumed he'd had it since birth.

A part of Maeve died that day, too.

Her heart was broken, just like Sam's.

. . .

Pope shakes his head. "Honestly, I am so sorry. That this happened to you, *and Sam*. No one deserves that."

Maeve had given him some of the story, but she kept most of the horrible details to herself. She shrugs and takes a sip of her water, unfazed. "Yeah, well. I don't know," she says, flatly. "It sucks."

Ever since Maeve started taking her antidepressant, she feels dead inside. It's hard for her to shed tears. But there is something about Pope's sincerity, the touch of his hand, and their intimate conversation that makes her hands tremble.

"Sorry," she says. "This is super depressing. We should get back to work."

"Please don't apologize," he whispers. "I'm just happy you shared, and I want you to know that I am here for you." He reaches into his drawer and pulls out a potato. "And I want you to keep this."

Maeve laughs, relieved. "What is that?"

"What do you think it is? It's a potato." He places it down next to her gently. "It's sturdy and strong. Doesn't bruise easily. You just... need a potato right now."

Maeve has no words, but she grins.

"Clearly, I am on to something," Pope says. "It made you smile."

She absorbs his gaze deep down in her belly. "Thank you," she says, her voice suddenly cracking. "It means a lot."

Maeve excuses herself to blow her nose and takes the potato with her. She places it against her chest as she walks away, like a security blanket. *Well, maybe he's not that terrible*, she thinks. But she's not opening up any more than this. *Back to being the vault.*

Chapter 9

HADLEY

When Hadley and Jack return from the Italian honeymoon, she commits to her new role as Mrs. Forrester. Married "late," Hadley has dreamed of this since she was a young girl watching Disney princesses get rescued by a prince charming. When she and Jack first met in college, she'd felt sure that they'd get engaged by graduation. But she was wrong. Jack's fraternity antics and lack of direction turned her off to the idea. And her mother, Constance, gave her an earful about husbands needing to have EP, or "earning potential." Jack partied incessantly, often forgetting to meet her, and he failed to secure a job after graduation. Hadley, on the other hand, lined up a job in May and had found an apartment. She decided it was time to break things off with Jack.

But after twelve years of bad dates, and a social media post indicating she was single later, they reunited. The rest is history. *Finally, I have my happy ending,* Hadley thinks.

But this is short-lived.

Now, her happy ending is a having a family.

Hadley went off her birth control pills three months before the wedding to help her body regulate, and she now performs daily ovulation checks. To distract herself from baby craze, Hadley spends time cooking and decorating her home on Fearing Road in Hingham. She mulls over wallpaper choices for her powder room and is torn between pale blue with white hydrangeas and sage with yellow lemons. She regularly tunes into the The Food Network and watches *Beat Bobby Flay* to gather new recipes from the best. She's particularly interested in recipes that feature a lot of fiber. Per her doctor's advice, she should follow a high fiber, Mediterranean diet to bolster her fertility. Between that, taking prenatal vitamins, regular exercise, and good sleep habits, her body will be the ideal vehicle for reproduction, a baby receptacle.

. . .

"Hullooooo?" Lizzie calls out, climbing the stairs. "Anyone home? Had?"

"Up here," Hadley shouts from her bedroom closet. Lizzie is no stranger to the pop-in. She shows up unannounced about three afternoons a week with a bottle of Sancerre and a range of emotions to process.

"Well, hello, *Mrs. Forrester*," Lizzie sings. "How was it? Tell all." She posts at the edge of Hadley's sleigh bed, dressed in a khaki mini skirt, white blouse, navy-blue jacket, and high heels. She grips two wine glasses.

"Amazing," Hadley says. "You have to see—"

"Can we open this? Sorry. I want to hear *everything*. I just need a drink, *stat*. I've had a day." Lizzie unscrews the wine top and pours herself a five-finger pour. "Okay, go. Resume. Sorry."

"Well, Rome was hot. *Very*. But the Hotel de la Ville was something else. I've never seen—"

Lizzie, again, interrupts. "Amazing. And how's Jack?"

"He's good. Um, he's back at work now. He's taking the five-thirty ferry home, so he should be here for dinner."

"Awesome," Lizzie says. Her eyes blink rapidly and stay closed a second too long.

"Okay, what's going on? Clearly, you are not listening and in some sort of state."

"Sorry. I totally want to hear all the delicious details of your honeymoon. I just—I can't stop thinking about the Wade run-in at your wedding. Have you talked to Macy? Did she ask about me? Did Wade say anything to you or Jack?"

This is so like Lizzie, Hadley thinks. It's always about her: "The Lizzie Show." Lizzie is the star, and Hadley and Maeve are the supporting characters—the Elaine and George to her Jerry Seinfeld. She recalls the time in college when she careened into the back of a truck on her bicycle, and Lizzie demanded in the emergency room that they discuss her make out with Billy Harrington at the Psi U kegger instead of the accident.

Hadley pours herself a glass of wine and sits on the chaise lounge next to her vanity. Her tabby cat, Snickers, joins her. "I did speak with Macy."

"What? Tell!" Lizzie's now dark saucer eyes appear to spring off her face like a creepy clown toy. "Does she hate me? Does she even know about me? About me and Wade?"

"Well, first things first, no. She doesn't hate you. However, I doubt she would ever tell me that, since she knows we're best friends."

"True."

"Second, I think you need to move on," Hadley says, scratching a purring Snickers behind the ears.

Lizzie tightens, folding her arms across her chest. "From what?"

"Wade."

"Wait, did *Macy* say that?"

"No. I am saying it. He's taken. He's with Macy. They are moving in together. Plus, you were married to Hank, since you've been with Wade, and that was also like twenty years ago!" Hadley's had this same conversation with Lizzie countless times, but it always seems to fall on deaf ears.

Lizzie sulks. "It was not *that* long ago. And you know Wade was the one who got away."

"Well? He got away. Wade's gone," Hadley affirms. "You know the definition of insanity?"

Lizzie shakes her head.

"It's doing the same thing over and over and expecting different results. You can't keep getting back together with him and thinking he will be a new Wade."

"Are you saying I'm insane?"

Hadley shrugs. She does think Lizzie is a bit insane, but this is what makes her loveable. She is flawed in the best way possible: She's unapologetically herself. This is something Hadley wishes she had the courage to be, but she knows that would look bad, and she's too self-conscious for that. Plus, Lizzie is a loyal friend to the core. She's just... well, *Lizzie*.

"Now what about Pope?" Hadley asks, clapping. "I *can't even* with that. How did it happen?"

Lizzie gazes at her phone, scrolling through emails. "I know, right? He's good. Yeah, um... I don't know. I just can't stop thinking about Wade. But yeah, Pope asked me out. We're going to dinner at Snug this week."

"Amazing! I am *so* going to spy from the bar!" Hadley shrieks. "Jack is super excited. I think you two could be a good match, and we could double date. I really didn't like his ex-girlfriend, Sarah."

Lizzie raises an eyebrow. "Was she a pill? I mean, issuing an ultimatum is super lame."

"She was worse than a pill. She was a tranquilizer."

Hadley can't wait to start throwing couples' dinner parties now that she's a wife. She can use all the new Shreve, Crump & Low dinnerware, Le Creuset pans, and Waterford crystal from her wedding registry. Her mother taught her how to be the ideal hostess.

Lizzie sets her drink down. "I've gotta go. Colby has a birthday party at Challenge Rocks, and I need to grab a present first." She hesitates. "The birthday girl actually asked for a Lululemon cross bag or Stanley cup."

"That's ridiculous. What is with these kids today?"

"Right? Do you think Buttonwood Books and Toys got in new Jellycats?"

"How should I know? I've been in Italy, and I don't have kids...yet."

"Well, don't rush it. Though, knowing you, you're probably already knocked up."

Hadley grins slightly, wishing it were true. *Not just yet.*

When Lizzie leaves, Hadley heads downstairs to prep dinner: New York strip steak, heirloom tomatoes, and corn. She is going to make a summer tomato salad, and Jack will man the grill.

Hadley walks outside to the patio to fluff the pillows on the furniture around the fire pit. She notices a group of boys across the street circling around on dirt bikes. Soon enough, she might have her own boy, she thinks. She *hopes.* Does she want a boy or a girl first? Probably a boy, so he can watch out for his younger sister. That's what she's always wanted. She will name the boy Hunter and the girl Payton. Or, if they are twins, Everly and Oakley. *Only a couple more days 'till the ovulation sticks turn maroon,* she thinks. *Soon, I will be a mommy in no time.*

Chapter 10

LIZZIE

When Lizzie arrives for her date with Pope, the bar at Snug is nearly full. Only two of the eight chairs are free. Pope is seated at the far end, near the wait station, with a pint of Guinness in front of him. The room smells of potato skins and Irish Stew. Lizzie is wearing skinny jeans, a black tank top, and platform sandals. Pope is dressed like he just came from work in a white linen shirt, gray pants, and suede loafers. *He looks scrumptious,* Lizzie thinks—*still not as good as Wade, but close.*

She places her hand on his shoulder. "Well, hello there," she says. Her nails are now manicured in poppy-red. She leans in for a kiss on the cheek.

Pope turns his face by accident, and they end up pecking on the mouth.

"Oops!" Lizzie squeals. "Got that out of the way!" She suddenly feels breathless.

"Oh, don't act all prudish, now," Pope says. "Too late. I've already tasted those amazing lips."

Lizzie blushes and tosses her lush hair behind her back. She prays it won't frizz in this heat.

"You look beautiful."

"Thank you. You, too," Lizzie gushes. "I mean, not beautiful...handsome. Isn't that what you say for men?" She laughs. "Sorry. I'm kind of nervous since it's our first date."

Pope grins. "But it's our second."

Lizzie grabs a stool next to him, shifting awkwardly. "Ah, yes! The wedding was our first!" She reaches for a menu and orders a Kim Crawford sauvignon blanc.

The bartender places the chilled, stemless glass on the dark wooden bar, and Lizzie sips while peering to her right to see if there's anyone she knows. As Hingham's most prominent realtor, she often runs into people she's either worked with or who seem to know her. Not to mention, her image is ubiquitous: *Greet Hingham* magazine, For Sale signs, and on grocery carts at The Big Y.

"Cheers," Pope says, lifting his glass. "I figured the Guinness would be good here."

"Have you never been?"

"Nah, I don't get over here much from the city, unless it's a special occasion to make it worthwhile. I prefer Southie." He gives her a nudge, and she giggles. "So how was your week?"

Lizzie exhales. "Stressful." Then she remembers that men really don't want to hear about your problems, so she changes course. "But overall good. The kids are in camp, and I have two new listings: one in World's End, and one on Turkey Hill." Having multiples listings is great, but it adds to Lizzie's stress. She currently has twelve listings.

Pope furrows his brow. "Why are there so many names here with a 'hill?' Like, Turkey Hill, Pear Hill, Baker Hill...How do you keep them all straight?"

"Well, the topography in Hingham is hilly! I don't know. Makes for better views of Boston, and that adds to the property values, so it all works out for little old me." She shrugs. "How was your week? How's Maeve?"

"She's good. You know, I feel bad because we got to talking, and I didn't realize she was a widow."

"Yeah, it's awful." Lizzie frowns. "Sam was a great guy. I feel so bad for her."

"Is she okay, you think?"

"Yeah. I think so. Why? Does she not seem okay to you? I know she was counting on that promotion that you stole."

Pope's eyes widen. "Promotion? Wait, I *stole* her job?"

"Well, I don't know that you *stole* it," Lizzie says. "That's just what *she* said." Lizzie wishes she could take a shot or hide under a table. She doesn't mean to spill the beans, but it always happens. *Shit!*

"She said that?"

"Maybe not, I don't know," Lizzie says, backpedaling. "I think—wait, no. I'm confusing her with one of my clients. Sorry. Don't say anything."

"I won't," Pope says. "I just feel terrible if that's what she thinks. No wonder she gives me such a hard time." He sips his Guinness and picks at the round, paper coaster beneath it.

Lizzie has a unique way of putting her foot in her mouth. One time, her friends got her a shoehorn for her birthday, claiming she could use it to unbury herself. It's like she just opens her mouth without thinking and whatever comes to mind spills out. Instead of "Ready, Aim, Fire," Lizzie is "Ready, Fire, Aim!"

"Well, I'm sure she's just being playful," Lizzie says. She reaches over and places her hand on Pope's lap. "Is this okay?" she asks.

He nods and places his hand on top of hers. A jolt of electricity travels up her forearm.

"So enough about Maeve! Sheesh! You're on a date with me!"

Pope chuckles. "Yes, that is true. Tell me more about you, Lizzie Mixon. I want your life story."

"Well, I'm not sure we have enough time for that. I didn't have nearly what I have now, which is perhaps why I'm so motivated. I want to make sure my kids have everything they want, and then some."

"Must be kind of difficult to achieve that here in Cha-Chingham."

"Tell me about it." Sometimes, Lizzie wonders why she didn't leave Hingham after her divorce. It's not easy for her to keep up, which is why she's a workaholic. Even though she's a top realtor, selling more than eighty luxury homes a year, she's still not at the top of the socio-economic ladder. "It's not terrible," she says. "I do what I need to do."

Lizzie inherited her work ethic from her parents. She didn't have to try hard to make friends in school, as the girls always wanted what she had: good looks *and* charisma. She was popular, but she was also smart and funny, the ultimate trifecta. The guys called her a unicorn.

"And you were married? For how long?"

"Seven years. You know the seven-year itch? It's real. It's like an itchy case of crabs."

Pope nearly spits out his drink.

"Sorry, that's gross. Too much?" Lizzie shakes her head. "Why do I mention crabs on a first date?"

"Second date."

She nods. "Right, well, I don't have crabs... just in case you're wondering."

"Do people even get crabs anymore?" Pope asks.

"I don't even know. But I kind of want to see one, you know?"

Pope blinks.

"Do they look like fiddler crabs?" She holds her arm in front of her body like she's wearing a sling. "I mean, do they walk sideways with a big claw through pubic hair?"

"I think we ought to get out of here; people are staring."

"Too much?" Lizzie says, scrunching up her nose. "Boo. I don't want the night to end."

"Does it have to?"

"Well, my kids are with their dad... if you want to come to my house for a drink? I have a dock, and we can sit on it and watch the sunset. It's a great view."

"I already have a great view," he says, grabbing her hand.

This is the first time she's felt it. It's rough, like he's good at cabinetry and manly things.

"But sounds good. Text me your address, and I'll meet you there."

. . .

When Lizzie gets home, the sun is setting, a fiery ball of orange and yellow. She walks to the end of the dock and sets up a couple of chairs for their date. She peers across the ocean at the Boston skyline. The Prudential Center stands tall amid bursting hues of pink. She thinks of Wade. She wonders what he's doing over there in Boston, and if he is picking out wallpaper with Macy for their new apartment. Maybe she's pointing out different choices with her teensy heart tattoo on her teensy wrist. *Barf. I hate her.* She will fight to get Wade back. But for now, Pope is a lovely distraction.

. . .

Wade and Lizzie's first apartment together was a brownstone on Strathmore Road in Brookline. It was just off the B line on the T, and they could hear the wheels screech by as it turned the corner from Commonwealth Avenue to Chestnut Hill Avenue heading to Boston

College. It was a two-bedroom apartment with a large living room and bay windows. Lizzie would read books, lying in the window while Wade watched football or swung his golf club in the air. One Sunday afternoon, they decided to sponge-paint the living room bright green. They stood on ladders, pressing the sponges lightly on the wall until it felt like a forest.

"I think we should get a zebra print couch to match," Lizzie said. "Then you can make some animal moves on me." She made a claw with her hand and cackled with laughter.

"Wouldn't it be more like a cougar, then? Seems more fitting."

Lizzie jumped down from the ladder. "Are you calling me a cougar?"

"No." Wade laughed. "Well, maybe a little."

"I'm not even thirty!"

"I see how you look at those BC guys..."

Lizzie grabbed a painted sponge and pressed it onto Wade's face, leaving a green square on his right cheek.

"What the hell?" he screamed. "You're dead!"

Wade soaked his sponge in the paint bucket and proceeded to chase Lizzie around the apartment. She shrieked with laughter and ran until she fell to the floor, and he landed on her, shoving his sponge on her forehead.

"I love you," Lizzie said, kissing his green lips.

"Love you most," Wade said.

. . .

Lizzie dangles her bare feet over the water, perched on the dock that is lined with weathered wooden planks. Her Boston Whaler is tied to the end, rocking back and forth like a cradle. Lizzie loves this time of day—gentle waves, cooling breezes, and sunsets. But tonight, something about the moment feels different. Maybe it's the company, or maybe it's the way the world has slowed just for a moment, but she senses the universe conspiring to make it unforgettable. She glances behind her at the sound of Pope's footsteps approaching. He's carrying a cashmere blanket and a bottle of Sancerre.

"Hope you don't mind I grabbed this from your porch," Pope says. "And I stopped at Hennessey's for some wine."

Lizzie reaches for the blanket and spreads it out on the dock, like she's readying for a picnic. "Perfect," she says. "Have a seat." She pats her hand to the right of her.

He sits and rests his hand on the small of her back. "This is gorgeous," Pope says, peering across the ocean. "I can't imagine this view every day."

"Yeah, it's not rotten. It's the reason I live in World's End."

"It does feel kind of like the end of the world. It's so private and peaceful."

They are silent for a moment, then Pope opens the bottle of wine. He pours her a taste. Lizzie swirls the grassy white wine around her mouth, giving it a thumbs up.

"To Hadley and Jack," Pope says. "For bringing us together. Cheers."

"I like that." Lizzie smiles.

They clink glasses, and he leans in toward her face, kissing her lightly. His lips are silky and soft, pouty. She wants more. Lizzie slides her tongue gently between his lips. He takes her by the shoulders and leans on top of her as she lays back on the blanket. She moans, feeling the weight of his body. Their legs intertwine. Desire courses through her veins. He continues to kiss her passionately, tugging at her hair, then sliding his hands over her arms, up her waist, her thighs. Wade who? She is lost in his touch.

But Pope stops there. "I think we should call it a night," he whispers, rising.

"Is something the matter?" Lizzie asks, leaning on her elbows.

"No, not at all. Quite the opposite. I just don't want to ruin things."

"Ruin?"

"Ya know, by doing too much at once. I think we should wait, is all. Savor it."

Lizzie gets up, dejected. "Okay, as long as that's all it is."

Pope looks her dead in the eye. "Honest," he says. "I just like you is all. I respect you."

Respect, Lizzie thinks. *That's a nice change from the last few guys I've met.*

She and Pope sit side by side on the blanket, talking and sipping wine until it's dark. She can't recall the last time she's had such a wonderful time. *What an unexpected twist*, she thinks.

. . .

On Sunday, Lizzie wakes at 8:00 a.m. to take Colby and Track to camp. The field is hot and muggy, and the plush green grass is freshly mowed and wet, ripe for mosquitoes. She wonders why she signed the kids up for weekend lacrosse camp in the first place, since they're also doing soccer and football camps during the week. The more sports, the better in Higham. It's like the children are born with a lacrosse stick in hand and a mouth guard instead of a pacifier.

"Did you read the new rules in Laxachusetts?" her friend Kim asks. She's drinking coffee from a mug. "They can check harder now." Kim is a mom friend, who's also a marathon runner. On this particular morning, Kim ran sixteen miles, from Crow Point to Derby Street then back to her house, all before practice.

"Wait, you ran that this morning??" Lizzie asks. She tugs on the front of her T-shirt, pulling it out from stretching across her tummy.

"Yes. That's why I look so hot and sweaty," Kim says. "I needed to just get it out of the way."

Kim is a slight shade of pink, and her frosted blond hair is tied back in a high ponytail. She's in running shorts, a sports bra, and a fitted tank. Her legs are a glowing bronze from beach days on the Cape.

"You are my hero, Kim," Lizzie says. She swats a mosquito on her ankle.

Paisley frowns. "I only ran ten miles."

"I only run when I'm late or being chased." Lizzie laughs.

She makes a joke of this, when truthfully, she feels like something is wrong with her for hating workouts. Why do they like running so much? All she wants to do in the morning is sit in a robe, drink coffee, and watch Netflix if she has free time.

They all giggle.

"Oh, stop, Lizzie. You're running all over town working! I *wish* I could say that," Kim says.

Lizzie wants to punch her.

"My husband ran about three miles with me, but then I dropped him off and kept going," Kim says. "I swear he duped me. He pretended to like running when we first met, and as soon as we got engaged, he became sedentary."

"Well, my *husband* spends all morning at Boston Golf," Paisley utters.

Why can't she just call him by his name? *We get it, you're married,* Lizzie thinks. *Just another thing that divides us.*

"Oh, I meant to ask—do you guys want to play pickle ball tonight? I reserved a court time. Shall we play couples?" Kim asks.

Lizzie grimaces.

"Oh, Lizzie, sorry. I mean, you should absolutely come, too."

"Well, I have been seeing this guy..." Lizzie says, trying to fit in.

A lacrosse balls lands at her feet, and she tosses it back onto the field.

Kim's eyes light up. "Shut up! Who? Bring him!"

The other parents on the bench turn and stare. There are three men in baseball hats and jeans, a mom on her laptop, and two younger children playing with dolls, waiting for their siblings.

"Too soon for couples' pickle?" Kim asks.

"Did you touch his pickle?!" Paisley laughs.

"Couples' pickle sounds like we are swingers!" Lizzie shrieks.

"Well, when in Swingham..."

Lizzie recalls the time that she and her friends decided to get to the bottom of the swingers rumor in Hingham. They went to the rumored hangout on a designated Thursday night and left their keys on the bar, which is supposedly the giveaway that you're looking to swing. But nothing ever came of it.

"No, I could invite him," Lizzie replies. She wonders if Pope has plans. It's last minute, and he'd have to come from the city, but he could easily take the ferry or the commuter rail. "I'll shoot him a text and let you know."

LIZZIE: *Last minute invite for couple's pickle ball. Wanna join? (pickle emoji)*

POPE: *Are we a couple now?*

LIZZIE: *Shut up, brat!*

POPE: *Sure, let me know the details, and I'll see if I can swing it!*

LIZZIE: *Will do. TTYL! (heart emoji)*

Chapter 11

MAEVE

When Maeve arrives at Hadley and Jack's house for dinner Saturday night, she's surprised to find Lizzie's car in the driveway. She assumed the dinner invite was just for her. Had this been a social event, she might have opted to stay home and order Thai food.

"Come in!" Hadley coos, arms outstretched for a hug. Her yellow, striped sundress complements her tanned complexion and coral lipstick.

Maeve gifts Hadley a bottle of chardonnay and follows her to the kitchen, which is all white except for a standout blue La Cornue range and a pink beaded chandelier. A citrus candle burns on the center island, next to Jack, who is picking at the magnanimous charcuterie board chock full of soft and hard cheeses, fig jam, honey, nuts, meat, olives, and crackers.

"Sweetie, make sure to leave some for the guests," Hadley chides.

Jack shoves a piece of rolled prosciutto into his mouth and wipes his hands on his pants.

"Guests? Is Lizzie here?" Maeve asks.

"Oh, yes! Lizzie and Pope are here, too. They are outside on the deck."

Pope? Please, no, Maeve thinks. Maybe she can pretend to get a stomachache and go home. Things at work have been somewhat awkward for her since she talked to Pope about Sam. She's embarrassed for being so vulnerable, even tearing up, especially in front of a male coworker, someone who threatens her job security. Maeve needs this paycheck. She still hasn't forgiven him for swooping in and stealing her job, but she's grown to like him a bit more, even if she doesn't want to admit it.

Maeve approaches Jack and gives him a hug. "Marriage looks good on you," she says.

Hadley grins and begins to regale her with highlights from their Italian honeymoon: the boat ride to Capri, L'Orangerie pool bar in Sorrento, and La Conca Del Sogno beach club in Ravello.

"And the food!" Hadley exclaims. "I mean, *so. Much. Food.*" She grabs a carrot stick and dips it in a bowl of hummus. "Do you want me to make you an Aperol Spritz, Maeve? It's what everyone drinks in Italy." She holds up her bright orange cocktail, chilled with ice and garnished with a slice of orange and a cherry.

"I'll just have wine. Those are too bitter for me."

"So back to the food," Jack says. "I don't think I had one bad meal."

"I put on like five pounds from all the pasta and wine. I look pregnant already!"

"That sounds really fun...I mean, the trip." Maeve says. "I definitely have Italy on my list."

She notices Pope and Lizzie cozying up by the firepit, holding hands.

"No need to get up and make a fuss," Maeve says. She doesn't want to be hugged. "I just saw you," she says, pointing to Pope, "And you, Lizzie, just stay seated and rest. I'm glad you're not working."

Lizzie grins. "Tell me about it. I've had back-to-back showings; the market is nuts."

"There seems to be a lot of inventory these days," Maeve says. Like most thirty-somethings, she enjoys creeping on Zillow and house shopping, even if she can't afford it and never intends to move.

Hadley lights the fire with an electric switch, as they "ooh" and "ah" when the chards of blue sea glass glow beneath the flames.

"Let's play a game," she says. "I have Trivial Pursuit, Boggle, or we could play charades!"

Maeve grabs a slice of Manchego and a wheat thin. "Please just poke my eye out first with that stick if you opt for charades," she says, chewing with her mouth full.

"Trivial Pursuit then!" Hadley says. She unpacks the blue box on the poolside table and distributes the plastic pie pieces. "Let's play couples! I call pink."

"Pope and I will be orange," Lizzie replies, smiling at him. "That okay with you, baby?"

Since when did Pope become her baby?

"Oh, I didn't realize we are playing partners," Jack says.

"Should I team up with Snickers, then?" Maeve asks, grabbing the cat and placing him on her lap. He purrs and kneads her legs with his claws. "Shouldn't he be inside with all these coyotes out?"

Every time Maeve sees a "Cat Missing" sign, she fears it was last night's feast. Just last week, she saw a coyote devour a wild turkey in her backyard.

"I bring him in to sleep."

"Well, it's just a matter of time before you don't care for old Snickers as much," Lizzie says.

Hadley and Jack exchange smiling glances.

I would never put Brutus last, Maeve thinks. She remembers when Rick joked that you should shoot the dog the minute the baby's head starts to crown.

"Working on it!" Jack says.

Everyone chuckles awkwardly as Jack carries on about how fun it is "trying" for a baby.

Hadley rolls the dice, moves her pink pie piece, and lands on a green square. "Science is not my strong suit," she warns.

Lizzie reads the card and shakes her head. "Okay, but this one is way too easy."

"Just read it," Jack says.

Lizzie sighs. "What species of fish is Nemo?"

Hadley peers off into the distance, wracking her brain for the answer. She twirls her thumbs.

"Come on!" Lizzie yells. "You can't tell me you don't know this."

"It seems like more of an entertainment question, not science," Pope says.

"Oh! I got it! A clownfish!" Hadley jumps up and down.

"Okay, you go again," Maeve says.

Hadley rolls the dice and lands on orange.

Pope reads a card to her. "Which American road runs from Chicago to Los Angeles?"

"Route 66!" Lizzie shouts. "I drove cross country on it after graduation!"

Pope picks another card. "Okay, next one. What does it mean to get an eagle in golf?"

"So easy," Jack mutters. "Two under par," he says, rolling the dice again before hearing the answer.

"Let's go swimming," Lizzie says, walking over to the pool. She kicks off her sandals and steps into the water. "It's warm! Like a bath."

Maeve joins her as Hadley peppers Pope with questions.

"So, it appears that you and Pope are getting serious," Maeve says.

Lizzie giggles. "He's so adorable! Isn't he?"

Maeve pauses to think about it. *Is he adorable?* She hadn't thought of him that way since she's been so busy resenting him. But maybe he's cute. She doesn't know. *Who even cares,* she thinks. She doesn't want to think of him in that way. Work is work, and no one should dip their pens in the company ink; it's messy.

"I'm glad it's working out," Maeve says. But she's not sure she means it.

Maybe she doesn't want Lizzie to date Pope. But why? *That's silly,* she thinks. She glances at Pope to validate that she is not the least bit interested in him as anything more than a coworker. He spies her and gives her a slight wave. She immediately turns back to Lizzie, worried she's been caught.

"We played couples' pickle ball with my friends Kim and Paisley at Cohasset earlier."

"I hate pickle ball," Maeve says. "Like, why not just play tennis?"

"Shut up, Debbie Downer. It was fun!"

Maeve considers if she is legit a downer. Soon enough, she won't have any friends left. These girls are kind enough to like her because they remember how "fun" she was back in college.

. . .

"Chug! Chug! Chug!" Lizzie chants, holding Maeve's legs up as she guzzles beer upside down in a keg stand. They are juniors and at an off-campus fraternity party. Maeve gulps Coors Light, occasionally spitting. She finally stands upright, cheering, with froth around her mouth and a wet, soiled shirt.

"Yaaaas!" she yells, flexing her arms like a heavyweight champion.

Maeve feels proud of her keg stand accomplishment, even if it is questionable and tastes disgusting. She leans her head on Lizzie and Hadley as they toast to their best friend with red Solo cups.

"To our BFF, Maeve," Hadley shouts over a Drake song blasting from the CD player. "I never thought she'd be the queen of keg stands when I met her freshman year, hiding her nose in a book in our quad, but she's surprised us in so many amazing ways. We love you, M-bomb!"

. . .

You could not pay Maeve to do a keg stand post-college. Well, that's not true, entirely. She did accept a dare to do one at Mimi Schlichter's bachelorette party after drinking four shots of Jägermeister at 21st Amendment. But that was then. Before Sam died. There is Maeve Before Sam (B.S.) and Maeve After Sam (A.S). Maeve B.S. was a lot more outgoing, hopeful, and optimistic. Maeve A.S. is more fearful, reserved, and insular. It took a lot out of her to lose her best friend and husband at such an early age over what seemed to be a nongenetic fluke. She is angry at the world, the universe, and the spirits in heaven for doing this to him. Sam was nothing but kind, and he didn't deserve to die so young. She didn't deserve for him to die, either. She was a rule follower, someone with good karma, or so she thought. She held the door open for strangers, gave her seat up on the T, returned lost money she found, and never compromised her integrity by cheating or lying (well, except for white lies to preserve a friend's feelings, such as, "No, Lizzie, you don't look stupid in that baby doll dress!")

"So have you two done the deed?" Maeve asks Lizzie. They're sitting alone by the edge of the pool.

"The *deed*?" Lizzie balks. "Are we in eighth grade?"

"Well, you know what I mean."

"Um, no, we have not had sex, done the deed, boned, whatever you want to call it," Lizzie says. "It's actually sort of strange. Like, he hasn't really tried. I mean, he came back to my house after our date on Thursday, and we just kissed goodbye at the door. We sat on the couch before that for like two hours."

"Huh," Maeve mutters. "I find that truly surprising, given how forward he is at work."

"Maybe he's like old school, like Richard Gere in *An Officer and a Gentleman*—well, minus the white uniform."

"And you aren't exactly Paula working in the factory," Maeve says. "I'm fairly certain Paula didn't have a Birkin bag."

"No, but she did rock that really sweet patchwork beret!"

They burst out laughing, the kind of laughter that hurts, that you only experience with your oldest and best friends.

"What's so funny over there?" Pope calls out. He stands and walks toward them. "This better not be at my expense."

"Only good things," Lizzie shouts, giving him a little wave.

"Well, make sure you tell your friend here that I'm not an asshole," Pope says.

"Oh, don't worry; I still think you're an asshole," Maeve assures him.

But then she thinks about it and realizes she doesn't believe that. She doesn't believe that at all. Could she possibly start to like him?

OCTOBER

Chapter 12

HADLEY

When her five-minute alarm sounds, Hadley runs into the bathroom to check the pregnancy test lying flat on the sink. She's been anxious to test since they had sex on days eleven through fourteen, and she splurged on the Digital EPT brand, so the results are crystal clear in writing. No wishy-washy faint lines. Is she pregnant? Or not?

"Oh, my god!" Hadley screams, running down the hall with the "pregnant" stick in hand. "I'm pregnant! I can't believe it! I'm pregnant!" Overjoyed, she first calls Jack, who is also elated. Next on the list, her mother, who immediately disappoints her and tells her it's too early. Last, she calls Maeve and Lizzie. They can't wait to be aunties! This is the start of her new life as a mom!

No one is surprised that Hadley got pregnant right after the wedding. She made it very clear that she wanted children from the get-go. Any time she saw babies, she would coo and try to hold them. Jack nicknamed her "Rumpelstiltskin," because she acted like she'd steal your first born. Snickers had been her only baby up until this point, and between his carpeted cat condo (five tiers tall) and the "A Spoiled Cat Lives Here" signs around the house on pillows, mugs, and doormats, he was her prized child... but not for long.

"Oh, Snickers," Hadley sings, holding him under his front paws, twirling him around, "we are going to be parents! And you will have a sibling!"

Snickers's eyes pop, like he sees a ghost—the ghost of his soon-to-be infant replacement.

"Will it be a boy or girl, do you think? I think it's a girl. I do. I've been nauseous, which they say means a girl. Oh, and I just read in *What to Expect When You're Expecting* that she's the size of a piece of rice! Can you believe it? Let's call her rice!"

. . .

Hadley spends the next few weeks nesting. She lies down on the couch for a nap every afternoon around three, careful to lay on her left side so as not to obstruct the baby's heartbeat (even if she hasn't heard it yet). She also starts an online registry for baby gifts (even though she just finished writing thank yous for the wedding gifts) and journals daily about her pregnancy symptoms. She is desperate to tell all her friends in Hingham the news, even though Constance warned her that she shouldn't announce it until the end of the first trimester. But Hadley can't hold back! Soon enough, she's telling the owner of Acquire Good and the salespeople at Artisans in the Square. When it's time for her eight-week appointment with the obstetrician to hear the baby's heartbeat, she can barely control her joy.

"Okay, hold still," the tech says. "This will be a bit cold." She inserts a wand into Hadley's uterus.

"Should I be jealous?" Jack asks.

Hadley erupts in a shallow laugh and begins to count the tiles on the ceiling, awaiting the results.

The tech continues to move the wand in circles while staring at the monitor. The room is dark and smells antiseptic. Hadley clenches her fists. The wait seems interminable.

"Just stay still," the tech says. "Let me move this around a bit more over here."

The sonogram machine whirs as they wait.

And wait.

And then?

There is nothing.

There is no heartbeat—just stagnant lights and shadows, a hollow cave.

. . .

Three weeks after the sonogram, Hadley still can't get out of bed. She reads books about fertility and loss, barely eats, and dresses in sweats. She joins a Reddit forum about miscarriages and journals her pregnancy journey. She doesn't care that the baby was only eight weeks and had no heartbeat. It was a baby to her, and she has the right to her feelings.

"It just wasn't meant to be," some said.

"It really was just a mass of cells," said others.

"There was something wrong with it, so it's for the best."

But this is no comfort. Hadley fears she will never conceive. She dreams up worst-case scenarios of infertility and repeated miscarriages. She maniacally researches treatments, sterility, sperm testing, you name it. She imagines a life with only pets and reads the book *Cooking for One*. Maybe she can adopt? Maybe a surrogate? She isn't sure. In any case, she's afraid to try again. But that really doesn't matter since she and Jack haven't had sex since she tested positive for the lost pregnancy. They've spent most of their time apart, and the few times they're together, a fight ensues, like the one during Sunday's football game.

. . .

Jacks is perched next to the Patriots game while Hadley needlepoints. She's sewing a pillow for the Hingham Women's Club "Festival of Trees" holiday fundraiser. She has already made a belt with golden retrievers sewn on it for the pet tree and a Santa stocking for the Christmas tree.

She places her needle down. "Do you think it's weird that Pope hasn't tried to have sex with Lizzie yet?"

Jack runs his fingers through his hair, fixated on the game. "What's that?"

"I asked if you think it's weird that—"

"No," Jack says. "It's fine."

"Well, do you think he's into her?" Hadley asks, picking the needle back up and pushing it through the hole. "Or is he maybe not over Sarah?"

"He's over Sarah. And yeah, I think he likes her. I don't know. We don't talk about it. I mean, you guys are brutal. If he tries to have sex with her, he's a pig. But if he doesn't, then there's something wrong with him."

"I didn't say that," Hadley retorts, even though she did assume something was amiss. She wants to poke Jack in the stomach with the needle. "I just wondered if he liked her is all."

Nonplussed, Jack stares at the television, intermittently clapping when the Pats score a touchdown.

"So what do you want for dinner?" Hadley asks.

"I don't care. You decide."

"Well, I was thinking maybe that spicy turkey chili I made?"

Jack doesn't reply.

"Honey?" she persists.

He turns to her. "What? I said I don't care, sweetheart. Jesus, can I just watch the game? This is why we don't like watching with our wives, because you talk too much."

Wow. "Fine, then I will leave you to it. I was just *making conversation*, something you've apparently forgotten how to do!"

Hadley excuses herself and goes upstairs. *What an asshole,* she thinks.

. . .

A few days and no apologies later, Jack tells Hadley he has to stay in the city with clients for dinner.

"Again?" Hadley asks, lying in bed.

"Yes, *again*," he says. "I have to work."

"Jeez."

"What?"

"You don't have to, like, imitate me. I was just *asking*," Hadley says. She pulls the covers up over her chest.

Jack approaches her. "Had..."

"No, it's *fine*," she says, pushing him away. "Just leave me alone."

"I have left you alone. For weeks. In your bed. That's all you seem to do. Did you forget I was even here? Why do you care if I stay at the office late or eat dinner in the city? It's not like I have you to come home to."

Hadley tears the covers off her head. "That is so not true! I make dinner for you every night! Fresh ingredients, new recipes!" She can't believe he's giving her a hard time. Does he forget what she's going through?

"I don't care about what's on the table, honey. I care about *who* is at the table. And *who* I care about is *you*. But you seem to have disappeared." Jack's lips begin to quiver. "It's like, when the baby's heartbeat stopped, yours did, too."

Hadley feels as though she's been punched in the gut. She has no words. Rather than manifesting some false reply, something cheery and reassuring, she says nothing. She lays back in bed and drags the covers over her head.

When she hears Jack leave, Hadley decides to Facetime her mom for comfort and reassurance. Maybe unpacking all of this, telling her about their fights, will help.

"Hi, darling," Constance says, her face magnified and too close to the screen. She's wearing bright pink lipstick that matches her pink caftan. "How's it going? Your skin looks dry, and you should comb that hair." Constance is in the kitchen, where she always is. "I'm making your father that Bolognese I sent you the recipe for last week. Did you make it for Jack yet?"

Hadley shakes her head. "Not yet."

"Hadley, honey, what's going on? Frowning causes unsightly wrinkles."

Hadley's voice shakes, and she starts to cry. "I dunno. Just all of this with the baby, trying to be the flawless wife... I feel like a failure." *I need a soft place to land*, she thinks. "And Jack and I have been fighting a lot."

"Now, Hadley." Constance sighs. "You know better than to sulk and wallow. Pick yourself up by your bootstraps and keep trucking. If you want to have a baby, you will. But you can't get yourself all worked up about it, because that doesn't help. And it certainly won't help your marriage if you sit around like a crabapple."

A crabapple, Hadley thinks. *That's all she has to say? I don't know why I ever tell her anything. She will always side with the man!*

When Hadley hangs up with Constance, she swears to herself that she will be different. When—and if—she's a mom, she will listen and soothe, not berate and judge. She will be the opposite of Constance. If she didn't have Maeve and Lizzie, she doesn't know how she'd survive. They are her soft spot, her home. She calls them to meet at Tosca and unpack everything bothering her.

. . .

"Just forget it," Hadley slurs. "I don't even want to think about babies anymore."

"I know it's difficult to imagine now," Maeve says. "But you will have your baby. It just may take some time."

Lizzie takes a bite of the porcini pizza. "Agreed." She chews. "And there are other alternatives to consider, including IVF. Like *everyone* now does it. Look at all the twins!" Hadley stares at the spinach stuck in her teeth. "I mean, now everyone has fraternal twins. We literally had one set of *identical* twins in my class in the '90s. This is not a coincidence."

Maeve shakes her head. "I don't see why people don't just admit it," she says. "Why do they pretend they didn't do IVF? Who even cares?"

"I don't know," Lizzie shrugs. "I think there is some kind of stigma, like how no one admits they lost weight on Ozempic."

"Pretty sure taking Ozempic and injecting fertility meds are not the same? Just saying." Hadley scoffs.

"Well, I am going to see if I can get some when I see my primary care doc next week," Lizzie says.

"Why the hell would you do that?" Maeve asks. "You do not need to lose weight."

"Well, everyone else is shrinking, so now I feel fat! If you can't beat 'em, join 'em. And I'm supposed to see Pope this weekend."

"Have you had sex yet?" Hadley asks.

"Nope."

"What is *going on?*"

"I don't know. Maybe he just respects me."

They erupt in laughter.

"Fuck you guys."

Hadley remembers the time she and Lizzie made a list of all the men she'd had sex with in their early twenties, their 'body counts.' They had been in their dorm room, smoking and listening to Dave Matthews Band. Hadley was proud that she could count all her partners on one hand, but Lizzie? Not so much. Lizzie had had sex with about twenty-five men by that time. Hadley felt this was too many, but who was she to judge? Truth be told, she'd had sex with one other man, and she'd only told Lizzie and Maeve about it. She'd made them swear on their lives not to tell Jack. If he knew, her marriage might be over, or so she thought. He had this pristine image of her, like she was on a pedestal. She doesn't want to destroy that, even if it's a mirage. This is why she admires Lizzie. There's no mirage about her. What you see is what you get.

"So how are things with you and Jack? Any better?" Maeve asks.

Hadley shakes her head. "A mess. We got into another fight."

"Oh no, again?" Lizzie says.

"It's like we can't *not* fight. We are legit exhausted, and we are taking it out on each other. Him more than me."

. . .

An hour later, they drop Hadley off at home.

"Call me if you need anything, Had," Maeve says.

"Same. I'm around all night. I'll come back and get you if you need," Lizzie says.

Hadley warms. "Thanks, guys. I think Jack should be home by now."

"K. Love you," Maeve says.

Hadley gets out of the car and hurries up the stairs to see Jack. With time and a few drinks, she's ready to make up. Maybe she has been hard on him. Maybe she will get dressed in the morning and not go back to bed. Yes, she will make him breakfast! Or they can go out to breakfast at Stars! She misses him and their connection. It's been so lonely these past few weeks.

But when she gets to their bedroom, Jack isn't home. The bed is cold and empty.

First, I lose my baby, and now I lose him?

Chapter 13

LIZZIE

The school bus drops Colby and Track off at the bottom of their driveway at 3:20 p.m., and they saunter inside. Both of their heads are down, and Track grasps the straps on his backpack as he strides past Lizzie, without a hello, to open the refrigerator and snack drawers. Colby tosses his backpack into the corner and follows his brother, in search of sustenance.

"Um... Hi!? How was school?" Lizzie says.

"We need more snacks," Track mutters.

"Like what? We just went to The Fruit Center yesterday."

"Those aren't real snacks, Mom. Stop trying to be healthy. I don't want a "leather wrap," fruit roll-up, or whatever the hell these are." He pulls out a box and places it on the kitchen counter. "Can we get, like, Oreos or Goldfish, or something recognizable that isn't organic and posing as a snack?"

"Jeez, you're *welcome!*" Lizzie sneers. "What is wrong with you, anyway? You can't just dump all over me because you had a bad day, Track."

He grabs a seltzer water and a bag of chips and heads upstairs.

"Do you want me to throw the lacrosse ball with you?" Lizzie calls out.

Track closes his door. "No, thanks," he shouts. "I'm playing video games."

"Colby, honey? How about you?"

"Maybe later," he says.

Sorrow closes up Lizzie's throat. Her babies, her tiny little ones, the lights of her life, don't seem to need her as much anymore. This seems to be the case more than not these days. It's lonely sometimes. *This reminds me*, she thinks. *I should text Wade. (And distract myself from my loneliness)*

LIZZIE: *Hey. It was nice to see you again at the wedding. I'll be in Boston for a conference at the end of the month. Wanna have lunch? 75 Chestnut?   xo L*

She hits *SEND*, and off her words go, into the universe. *Okay*, she thinks. *Rip the Band-Aid.*

But after she hits *SEND*, Lizzie wants to puke. She puts her phone in her purse. He can always say "no, thank you," since he's dating Macy. Or maybe he and Macy have ended things by now. One can only hope! 75 Chestnut was Wade and Lizzie's spot when they lived together in Brookline. They'd meet after work on the Boston Common and walk down Charles to Chestnut Street. She wonders if he wants to go there as a sort of sweet memory, or out of sheer convenience—Macy lives up the street.

. . .

Two years into their relationship, Wade and Lizzie were skating on the Frog Pond in Boston Common. It was a blustery day, and Lizzie was dressed in blue cashmere mittens to match her cashmere pompom hat that that Wade's mother had given her. She gripped the side of the wall as she stepped onto the ice, using her toe pick as a stop to prevent a fall. Wade was already circling the rink like a pro, having played ice hockey. He wanted to play in college, but his parents didn't support doing a gap year for hockey. Children seemed to be skating better than her, clad in snow suits and using milk crates for support. Wade slid up behind Lizzie, grabbing her hips and making a T-stop.

Lizzie shrieked, wobbling forward. "You're going to kill me!"

"Relax. I've got you, babe," he said. Wade snuggled his square chin into her shoulder bone and whispered in her ear, "I've always got you."

Lizzie warmed, despite the cold air chapping her pink cheeks. She and Wade held hands and circled the rink several times, gliding like a pair of swans.

"I might be getting kind of good at this." She laughed. She peered at the center circle of the ice, noticing a woman, dressed in a skating skirt with a white, furry sweater and earmuffs skating backward and leaping into the air for an axel.

Lizzie marveled and made a muffled clap in her mittens when the woman landed. "Amazing!" she shouted. "Let's go get a hot chocolate, and perhaps with a shot of Baileys!"

They walked across the Common to Charles Street, passing Deluca's and Figs. They made a left on Chestnut Street and arrived at 75 Chestnut. When they entered the restaurant, it was bustling with a bar crowd. It was like a cheery living room, with drapes, candles, dark wood, and floral wallpaper. It smelled of French onion soup. The balmy air soothed her cold face and itchy, frosted thighs.

"Don't scratch them," Wade said. "You will make it worse."

"I like when I can see those red fingernail lines later, like I was attacked by Freddie Krueger."

"You're a freak," he said.

"Nah, now that we're here, I think I want a dirty martini with blue cheese stuffed olives."

Wade made a vomit face. He couldn't stand blue cheese, which Lizzie found unfortunate, because they could never split the wedge salad, one of her favorites.

One martini and forty-five minutes later, Wade and Lizzie were nearly sitting on each other's laps at the bar. Their legs were touching, with each other's feet on the footrests, and they were holding hands, gazing into each other's eyes.

"Two love birds," an older gentleman next to them said.

They laughed.

"Aren't we adorbs?" Lizzie asked.

"Reminds me of me and my wife. We used to sit here, just like you two, every Saturday afternoon."

Lizzie presumed his wife had passed but didn't want to ask. "That's really nice," she said.

He tipped his hat at her and resumed reading the *Beacon Hill Times*. Lizzie turned to face Wade. "That is so sweet and makes me sad," she said. "I hate death. It's the worst."

"Happens," he said. "Just nature." His pragmatic responses irked her. She felt he lacked a certain depth.

"Well, I certainly don't want to acknowledge it. I have too much to do," she said.

He sipped his vodka soda. "In life?"

"Yes! I have, like, goals! Plans!"

"And am I part of those plans?" he asked.

Lizzie seemed to stir the pot every time she drank. "Maybe, maybe not!" She laughed, but Wade didn't find this funny.

"What?"

Lizzie knew "what," but she liked to play games, even at the expense of Wade's feelings. It made her feel like she was in control, the one in the driver's seat. "I just don't know! Is that bad?" she asked.

"I'm not going to answer that," Wade replied. "How would you feel if I said that to you?"

Lizzie bit into an olive. "I'd be fine with it," she said chewing.

"I'm going home," Wade said, standing to pay the bill.

"Stop! We're having fun!" Lizzie pleaded.

"No, *we* are not having fun. I *was* having fun, until you ruined it by being snarky and cruel."

"Oh, come on, sweetie. I was kidding!" She tugged on his arm.

"Fine," he said, sitting back down. "But don't do that anymore. I don't like it. Happens too often, especially when you're drinking."

"I'm sorry!" she said, louder. "I just feel like maybe we are not a match sometimes." *Tit for tat. Cat and mouse.*

Lizzie couldn't help herself. She continued to peck away at Wade, as he grew uncomfortable and upset.

"What the fuck do you want, Lizzie?" Wade whispered, putting on his coat to leave. "Do you even know what you want?"

She didn't have an answer.

"I can't do this anymore."

"Are you leaving me?" she asked.

"I don't know."

. . .

Later that evening, it's Back-to-School Night, and Lizzie checks her phone *again* for a text back from Wade. She wonders if it was a mistake to send it. Acting on impulse is not one of her best traits. *It's ready-aim-fire, not ready-fire-aim!*

"Helloooooo!" Cassidy shouts, scampering down the hall in a Lily Pulitzer dress and pearls.

Lizzie tenses up. "Hey! Sorry I never called you back. I've been crazed."

"No worries," Cassidy says. "I did hear you've been a bit busy..." She covers the side of her mouth with her hand. "Someone named Pope?"

"Oh god. Who told you that?"

"Honey, it's basically in the *Hingham Anchor* at this point."

Lizzie grimaces. She likes Pope; she does. But she can't seem to fully invest. With her feelings for Wade, she just feels detached.

"Well, we're just dating, taking things slow," she says. "In fact, I'm not sure we're even dating."

Cassidy frowns. "Bummer! I was all excited for you!"

I don't believe that for a minute, Lizzie thinks. Cassidy is her competition. Every year, she comes a few houses shy of winning the title of #1 realtor in Hingham, right behind Lizzie. She keeps Lizzie on her feet.

"Yeah, well, be excited that I just sold a house in Cohasset on Jerusalem Road for $4.8 million. That's something to cheer about." Lizzie knows this will go up Cassidy's ass sideways.

Cassidy's face tweaks. "I am in love with that house. Stunning. Who bought it?"

"Some couple from New York. They want it as an investment property." Lizzie rolls her eyes. *She is loving this game.*

"Figures," Cassidy says. "Well, I have to scoot to Bronwyn's classroom. Mike's meeting me in there. So good to see youuuuuu."

. . .

Lizzie sits next to her ex, Hank, in a tiny chair, better suited for an elf, at Colby's desk. The desk is neatly organized with Colby's folders, pencils, glue, and scissors in the compartment. His name is stenciled on a laminated sign.

Lizzie whispers to Hank, "He's so tidy. Takes after you."

Hank doesn't acknowledge her, which prompts Lizzie to wonder if he's still angry. The divorce was drawn out over two years, and many unkind words were exchanged. It was ugly. It's taken a while to get back on solid footing as coparents. He's iced her out emotionally, but who has time for that with two boys? They just need to be good parents.

She nudges him. "Are you good?"

"Yeah, fine. Just trying to listen," Hank says.

"K. Let's catch up after."

The teacher stands at the front, talking about the children's daily routine: pledge of allegiance, ELA, math, snack, science, lunch, recess, social studies, Spanish, and release. A tired hamster lurks in the corner, eyes like slits, sitting in his bowl of food. Lizzie's phone vibrates in her purse. She checks, and it's a text from Wade!

WADE: *75 Chestnut works. 1:00?*

Lizzie's veins course with excitement. She peers over at Hank, ensuring that he didn't see the text. Not that it would matter, since he's been in a relationship with "that Heather girl," but she's trying to be mindful. Truth be told, she really doesn't care about Hank and Heather. In fact, the happier Hank is, the better their relationship. It takes the spotlight off her. She knows Hank secretly hates her for divorcing him, but she did him a favor. She set him free, so he could find someone who truly loved him. She never got there.

Lizzie slides her phone back into her purse like she's hiding a passed note in class. *Wade wrote back! What should I wear? What if this is our time? Maybe it is. I mean, we are thirty-five now. I think I was just too immature to be in a real relationship back then.* These thoughts pulse through Lizzie's brain as the teacher blabs on.

When the classroom night ends, Lizzie and Hank head to Track and Colby's lockers. She opens Colby's and spies a photo of his Boston Terrier, Boomer, hanging from a magnet inside. Her heart clenches at the sight of the dog. Boomer was one of the compromises in the divorce settlement: He'd stay with Hank, because Lizzie didn't have time for him.

"How's Boomer?" Lizzie asks.

"Great. I walk him by Weir River Farm daily. He loves it."

"That's a good spot," Lizzie mutters.

"Hey, I've been meaning to talk with you," Hank says.

"What's up?"

"Well, I'm not sure this is the best time..."

Lizzie's stomach drops, anticipating the worst. "What? Now, you have to tell me."

Hank inhales. "I proposed to Heather this weekend, and we are going to get married next spring."

"Congratulations!" Lizzie says. She doesn't really mean this. *How did he get remarried so fast? He's winning... Maybe he didn't love me as much as I thought he did.*

"Thanks. I waited to tell the boys because I wanted to talk with you first. But since word travels fast, I wanted to let you know as soon as possible."

Lizzie's shoulders tense. "Of course, yes."

Lizzie's insecurities surface, and she starts to play the comparison game. What if Heather is a better wife than she ever was? Or what if the boys like Heather more? And does he love Heather more than he loved her when he proposed?

Her mind whirs and sizzles as she hurries to her car. She can't get in fast enough. The moment she closes the door, she drops her head into her hands and bawls, a big, hearty sob. She crouches down so no one in the parking lot can see. Her heart is heavy, with pain in in her chest. *Repeat the mantra...I am not a loser...I am the number one realtor on the South Shore.*

Lizzie glances in the rearview mirror at her face, red and splotchy, her nose running. Mascara trails beneath her eyes. *I can't go home to an empty house,* she thinks. She imagines her boys watching a movie right now with Heather. Heather and her engagement ring. It's probably more than four carats! And maybe he went with rose gold instead of platinum this time? No, he's too boring for that. He probably got Heather the same exact ring he got her: a white gold, emerald cut diamond. He's so predictable.

Lizzie isn't sure why she can't just be happy. It's like she has to make herself miserable, despite her countless blessings. She has two wonderful children, her health, beauty, a thriving business, and great friends. But for some reason, she can't get out of her own way. *WHY DO I DO THIS,* she thinks??

Pull it together, Lizzie. Flip the script. Things are not that bad. In fact, maybe they are better than ever. She has a date with Wade, after all. Maybe he will give her another chance? *Then, I will be happy. Only then...*

Chapter 14

MAEVE

After work, Maeve and Pope meet at the Tackle Bar, their new account, to draft a press release about the opening.

"This place reminds me of Bass Pro Shop," Maeve says. "I love that store."

"Oh, my god, have you had the hot dogs there?" Pope asks.

Maeve laughs. "I love that of all the things to like at Bass Pro, you mention the hot dogs."

"What? They're solid!" Pope chuckles.

Various fishing lures and buoys hang from the ceiling on one side. On the other, it's a football theme, with Tom Brady's Patriots jersey featured in a frame on the wall with his autograph. The tables have little tackle boxes on them, securing the salt and pepper shakers.

"Think there are enough TV's in here?" Maeve jokes. "It's like being in Sears."

"Is Sears even open anymore?"

"Good question. I think there's one at South Shore Plaza? But I'm not sure."

Maeve reaches for her laptop. "Okay, let's talk press. Who are you reaching out to?"

"The Globe, Herald, Boston Magazine..." Pope scrolls through his list.

"What about *The Patriot Ledger?*"

"Got it."

Maeve chews her cuticles. "I think we should send to all suburbs, too. I have South Shore. Can you cover North Shore?"

Pope types. "Yep. I can do Central, too. *The Telegram* and *Gazette—*"

"How about the Cape? *Cape Cod Times? Falmouth Enterprise?*"

Pope nods, still typing.

Maeve's buzzing. This is her *thing*, publicity. She can rattle off the names of all the editors at the major newspapers in New England, not to mention the bloggers and smaller periodicals online. "We need to have a comprehensive spreadsheet with tabs of the different regions, listing dates, and times sent, contact information, and results. Rick will want this by end of day."

"Already on it."

Hm. Maybe we do make a good team, Maeve thinks.

Pope pulls out his phone and begins texting.

"So, how's it going with Lizzie?" she asks. She wonders if the text is from her.

"Good."

Good? That sounds...generic.

"You dating anyone?"

Maeve shakes her head. "Nope. Not interested."

"Not interested in dating *ever* or just right now? I mean, I'm sure it takes time. Sorry."

"I haven't decided," Maeve says. "I mean, I guess if the right person comes along, I'd be open to it? Just isn't a priority right now."

Pope nods and rolls the wet straw wrapper between his thumb and index finger. He takes a sip of his beer. Silence ensues. "I'll start drafting the release," Maeve says. She pulls her laptop out of her bag and begins to type. A waiter arrives with two shots of tequila.

"From the owner," the waiter says.

Maeve exchanges glances with Pope and shrugs. She downs the shot in one gulp, channeling her youthful days in college. Moments pass as the tequila takes effect. "So how many people have you had sex with?"

Pope nearly spits out his drink. "What's that!?"

"You heard me," Maeve says. "What's your body count?" She's trying to discern whether Pope is a gentleman, as Lizzie suggests, or maybe he's just not *that into her. I mean, if he's had sex with a lot of women, then he would have tried it with her by now, right? Or maybe he just likes her so much that he's waiting out of respect. I need to look out for my girl and get answers.*

Pope starts counting on his fingers. He holds up eight.

Maeve's eyes widen. "You can count them on two hands? That's sort of... shocking."

"Hold on, now," Pope says. "Not all guys are dogs, you know." Pope shoves the saltshaker across the table at Maeve, like he's playing shuffleboard. She catches it. "Well, then, it's only fair that I ask: what is your body count? How many men have you been with?"

Maeve stares blankly. "How do you know I only sleep with men?"

"So you sleep with women, too?"

"No, I just was trying to be mysterious," she says, skating the saltshaker across the table at him. It lands on the floor.

Pope leans down to pick it up and tosses salt over his right shoulder. "You don't have to try," he says. "You are a mystery."

Their food arrives. Pope ordered the fish and chips, and Maeve chose the seared tuna tacos with a wasabi soy slaw and pickled ginger. She bites into it, and white juice drips down the center of her chin like a soul patch.

"Good?" Pope asks.

"Mm."

They eat in silence for a few moments. She takes a sip of her drink. "So do you miss Cleveland?"

"I do," he says. "Not always. But I miss the people, and it's just an easier way of life there. Like, everything is a bit slower and nicer."

"Really? In *Cleveland?*"

"Okay, it's not downtown. It's the suburbs of Cleveland, just like Wellesley or Hingham. There are not aliens there. Jeez, all you Boston people are so judgmental. Massholes."

"I'm sorry," Maeve says. "You seem cool, and you're from there, so maybe I'm wrong."

He smiles. "Oh, I'm cool now? I thought you hate me."

"I do." She grins.

"Okay, just making sure."

"Can I have a fry?" Maeve reaches over and grabs a fry from Pope's plate. She bites off the tip. "Psyched we got this account. Cheers!"

"Cheers," Pope says, holding up his glass.

"To many more." She takes a beat to think. "New accounts!"

Pope smirks. "Really?"

"Just... cheers, damn it."

They clink glasses and exchange a heavy glance.

"Cheers, Maeve."

This is fun, Maeve thinks. *I wonder what it would be like to go on an actual date. Maybe I do want that. Maybe it's time. I deserve love again, too, right? But wait... is it too soon?*

Chapter 15

HADLEY

Hadley wonders if she jinxed herself all those years in her twenties when she didn't use the last match in the matchbook to light her candles. The superstition that you get pregnant if you use it might have ruined her chances of motherhood. If it's not that, then she's not sure what it is. She's been taking prenatal vitamins, and both she and Jack were tested for fertility issues. Her doctor says she should just try to relax, that stress may be thwarting a successful pregnancy. But how can she relax when she's counting days, peeing on sticks, and forcing sex? It seems counterintuitive!

"Let's go away for the weekend," Jack suggests. "We can head down to the Cape."

Hadley considers it. "Yeah, that sounds fun, I guess. Maybe we can invite the girls?"

"Well, if that's the case, let's invite Pope, too. No? Aren't he and Lizzie still dating?"

"Yeah, that's a great idea!"

"What about Maeve?"

"I'm inviting her."

"Will she mind? With Pope there?"

"I'll ask, but I feel like they have been getting along," she replies. "Let me test the waters and get a feel."

. . .

Hadley and Jack are first to arrive at their Cape house in West Falmouth for the Columbus Day weekend. Lizzie, Brandon, Pope, and Maeve will arrive soon. Just what the doctor ordered, rest and relaxation! Hadley unpacks the groceries: avocadoes for guacamole, chips and salsa, hummus, gouda cheese, salami, almonds, strawberries, smoked salmon, and bagels. She will pick up steaks, soup, and salad from the West Falmouth Market.

"Where's everyone going to sleep?" Jack asks. He's stacking wood in front of the fireplace. "I presume Pope and Lizzie in the same room? Or will Brandon bunk with her, as usual?" Hadley's used to Brandon being Lizzie's plus-one. The only reason he couldn't be her date at the wedding was because he was in Provincetown for Bear Weekend.

"I dunno. I mean, let's just see where they put their bags."

Hadley takes inventory of the house, refreshing soaps and towels and opening windows. She heads to the garden to cut some fresh dahlias, mums, and purple pansies for the tables. The air is crisp, the perfect time for her to break out her puffy vest and new boots. She inhales and closes her eyes, absorbing the saltmarsh breezes. Her shoulders soften, and her muscles relax. As Hadley cuts flowers, Lizzie and Brandon pull into her clamshell driveway on Gilbert Lane. They had a showing in Plymouth and drove down together from there. Pope's coming with Maeve from Boston.

"*Bonjour!*" Lizzie calls, grabbing her bags from the back seat. "I brought treats!" She holds up two bottles of Miraval rosé on either side of her head like earmuffs. Brandon's carrying appetizers from The Bloomy Rind.

"Pour me a glass now, sweetie," Brandon says. He walks over to Hadley and gives her a big hug. "Hi, honey! So happy to be here. I missed you! And you're a *missus* now. So exciting."

Hadley laughs. "Yes! Do I look different?"

"Just gorge, as always." Brandon winks. "And can we discuss those chunky boots? To die for."

"Thanks," Hadley says, turning them side to side.

They make their way to the kitchen while Jack starts the fire in the living room. A distinct chimney smell permeates the air.

"This is so fall!" Lizzie coos. "The smell of fire, mums, cool air... I am in heaven."

"Just as long as you don't say pumpkin spice," Jack says.

They giggle. Hadley despises the smell of pumpkin spice candles.

Hadley pulls Lizzie aside. "So, you want to stay in the same room as Pope, I presume?"

She nods. "Obviously."

"Okay, I wasn't sure since you usually stay with Brandon."

"Well, lucky for me, I have a date this time! And maybe I'll get some action," she says, shimmying.

Hadley wrinkles up her nose. "I'll put you guys away from me."

Chapter 16

LIZZIE

Lizzie grabs her suitcase and heads upstairs with Brandon to unpack. She tosses her luggage on the bed of the room to the left of the stairs. Aside from the primary bedroom, this is clearly the choice room, complete with a private bath, stand-alone tub, bird wallpaper, and a view of Oyster Pond. Brandon sets his bags down in the "history room," which has centennial wallpaper with cannons and ex-presidents. There is no view. Maeve, she learns, will be in the room off the kitchen, with its own private deck.

"Hello? Anyone home?" Maeve calls out.

"In here!" Jack says.

Maeve joins him in the living room and gives him a kiss on the cheek. "Where should I put my stuff?"

Jack turns toward Hadley on the stairs for the right answer.

"You're in the bedroom off the kitchen," she says, hopping down in socks and sweats.

"Aw, you look so cozy," Maeve says, hugging Hadley in her soft, cashmere sweater.

"Am I in the she-shed?" Pope asks.

Lizzie runs down the stairs to greet him. "Hi-iiii," she says, kissing him on the cheek.

"Nah, that's too big for you, Pope," Jack says. "We have something special in mind..."

Pope embraces Lizzie, and they walk to the kitchen where Hadley and Brandon prepared a charcuterie board and crudité.

"You must be the one and only Brandon." Pope grins.

Brandon blushes and whispers in Lizzie's ear, "You're right. He's hot." He offers a handshake to Pope. "Nice to finally meet you."

"Brought you a bottle of the good stuff," Pope says, handing Jack a bottle of Knob Creek.

. . .

"It's so weird that we didn't meet before," Lizzie says. "Like, have you been coming to this house, too?"

"Yep. So crazy. Had a lot of fun times here. Too much fun." He rolls his eyes. "Wanna take a walk to the beach with me?"

Lizzie nods, following him to the door.

"Okay, I'll just stay here with my salami." Brandon chuckles. "You know how I love a good salami!"

"No, come with." Lizzie laughs, grabbing two of his fingers.

Brandon obliges and throws on his navy peacoat and hat. They exit the house and wind down the dirt road. Very few cars pass, except for landscaping trucks, which are there for a fall cleanup. There's a murky frog pond with lily pads to the right and a finger dock extending into it with two empty Adirondak chairs. The air smells of marsh, salt, and sand—the perfect Cape Cod scent. When they reach the end of the road, they spy a sand path parting the tall green sea grass.

"Watch for ticks," Pope warns, pulling his socks over his pant legs.

"Ew!" Lizzie shouts, batting at the grasses, chopping them with her hands like a machete. "I hate ticks."

There's a small cottage to their right, appearing somewhat abandoned. Parasitic vines line the weathered gray shingles like something out of a Dickens novel.

"I wonder who lives there," Brandon says. "Looks like a murder cottage."

"Should we call Keith Morrison?" Pope jokes.

Brandon holds up his hand. "I love *Dateline*. Ob-sessed."

They spy a private beach sign.

"Is this kosher?" Brandon asks, peering behind him.

"It's fine," Lizzie affirms. "During the summer months, it's a no-no. But in the winter, the beaches are everyone's. At least that's what the locals think." Lizzie takes off her shoes and socks, feeling the wet, brown sand between her toes. It's low tide, and a family of piping plovers hops along the edge of the shore, dodging slipper shells and slimy green seaweed.

"Look at that osprey nest," Pope says, pointing to a large nest atop a wooden pole in the middle of the salt marsh.

"I didn't realize you were a bird enthusiast." She laughs.

"I'm such a dork that I even have a birdsong app on my phone."

Lizzie and Brandon bust out in laughter

"Oh, my god. I am so in love," Brandon says.

"Me, too," Lizzie says, grabbing Pope's hand. *I wonder if he really believes this*, she thinks. *I mean, could I love him?*

They stroll down the beach, collecting shells and sea glass. "Ooh! I found a purple piece! I have to show Maeve. She collects sea glass!" She hides the piece in her coat pocket.

"Really? That's cool," Pope says.

"Yeah, she's really into it. Each color has some kind of meaning. She makes jewelry out of them on the side. You should ask her about it."

"I will," Pope says.

"Are you guys getting along, like at work?" Brandon asks.

"I think so?" Pope says. "But you'd have to ask Maeve."

"No thanks. I'm too scared," Brandon says.

Pope smiles. "Aw, give her a pass. She's had a hard run."

Lizzie's heart melts. "You're a good guy, you know that?" She leans in and puts her head on his shoulder.

"Thanks," Pope says, wrapping his hands around her waist.

"Hey, what about me?" Brandon leans in for a hug.

They all laugh and take a seat. Lizzie digs her toes in the cool sand like a hermit crab. She glances at Pope, who is looking off in the distance. He appears so peaceful and calm. Happy—something she is not. Could she possibly fall for him and forget Wade?

Chapter 17

MAEVE

After dinner, Brandon, Lizzie, and Jack go outside to smoke weed. Hadley heads upstairs to bathe. Pope and Maeve sit inside by the fire, drinking a spicy malbec. The fire crackles and sparks.

"Want to play backgammon?" Pope asks, unpacking the leather suitcase.

"Sure," Maeve says. "I'll be white."

They set up the tiny, round pieces on the leather board and shake the dice in the felt cups. Maeve rolls two sixes and goes first.

"So, tell me what purple sea glass means," Pope asks, as Maeve moves her white piece across the darts.

She sips at her red wine. "Huh?"

"Sea glass," he says. "I heard you collect it and know the meanings of each color? Lizzie told me. She found a purple piece on the beach today."

"Oh! Yes! Wow, purple is rare," Maeve says. "Well, purple sea glass is originally blue, but manganese and UV rays turn it the shade of violet we see."

Pope's eyes widen.

"Yeah, I'm kind of a nerd."

Most evenings, Maeve walks Brutus to the end of Downer Avenue to take him swimming. It's a quaint walk with ocean views on one side and sprawling homes on the other. As she tosses him the ball, she collects sea glass to make jewelry: green is good luck, red is rare, and white means an angel is guiding you. Sam is her angel.

"That's kinda nerdy." Pope chuckles. "But to be honest, I also let my nerd flag fly today when I showed Lizzie and Brandon my birdsong app."

"You have one, too? That's so funny! I thought I was the only freak who wanted to know if there was a warbler or a tufted titmouse in my yard!"

Pope cracks up. "Tufted titmouse!"

"Are you laughing at the 'tit' part, or at me?"

"Well, both," he replies. "Honestly, I'm just pleasantly surprised by all of you." His blue eyes twinkle in the firelight.

Maeve concentrates on the backgammon board, averting her gaze. "Your turn," she says. "Oh, and thanks." Her mouth forms a slight smile, and she's not sure if it's the wine or Pope that is making her tingly.

. . .

As the night wears on, everyone gets progressively more drunk and high. Lizzie and Brandon, in particular, are hammered and shouting '90s pop rock on the karaoke machine. Pope joins in for a duet of "Islands in the Stream" with Lizzie, and he and Brandon sing "More than Words" together. Maeve grabs the mic for a Pat Benatar solo of "We Belong," and she and Lizzie sing The Bangles' "Walk Like an Egyptian," complete with the King Tut moves.

Pope whispers in Lizzie's ear, "Want to head up to bed soon? Pull an Irish goodbye?"

"No way! I'm having too much fun!" Lizzie shouts, researching kara-oke songs on her phone, swaying her hips back and forth to the music.

"How can you go to bed now?" Brandon screeches. "We are just getting started!"

. . .

A few minutes later, Maeve retires to her bedroom off the kitchen. She locks the door behind her and sits on the side of the bed. There is a photo of Jack and Hadley skiing at Sugarbush on the nightstand, along with a lavender- and honey-scented Yankee candle and a glass box. She reaches over to see what's inside, and it's a bouquet of almonds in a netted sash from their wedding, which has their names and the wedding date inscribed on the bow. Maeve recalls that day, when she first saw Pope while standing beside Hadley at the altar. He was the last person she wanted to see.

But tonight is different.

Tonight, she can see what others see in him: wit, charm, sensitivity.

Oh stop, she thinks. *First of all, he works with you. And second, he's dating Lizzie.*

She changes into her sweats and skips brushing her teeth and washing her face. She turns out the lights and lies in bed, listening to the thump of the karaoke machine and Lizzie and Brandon's muffled shouts from the living room. She closes her eyes and hopes to dream of Sam, but instead, she has a sexy dream about Pope.

About an hour later, Maeve jolts awake to the sound of Lizzie shouting at Pope. *It was just a dream*, she realizes. Holy shit. It was a crazy dream. And she's in Hadley's house on the Cape. *What is Lizzie yelling about?*

Maeve unlocks her bedroom door a crack and peeps out. Pope and Lizzie are at the kitchen table. Lizzie is slurring, and she's blinking her eyes a lot, a sign she's wasted.

"I feel like you don't even really like me! Why haven't you had sex with me?" Lizzie shouts. She pulls her chair closer to his.

"Lizzie, sweetheart." He laughs. "It's not that I haven't wanted to; I was taking things slow."

She tosses a stale wheat thin from the charcuterie board at him. "Bullshit! You don't find me attractive."

"Not when you're like this," Pope retorts. "But in general, I do. Of course. Hey, let's talk about it in the morning."

Maeve is cringing. She needs to extricate Lizzie stat, before she takes a nosedive.

"No time like the present," Lizzie says. Then she gets up from her chair, outstretches her arms, like a helicopter, and twirls around the room. "Time… what is time, anyway? Time… time for me to meet up with Wade soon!" She catches herself, looks at Pope, and covers her mouth with her hands.

Maeve's eyes widen. Wade?! Why is she seeing Wade? And why, more importantly, is she telling Pope this? She is going to regret this! Maeve grabs a robe hanging in the closet, ties it around her waist, and jumps to Lizzie's rescue. She can't let her sabotage everything with Pope. She dashes into the kitchen in her bare feet and grabs Lizzie by her shoulders.

"Look at me," she whispers. "You need to go to bed. Now."

"Maeve! You're up! You Irish goodbye'd hardcore! Let's do a duet!"

"Not now, Lizzie," Maeve says, trying to escort her upstairs.

"Don't worry about it, Maeve. I've got this," Pope says.

Maeve shakes her head at Lizzie. "Follow me," she says.

"Whaaat? What did I dooooo? You're being mean! Stop!" Lizzie wails.

"Nothing, honey. Just come upstairs. It's time for you to sleep," Maeve whispers.

"I think I'm going to grab a couch down here," Pope says.

"Nooooooooo!" Lizzie shouts, freeing herself from Maeve. "You hate me! Why do you hate me?" She runs over to Pope and throws her arms around him in an embrace.

"I don't hate you, Lizzie. But I'm not in the mood to talk about this anymore, or to hear about how you have plans with your ex. I thought you were over that."

"Who? Waaade???" Lizzie laughs loudly. "Wade..."

Maeve grabs Lizzie and pushes her to her room unwillingly, like she's a toddler refusing to go to bed. She closes the door. "Go to sleep."

"I wasn't done singing," Lizzie says, flopping down on the edge of the bed.

"You'll thank me in the morning that I dragged you out of there."

Lizzie blinks. "What? Why?"

"You are sabotaging your relationship with Pope! You're screaming about Wade!"

Lizzie falls back. "But I love Wade."

"Really? Do you really *love* Wade?" Maeve asks. *I can't do this again with her*, she thinks.

Lizzie closes her eyes, nodding.

"Well, I don't think you do. I think you love the idea of Wade. If you actually got him back—which, by the way, you shouldn't—you'd end up breaking up with him again."

"Uh-un," Lizzie mumbles, shaking her head, eyes shut.

"Pope is a good guy. Give him a chance."

Lizzie snores.

"You'll see."

I see.

. . .

The next morning, Maeve spots Pope packing up his car from her window. It's early. Lizzie is still asleep. She puts on a sweatshirt and goes outside.

"You heading out?" she asks, arms folded across her chest.

"Yeah, I gotta get back. May go into the office. I have some stuff to catch up on."

Maeve knows this isn't true because they tied up most of the loose ends together before they left for the Cape. Rick insisted on it. "Are you okay?" she asks.

Pope closes the trunk and sighs. "It's all good," he says.

"She can be a lot, but she doesn't mean it."

Pope nods. "I know."

"Well." Maeve shrugs. "Text us when you get back."

Maeve watches Pope as he drives away. He rolls the window down and stretches a hand out when he reaches the stop sign at the end of the street. *He sees me*, she thinks, embarrassed. But does he really *see me*?

Chapter 18

LIZZIE

It's Hingham Friday Night Football, and Lizzie brings Colby and Track to meet some friends at the field. Hundreds of students and families line the bleachers under the night sky, with bright lights illuminating the football field. The Hingham Harbormen are playing their rival, Hanover. Young kids scurry underneath the bleachers and gather by the snack bar while parents watch the game and drink clandestine cocktails.

When Lizzie arrives, her friends are mid-discussion about food and diets.

"I recently boycotted swordfish because the catch sizes were too small," Julie says, proudly. "But it did not have an impact."

"I am fairly certain I saw a swordfish sandwich on the menu last week at The Catch, so you're not wrong there," Mallory says.

Lizzie takes a sip of her sauvignon blanc. "Wait, but my doctor told me to go on the Mediterranean diet, and swordfish was recommended. Should I be boycotting it?"

"That is terrible," Julie says. "Yes. And get a new doctor."

"Maybe just try Keto? I lost weight on that," Paisley replies. "No carbs, but not a ton of fat either, like they used to say."

"I do intermittent fasting, sixteen hours," Mallory says.

Lizzie frowns. "I feel like I'm starving when I do that. And I can't drink black coffee in the morning. No way."

"I just walk in Bare Cove with a weighted vest. Screw diets," Kim says.

"Oooh, I have been wanting to get a weighted vest," Lizzie says. "Does it make a difference?"

Hingham scores! "Go Hingham!" Lizzie shouts. "So, any new tea in town? I feel like I've been MIA."

"Well, there are a couple new splits and a few cheating rumors," Paisley says.

Lizzie's eyes widen. "Really? Like whom?"

Paisley leans in and whispers, "Jessica and Tim Wright and Veronica and Morgan Sullivan, for starters."

Julie shrieks. "What?! I mean, I'm not surprised by Jessica and Tim. She legit hates him and shames him at every party. But Veronica and Morgan? That's wild."

"Yeah, apparently, he's hooking up with some teacher from Cohasset. I guess they met through the club?" Paisley says.

"Ew, do you know her?" Lizzie asks. "I'll have to ask Brandon about that. He knows Morgan, and we sold them their house in Bradley Park a while back."

"Well, you might be selling again!" Julie says.

Hingham scores another touchdown, and the cheerleaders shake their pompoms and dance: *"H-I-N-G-H-A-M! We're the Hingham Harbormen! Goooooooo Hingham!"*

Lizzie scans the crowd for Colby and Track, who are at the snack bar surrounded by several girls dressed the same in leggings, Uggs, and baggy sweatshirts. They are eating nachos and licorice. She spies several of her former clients and waves to them.

"Hurricane Cassidy is approaching," Lizzie warns. "Brace yourselves."

The women shift to the left to make room for Cassidy, who plops down beside them in knee-high, truffle-colored boots with heels, a counterintuitive shoe choice for bleachers.

"What did I miss?" Cassidy asks. "I could not get my kids out of the house, for the life of me!"

"Oh, not much. Just the latest diets and divorces," Lizzie mutters.

"You mean Tanner and Missy?" Cassidy asks.

"Them, too?!" Julie gasps. "When did that happen?"

Cassidy peers behind her to ensure no one can overhear. "Well, keep this on the DL... I only know because my housekeeper told me about it."

"What did she hear?" Julie asks.

"Apparently, they are packing up to move, and she overheard Missy on the phone with her lawyer."

"Isn't that like a HIPAA violation to reveal that info about your clients?" Lizzie asks.

"Not sure housekeepers qualify for HIPAA," Cassidy says. "Unless the 'H' stands for housekeeper!".

The ref blows the whistle, and the music blares as the announcer shouts, "SCOOOOOORE!" The cheerleaders twerk and tumble.

"If I tried that move, I'd slip a disk," Lizzie says.

"I'm pretty sure I tried that move last night." Mallory laughs.

"T.M.I.!" Paisley yells.

"So how are things going with Pope?" Cassidy asks, waggling her eyebrows.

"Good," Lizzie lies.

"I am just so tickled about it!" Cassidy says. "I need to see this man!"

"He's hot," Paisley says.

Lizzie considers this. *He is hot*, she thinks. *And nice*. So why can't she just get over seeing Wade? Lizzie changes the conversation to the usual: kids and sports.

"I'm super stressed," Mallory says. "Tim may have shattered his tibia playing football last week, and it could really ruin his chances of playing for a D1 school."

"What's so wrong with D3?"

Mallory rolls her eyes. "It's not the same. *We moved here for the sports.* We've put in so much time."

Julie nods. "Tell me about it. We have four games this weekend. Alan and I are like ships passing in the night. He takes Cole to football, and I'm driving all over New England for Wren's soccer."

Lizzie wonders if she should enroll Colby and Track in more sports. But she has open houses on weekends, and she doesn't have a partner to share the driving with. *Divorce sucks*, she thinks.

The Hingham Harbormen score the winning touchdown.

"G-O—OOOOOOOOO HINGHAM!!!"

. . .

Lizzie parks in the Boston Common garage and exits on Beacon Street. The air is crisp, and orange, yellow, and brown leaves pepper the brick sidewalks. A street musician plays Irish music on the bagpipes with a Venmo sign in front of his tip bucket. Lizzie veers to the side and spots Wade perched in front of Starbucks. His dark hair has grown since she last saw him at Hadley's wedding, and it covers the tops of his ears slightly, like baby earmuffs. He reminds her of the guys she dated in high school, minus the dirty, white baseball hat that's curved at the front. Lizzie crosses the street and tightens the sash of her wool coat.

"Hey," she says, leaning in for a hug. His familiar smell transports her back to their Brookline apartment. He smells like home, a favorite stuffed animal.

"Hi." Wade smiles.

God, he's gorgeous. Regret for all the pain she's put him through courses through Lizzie's veins. They stroll down the cobblestones, past Café Paradiso and toward Chestnut Street.

"Hungry?" he asks.

"Starving," Lizzie lies. She has zero appetite with her nerves. She just wants things to go smoothly. She's thought about this date for weeks.

"How was the conference?"

Lizzie cocks her head to the left. "Conference?"

Wade chuckles. "Isn't that why you're in town? You said you had a conference."

"Oops, busted." Lizzie laughs. "I just wanted to see you." She shrugs. "Is that bad?"

He shakes his head and laughs. "No," he replies. "I wanted to see you, too." They pass a young couple in their twenties, holding hands and dressed in matching Harvard hoodies.

Wade sighs. "I felt sort of bad after running into you at Hadley's wedding."

"Me, too!" Lizzie says. A combination of relief and hope wash over her.

"How's... what's his name? Pope?"

"He's fine." She hesitates. "I mean, I think?"

"No more Pope?"

Lizzie doesn't answer. "How's Macy?"

"Good," Wade says.

She raises and eyebrow. "Intriguing."

Wade laughs, flicking her on the arm. "What's that supposed to mean?"

"Ow!" Lizzie says. Her body is tingling. "Yeah, she was kind of all up in your grill and peeing on you at the wedding!"

"She can be a bit clingy," he admits. "But I think you make her nervous."

"Tell her to get a spine," she yells, punching him lightly back. *I wonder if he is nervous*, she thinks.

"Have you always been this loud?"

Lizzie remembers how Wade used to say she made him hard of hearing from cackling so loudly in his ear while resting her head on his shoulder. She loved cuddling with him, being the inside of the spoon.

When they arrive at 75 Chestnut, Wade opens the door for Lizzie. She strolls over to the end stools at the bar, closest to the window. "Shall we sit in our old spots?"

"I don't know. I kind of have P.T.S.D. from those."

Lizzie shushes him with her index finger. "Oh, are we going to talk about that? Because it seems to be your favorite topic."

"Forget it," Wade says.

Lizzie knows what he's referring to: The last few times that she and Wade saw each other, aside from Hadley's wedding, it always ended the same way—with her sobbing after picking at the scab of their relationship, prodding him as to why it ended.

"And as an FYI, these stools? I did *NOT* walk away," she affirms. "*You* went home and left me here, if you recall."

"I'm not talking about that night, Lizzie. I mean, in general." He shakes his head. "Whatever, it's water under the bridge, now."

"Is it?" she asks, taking a seat.

Lizzie feels her throat close as her eyes well up. *I am such an idiot,* she thinks. *Why did I think this was a good idea? I always do this—come back for more? But it's my fault. I know, I know...I have to hold it together, or he will never agree to see me again.*

"Oh, Lizzie. I will always love you," Wade says, rubbing her back gently. "I don't want to see you cry."

She wipes the tear from her cheek and tries to focus on the blurry drink menu. She looks up at him. "Love me *most?*" she asks. That's what he always used to say: He loved her *most.*

She was the most important to him. He chose her.

"Let's order drinks," he says, motioning to the bartender. "What are you having?"

He didn't say he loved me most. Lizzie wonders if it's too late. Maybe she's lost him.

"A Painkiller," she jokes.

"Let's make that two."

NOVEMBER

Chapter 19

HADLEY

Hadley is busy organizing. *Perhaps, if I build an appropriate nest, the baby will come next,* she thinks. Maybe do it in reverse: nest before baby? *That's an idea.*

She sets aside the morning to get her desk work in order. First things first: change all passwords (not that she can remember half of them anyway). She makes a list of each of her accounts on her new monogrammed stationery. There are far too many. Next, she prints labels for her shelves with her label maker.

After nearly three hours, Hadley checks this off her to-do list and prepares lunch: Greek salad with grilled chicken and a side of marinated olives from EuroMart. Jack is at work, so she just makes lunch for herself. For dinner, however, she will prepare a more lavish meal for the two of them, comprised of pork loin, mashed potatoes, and artichokes. For dessert, she will serve Key lime pie.

Now November, the days are shorter, and the temperature has dropped. It's time to prepare for holiday festivities and decorations. Currently, her front walkway is decorated with pumpkins and gourds of all shapes, colors, and sizes, as well as bales of hay, mums, and fall planters. Thanksgiving is one of her favorite holidays, but Christmas ranks the highest. Will she have an all-silver tree with white lights and hydrangeas this year? Or perhaps she should go with a metallic theme, comprised of Christopher Radko ornaments and colored lights. She calls her mother to discuss.

"Hello?" Constance answers.

"Hi, it's me."

"Oh! Hadley, darling! How are you?" she sings.

"I'm fine, just planning for Christmas and wondering if you had any thoughts on my tree decor." Constance is known for her exquisite taste, and in particular holiday décor. Her house on Juniper Lane is famous for its memorable, sixteen-foot, illuminated tree in the upstairs window and the manger scene on the expansive front lawn. Constance is a devout Catholic and doesn't miss a Sunday church service, so it is only right that her manger scene impresses. Hadley remembers the rotten New Year's Day after some neighborhood kids stole Constance's baby Jesus from the manger. It was later found smashed into pieces in front of a gas station. Now, Constance keeps a security camera in the manger and a lock on the baby Jesus.

"Well, sweetheart, I am sure I have *lots* of thoughts, but given that's it's right near Halloween, I wonder why on Earth you are considering this now. Do you have too much time on your hands?"

"No," Hadley defends. "I just want to be prepared, and if I must order anything in advance, then I want to get a head start. You know how busy it gets around the holidays, with mail delays and all."

"Well, honey, how about a baby-themed tree? Hm?" Constance giggles. "I have some little items we can put under there!"

Hadley's heart sinks. Everything with her mother seems to be about the *non-baby*, the baby that can't come-to-be. And how can she suggest a baby tree? Is she seriously that blind?

"Just as like keepsakes for later, if not sooner! How are things going with *all that?*"

All that, Hadley thinks. *All that?* It's a lot heavier than the rather dismissive "all that." *All that* has been basal temp and menstrual cycle monitoring, prenatal vitamins, and acupuncture. *All that* has been meditation and deep breathing exercises. *All that* has been countless books and blogs on pregnancy and loss. *All that* is a combination of deep hope and dark despair.

"Fine," she says.

"Just fine?"

"What do you want to hear, Mom? Nothing is happening! I am barren! I am sad and rotten inside! Is that better?" she cries.

"Oh, Hadley, honey. No, of course not. I'm sorry to have bothered you."

"Are you though? Because it doesn't feel like it. Why are you suggesting a baby-themed tree when all I want to do, more than anything in the world, is to have a baby, and I can't! Since you know this, that suggestion seems rather hostile. Don't you think?"

Hadley hears her father grumbling in the background. Constance whispers to him. "Now, darling, I certainly didn't mean to upset you."

"Well, you did. And now I have to go." Hadley hangs up the phone and turns it on silent as Constance tries to ring back. Hadley knows she will leave an undoubtedly sycophantic message. She's not going to call her back. She can let it fester and attend to her father. That's what she taught Hadley growing up: women should please a man and not ruffle feathers. Men don't like waves on a boat, she'd say. *Be pleasant, calm, and attentive; pretty, smart, and nice.* When your man gets home from work, have a cold drink ready for him at the door and be sure to listen to him about his day; he doesn't care to hear about yours. Make light conversation, wear makeup, and keep the house tidy.

These are all the lessons she bestowed. But these traditions didn't bode so well for Hadley when she was in college or on the dating scene in Boston. She either seemed cuckoo or overeager, neither of which were attractive.

. . .

14 YEARS AGO

Hadley, Maeve, and Lizzie just graduated from Boston College. They were hanging out in Hadley's Beacon Hill apartment before heading to the bars for the night.

"Are you serious with those Beanie Babies on your mantle?" Lizzie asked, tossing them to the side. "You can't bring guys back here with them."

"What's wrong with Beanie Babies? They're cute."

Maeve took a swig of her Corona. "They are not cute. They are sophomoric and dorky."

Hadley frowned. Her apartment was decorated as if she were still in high school, complete with Disney memorabilia, cat posters, and a Laura Ashley floral dust ruffle. "This place is like a dick shrinker."

Hadley chuckled as she curled her hair in the mirror. "Are we going to Sonsie tonight or Eastern Standard?"

"Eastern Standard has cuter guys."

Hadley worked during the day in an entry level position in direct mail marketing at Kessler Financial Services on Boylston Street. Maeve was a reporter for the *Beacon Hill Times*, and Lizzie had just passed her real estate exam. They spent their days at work and their evenings out at bars and trolling for prospects.

"I just think you need to fix your game," Lizzie explained to Hadley. "It rings a little despo."

Hadley grimaced. "I am not desperate! I just had a recent break up with Jack!" She coated her bouncy party curls with hairspray and applied pink lipstick, which left a bright ring around the top of her beer bottle. "And I'm not taking dating advice from you, Lizzie."

Lizzie shrugged in agreement. "Probably a good idea."

Maeve moved about the room, tossing dance trophies, a Cabbage Patch doll, and anything Disney into a bag. She then hid it in the back of Hadley's closet. "Okay, I think we are good here now," she said. "My work is done. Just try to be more New England and less Southern Belle. Make sense? Dorothy, we are no longer in Kansas anymore."

"I'm from Virginia," Hadley huffed. "So go fuck yourself."

"Better!" Maeve shouted. "Now you're in Boston!"

"You can go fuck yourself, too."

. . .

PRESENT DAY

But Hadley doesn't like the New England way; she never has. And now, at thirty-five and married, she will do it her way. She wants to maintain the Southern Belle traditions and a hopeful, less cynical nature. So what if she is accused of being unambitious, arcane, or pathetic? She knows who she is, and she is confident in that. And guess what? Jack loves her for that, *so there.*

Hadley walks upstairs to her bedroom and sits on the loveseat. Snickers jumps into her lap. He purrs as she rubs her two fingers in between his furry ears. *Little Snickers, my first and maybe last baby.* She contemplates more projects as he looks about the room: color coordinate the closet; make labels for Jack's shirts (weekend shirts, golf shirts, work shirts); create a list of items to sell on Hingham Yard Sale (old golf clubs and tennis rackets) and sort the printed photos for framing. It is going to be a busy week, just as long as she keeps moving. *A rolling stone gathers no moss... Stay busy. Don't stop.*

Chapter 20
MAEVE

On Maeve and Sam's wedding anniversary, November 3rd, she and Brutus are making a cake. Well, to be fair, Maeve is baking, and Brutus is panting at her feet and licking drips of frosting that fall to the floor. She has made this same carrot cake—Sam's favorite—since their first anniversary, when they celebrated together in their new home. Now that he's passed, she still bakes the cake but enjoys it alone with a framed photo of Sam and Brutus by her side.

Sometimes, Maeve talks to Sam, asks for his help, or for a sign from him that she's doing things right. The sign can be anything from finding a white piece of sea glass (her angel is watching) to a strong gust of wind on the beach just as she whispers his name. He is always with her, inside her heart and at the forefront of her thoughts. She wants to keep it that way. That's why she has no room for dating. Should she move on with someone else, she worries she will forget him, or that he will be upset, frowning down upon her from heaven, disappointed. After all, his death was sudden, so she never had that conversation that spouses get to have about moving on when they know they're going to pass. She was never granted permission, and it doesn't seem fair to ask.

Since the weekend on the Cape, Maeve is conflicted about her feelings for Pope. Like, what even are they? Are they feelings or just lust? Her dirty dream, their conversations by the fire, and his diminished relationship with Lizzie have muddled things. *I mean, I don't like him, right?* First of all, he stole her job. Secondly, he talks too much and too loudly all day. Third... what is third? She can't recall, but she knows there is a third reason, if not more.

Speaking of Lizzie, she called Lizzie this week to check in. She pulled her best wing woman attempt that evening on the Cape, and she never got a thank you. Perhaps Lizzie was too drunk to remember Maeve dragging her dead weight into bed while she was extoling her undying love for Wade.

Maeve places the cake in the oven and sets the timer for fifty minutes. She goes into the dining room and lights some candles. Her favorite is the cucumber mint one she made in a soy candle-making class at the Hingham Historical Society. She wonders if she should sign up for another class over the winter, like maybe floral arrangements or wreathmaking. Then she thinks about Hadley, who always has the best wreaths at Christmas. She decides to give her a call.

"Hey there," Maeve says. "What are you up to?"

"Oh, my god. I am just drowning in tasks and up to my ears in holiday nonsense. But I'm glad you called because I'm thinking of hosting a friendsgiving this year! Would you come?"

"Sure, but you're not going to your mom's? You always do."

Hadley sighs heavily. "Let's just say I put Constance on pause."

"Okay..." Maeve chuckles. "Should I ask?"

"No."

Raised by her grandparents, Maeve doesn't know what it feels like to have a "mom," per se. She never met her father, and her mother was killed in a car accident when she was a baby. She has no memories of her, just some photos her grandma shared. She shares her mother's dark curly hair and small ears. She always wanted a sibling, but her friendships with Hadley and Lizzie fill that void.

"Gotcha. Well, send me the details for the party."

"Okay. What are you up to?"

"Well, today is my wedding anniversary, so I'm baking a cake and celebrating."

Hadley is quiet. "With whom?"

"Sam!"

"No, I mean, who are you celebrating with?"

"Oh, sorry. Just me and Brutus."

"Do you want company? I feel bad you're there alone. Are you okay?" Hadley asks. "Yeah, I'm fine," *Not really, I'm lonely and depressed.*

"What year is it again?"

"It's our eighth anniversary," Maeve says.

"What is that? Copper?"

"Bronze."

"Aw...I'm sorry, honey. Do you want to come here? We can have the cake together!"

"Thanks, but I'm good. I need to get to bed early because we have a long day at work tomorrow."

"K. Wait, has Pope said anything to you about the Cape weekend and how things are going with Lizzie? I feel so bad for him."

"He hasn't mentioned it yet, and I feel weird asking. I called Lizzie to see how things went with her Wade meet-up. Did you talk to her?"

"No, but Pope spoke to Jack, and apparently he is *not* happy."

Maeve's heart jumps. "Really? He said that?"

"Yes. I think he's over it...over her, I mean."

"Oh, I feel bad," Maeve says, despite her sudden mood elevation.

"Don't. She did it to herself," Hadley says. "She self-sabotages! I swear. First, she divorces Hank, now she offends Pope, and all for Wade, who is *factually* dating my cousin! It's ridiculous."

"Does Macy know?"

"No, and I'm not planning on telling her. She'd be really upset. She's like planning their engagement."

"This is not good," Maeve says. "Lizzie needs an intervention."

"She really does."

"Well, send me the details about Friendsgiving, and I'll talk to you soon."

"Sounds good," Hadley says.

"Thanks. Love you."

"Love you, too."

When Maeve hangs up the phone, she does a little dance around the room without even realizing it. Brutus barks and stands on his hind legs, joining her. She grabs his two front paws and circles around with him, singing, before breaking down in laughter when she sees her reflection in the mirror.

"Oh, Brutus." Maeve laughs. "What are we doing?!"

She exhales and plops down on the sofa. Brutus jumps up and lies on her feet. His golden coat is warm on her toes, like a blanket. She closes her eyes and thinks about Pope and Lizzie, and then about her and Pope, about her dream. *No*, she tells herself. She slaps her hand against her forehead. *Stop it.* But she's giddy. She can't stop. She smiles and feels hopeful, excited. *What a turn of events.*

Then her oven timer goes off.

BZZZZZZ!

Is this a sign? It's Sam. He doesn't want me to forget him.

She jumps up and takes the cake from the oven, then sets it down to cool. A mixture of spice and carrot emanates in the air.

"Don't worry, Sam," she whispers. "I was just being silly." She takes off her oven mitts. "Happy Anniversary, baby. Miss you."

. . .

The vibe is off at work the next day. Maeve senses something ominous when she sees her landline blinking. It's marked urgent, and from Rick.

RICK: *Uh, hey, Maeve, give me a shout when you get in. It's important. Thanks.*

Maeve's stomach flips. She hates messages like this from Rick. It means the rest of the day will be shit because he's in a piss mood. There's a joke in the office that Rick's moods dictate how the day will unfold. If Rick's happy, everyone in the office is happy; if Rick is angry, everyone pays. Rick's assistant, Audrey, even has a flip calendar at the edge of her desk with different faces and emotions: frustrated, curious, elated, belligerent... Unbeknownst to Rick, she flips the calendar to the appropriate emotion daily, so everyone knows what to expect. It's an inside office joke. The other one is that when Rick is on the floor, or gets back from an offsite meeting, Audrey will send an instant message to all: "The eagle has landed." This means *shut the hell up, look busy, and steer clear of water bubbler convos.*

Maeve hangs up the phone and heads directly to Rick's office. Audrey is seated out front, and her desk calendar is set to "cantankerous." *Great,* she thinks. *Buckle up.*

"Hey, Audrey," Maeve says. "Is he in?" She rolls her eyes.

Audrey chuckles softly. For fifty-five, she appears closer to thirty-five. Her hair is in a topknot, and she has on bright red lipstick and a scarf draped over her shoulders.

"Yep. Just waiting on Pope," Audrey says.

Pope walks up behind her. He smells fresh, like he just showered. He sighs. "Hey."

"Do you know what this is about?" Maeve whispers. "Are we in trouble?" She wonders if she has coffee breath. Maybe she should have eaten a mint.

"You both can go in," Audrey says.

When they walk inside, they sit down in the two chairs facing Rick's desk. His desk is extremely long, like he's at King Arthur's table. It's too big for him physically, but it matches his magnanimous ego. He's reading the newspaper and removes his glasses when he sees them.

"What happened with the Royal Lobster account?" he asks sternly.

"I don't know what you mean," Maeve says.

Pope interjects. "There was a miscommunication."

"Nobody showed up at the opening. It was a disaster!" Rick shouts.

Maeve attempts to catch up. She's not sure what Rick is referring to. She and Pope organized the Royal Lobster grand opening in Downtown Crossing, and it went off without a hitch. *Didn't it?* Sure, there were not as many reporters as they had hoped, but why would *The Globe* care about the opening of a Royal Lobster when there are more important things to cover, like the mayor's new housing policy or the homeless tents on Mass Ave? Sometimes she really questions the significance of her job. Today is one of those days.

"Well, to be fair—" Maeve says.

Rick cuts her off and puts his hand up in the air like a stop sign. "There is no fair here, Maeve," he says. "There is success and failure, and this was an absolute failure. It was worse than failure. It was epic flop! On both your parts," he chides. "You had months to plan this and ensure there would be press coverage, and there isn't one damn piece about it in *The Globe*, the *Herald*, on Boston.com, *nothing*. Larry is furious." Larry is the CEO of Royal Lobster, a cherubic man whose face is red, like a lobster. He's got that salty dog drinker face and a bulbous purple nose, like he's had too much gin.

"We can fix this," Pope says. "I was already on some calls this morning with the *Herald*, and I pitched a story idea with a different hook."

"Too late," Rick says. "They dropped us. We lost the account."

Maeve is shocked. "What? That's ridiculous! One mishap, and they drop us?"

"It's tough out there, and there's no room for mistakes," Rick says. "Listen, I have a ten o'clock, so let's unpack this later. Have Audrey set up some time for us to regroup later in the day and see what you can do to salvage it, if anything."

"Thanks, Rick," Pope says. "Will do."

"On it," Maeve says.

Maeve and Pope exit Rick's office and head back to their desks.

"Well, this sucks," Maeve says.

Pope doesn't reply.

"You okay?"

"Umm... let me see," Pope says. "Am I okay?" He pauses. "No. In fact, no, I am not okay."

Maeve stops walking and reaches for his arm. He moves it aside.

"I don't feel like talking about it right now," he says. "But I am disappointed that you didn't reach out to Jackson Wright at the *Globe* about the opening."

"What do you mean? I did!" Maeve retorts. *Disappointed. She hates that word.* She wracks her brain, trying to recall if she did in fact reach out to him. Jackson Wright is the food reporter at *The Boston Globe*, who covers all the important restaurant openings.

"Are you sure? Because I just got off a call with him this morning, and he had no recollection of speaking with you."

"I mean, I think I did? I will go through my emails and—"

"Forget it, Maeve," he says. "We must triage here. We don't have time for you to be surfing through your emails."

This stings. Now Pope is in "boss mode" and blaming her? "Well, what can I do to help?"

He huffs. "I'm not sure yet. Let's circle back later this morning. I have a lot on my plate."

"I'm sorry," Maeve says.

"Yep," Pope replies. He hustles to his desk, leaving her behind.

She feels embarrassed, belittled, and upset. She knows she is good at her job. *Right?* She starts to wonder. Maybe there's a reason she wasn't promoted and had to share the job with Pope. She can't handle it herself. Maybe she did fuck this opening up. Maybe she doesn't deserve a raise.

Shame and doubt course through her veins. *I don't deserve to be here*, she thinks. She is mortified. Not only is Rick mad at her, but Pope is as well. She desperately wants to engage with him, to talk it through, but she knows she should just return to her office and hold her head high. *Don't act like a dumb crybaby*, she thinks. But she can't help herself. She scurries off to the bathroom, locks the stall, and sobs.

Chapter 21
LIZZIE

It's been a week since Lizzie saw Wade, and she can't get her mind off him. She felt all the feels, like the connection is still there. Sure, after they got settled, Wade didn't want to talk about their relationship, past or present, but she senses that things with Macy are on the downslope, despite what Hadley tells her. She stifles a laugh at her desk, thinking about when Wade tossed a half-eaten olive from his martini at her, and it accidentally landed in another lady's drink at the bar.

"What is that shit-eating grin on your face?" Brandon asks. He's slurping on a green juice from The Daily Press. "Did you get laid last night? Did Pope forgive your meltdown on the Cape?"

"No, I'm just thinking about Wade."

"So, who is it going to be? Pope or Wade? I feel like we are on *The Bachelor*. Who will get your final rose, Lizzie?"

She scrunches her nose. "I mean... I kind of feel like we are done with Pope," Lizzie says.

Brandon frowns. "Really? I like him for you though! *For us!*"

Lizzie laughs. "I know you think this is about *you*, but I'm the one who is actually dating him."

"Lame," Brandon whines. "Fine. But I don't support this Wade thing. I think that ship has sailed. The horse has left the barn, sweetie."

"Don't say that," Lizzie says. "Am I a barn animal in this scenario? I already feel chubs."

"Well, I was going to call you Miss Piggy, but that's more about your sex drive than it is about your figure."

"Shut up!" Lizzie shouts, tossing her mechanical pencil in his direction.

Brandon weaves and bobs his head, dodging like a boxer.

"I have not even had sex with him! Remember?" *And I'm not sure that whole respect thing isn't bullshit. Maybe he never wanted to have sex with me.*

"Yes! How can I forget? How can *anyone?* You shouted at him about it for an entire night!"

"*As if* you even remember. You were legit passed out in your own spittle on the karaoke machine."

"Truth." Brandon laughs. "Well, so are you going to dump him? I feel bad, but I can't say he doesn't see it coming. In fact, I'm surprised he hasn't dumped your ass first after your shenanigans with Wade."

"Well, truth be told, I haven't heard much from him," Lizzie replies. "Maybe he *did* break up with me, and I just don't know it."

Lizzie checks her phone. There are no messages. *Is Pope done with me? Maybe there is no need for a conversation?* No. She can't do that, because she will inevitably see him again at Hadley's Friendsgiving or at one of Maeve's work events. Better to tie it up with a bow and be an adult, than to leave it messy and unfinished. She decides to text him.

LIZZIE: *Hey, long time, no see! Any chance we can get together and talk?*

She waits for a reply, but it doesn't come for another hour—a painfully long hour.

POPE: *Sure. What works for you?*

LIZZIE: *I can come to you. I'll take the ferry in. Want to meet at Davio's at the Seaport? Tomorrow around 6?*

POPE: *Sounds good. See you then.*

Hm. Very blustery and cold, Lizzie thinks. She sets the phone down and peers at Brandon through her office wall window.

"We are meeting tomorrow," she shouts.

"You and Pope?

"Yep."

"Should I hide?"

Lizzie giggles, even though she feels bad for hurting Pope's feelings. It wasn't wholly intentional. She just wants to win Wade back. "Wish me luck."

· · ·

When Lizzie arrives at Davio's, Pope is already seated at the bar. He looks disheveled, with a several-day-old beard and one side of his shirt collar tucked into his sweater. He has a dirty martini and a *Boston Herald* in front of him.

"Hey," she says, resting her hand on his shoulder.

He turns to her with his steely eyes. "Hey."

"Are you okay? You look like you've had a day."

"I have had *a week*," he says. "Things at work are gutting me, and we lost a major account."

"Oh no! Which one?"

"Royal Lobster," Pope says. "So, you haven't spoken to Maeve, I guess?"

"No, what's up? Is she okay?"

"Yeah. I don't know. It's been rough is all I'll say."

Lizzie sits down next to him and orders a Bombay Sapphire and soda with three lemons, minus the carcass. She learned this order from Dorit on an episode of *Real Housewives of Beverly Hills.*

"So!" She smiles, lifting her glass in the air. "Cheers?"

"What are we cheering to?" he asks.

"To a shit week?"

"To a shit week," he says.

They clink glasses.

"Well, I wanted to meet because—"

Pope stops her. "It's okay, Lizzie. You don't have to say it. I already know why we're here."

She winces. "You do?"

"It's not working," he says. "I see that."

"I'm so sorry." She frowns, reaching for him.

"Don't be sorry. I should have known, since when I met you, I was a decoy for the guy you still had feelings for."

"Oh stop," she says. "I had feelings for you, too!" *Not really.*

Pope smirks. "*Had.*"

"*Have,*" she replies. "No, I don't know. It's complicated. I just think we are better friends." Her skin is tingling, and her face feels like someone lit a fire under it.

"It's not that complicated," he says. "You're not over Wade. You said as much to me, if you recall."

She sighs and places her hand on her forehead. "I know. I'm sorry. I'm a terrible person. I feel bad."

"You're not a terrible person, Lizzie. But you're not in a place to be my girlfriend."

Lizzie shudders. "Aw, you just called me your girlfriend!" She grabs his hand, wondering if she's making a mistake. *Why am I dumping this amazing man who respects me and calls me his girlfriend? What is wrong with me?*

"Well, not exactly," he says. "But, yeah, I was into you."

"*Was?*"

"Lizzie, you and I both know this is over," Pope says. "We gave it a whirl. Just wasn't meant to be."

"I thought I was the one who called this meeting!" She laughs uncomfortably. "That's what I was going to say!"

"Made it easy for you," he replies.

"Thank you for understanding, Pope. I never deserved you."

He chuckles. "Nope, you never did."

Deep down, Lizzie wonders: Is she undeserving of love?

. . .

Now that she's no longer dating Pope, Lizzie fills her free time with tennis and friends. On Friday, she meets them at the country club for a boozy girls' lunch. It's a monthly tradition to meet up before the kids get home from school to catch up, drink four-finger goblets of wine, and share a Bang Bang cauliflower platter. The sun filters through the floor-to-ceiling windows, casting delicate shadows over the pristine white tablecloths. The room smells faintly of fresh-cut lilies and grass. The waitstaff, dressed in crisp black-and-white uniforms, moves with efficiency.

"Honestly, it's exhausting." Catherine sighs, dabbing the corner of her mouth with a napkin. Her blond bob is sharp and edgy, like her sparkly diamond earrings. "Between the education foundation gala and that insufferable town hall meeting about the new high school track, I haven't had a hot minute to myself."

"I skipped the town meeting. If I have to listen to one more person drone on about too much homework in the middle school, I might scream. I'd rather they do homework than zone out on TikTok," Paisley says.

Lizzie rolls her eyes. "Agree. I'd rather just read about it on Hingham Hub."

Catherine smirks. "Well, I think it's important to show up and vote. Also, you missed quite the spectacle. Diane Pembroke had a full-blown meltdown about the yacht berths. Something about 'preserving the integrity of the shoreline.' It was like watching a soap opera but with more Botox and less self-awareness."

"Oh, boy," Lizzie says, shaking her head.

The waiter arrives with their Bog salads—delicately arranged plates of organic greens, cranberries, a sprinkling of goat cheese, and almonds.

"I don't know why I always order salad. I leave starving," Paisley says. "Should we get fries, also?"

"That's the point," Jill says, tightening her silk scarf tied with surgical precision. "We eat salads, and the rest of the calories are in the wine." They laugh.

"So, what else is happening?" Lizzie asks, chomping on a bed of arugula.

"Oh! I ran into Elise Harper at mahjong last week," Catherine says. "She looked...tense."

Maddy grins. "Oh, I'm sure. You know her husband's new 'assistant' just moved into their guest house? She's about twelve and a half and somehow manages to make Lululemon look like lingerie."

"Poor Elise," Catherine says. "Though, really, she should have seen this coming. David was never the 'grow old together' type. He's the 'trade you in at forty-five for an upgrade' type."

"He's hardly the only one doing that," Paisley murmurs, slicing through a piece of lettuce. "I feel like half the men in Hollywood swap their wives for someone who argues that being an influencer is actually a career."

Jill reaches for the wine and pours herself a five-finger pour. Paisley gives her a look. "What?! Paul told me to take an Uber," she says defensively. "I think I can only have two, because Tommy has soccer practice at five, and Lily has a birthday party at Starland."

"Well, I think that's about four, so you're good." Lizzie laughs. "But you look adorable. Where did you get that scarf?"

"That new store on Centre Street," Jill says.

Maddy frowns. "Oh, I was just in there and didn't see those."

"I don't go in, because I know I'm going to spend my entire allowance," Catherine says.

Lizzie almost chokes on her ice. "You have an allowance? Are you fourteen?"

"Shut up! Chris gives me an allowance for clothes each week, so I don't max out our credit cards. It's only a thousand."

Lizzie's mouth drops. "Seriously? That's a lot!"

"Well, what do you spend on clothes in a week?" Catherine asks.

"Um, sometimes nothing? Sometimes more! I don't know. But I sure as hell don't have a budget just for clothes." *No wonder she always looks like a million bucks. Well, now we know it's more like a thousand bucks. A week.*

"I didn't see you at Tavern Night, Lizzie," Catherine chides. "It was legit the largest fundraiser the Hingham Historical Society has ever had. We sold 400 tickets!"

"That's awesome," Lizzie says. "Sorry I missed. I had to go into the city."

Catherine leans in. "To have a sexy dinner with that guy? Pope?"

"Actually, no. To end things. It wasn't very sexy."

She frowns. "Wait, what? What happened? We were so excited about that."

Lizzie can't believe her dating life is so enthralling to her married friends. They tell her they want to live vicariously through her, but she knows this is not, in fact, true. Who would want to be a divorced, single mom and back on the dating scene? She knows not one of these women would trade their marriages to be on Hinge or Bumble.

"I just wasn't feeling it," Lizzie says. She is not going to mention Wade.

The server arrives with two orders of Brussels sprouts, crab cakes, and fries.

"Too bad," Paisley says, reaching for a fry. "Who else do we know for her, guys?" She looks around the table as the women brainstorm.

"What about Greg Simons? He's single," Paisley says.

Lizzie puts down her salad fork and covers her mouth with her hand while she chews. "I mean, am I ugly and I don't know it?" *Why do they insist on setting me up with these dorks?* "Thanks, but no thanks."

"He's adorable! And if you give him a chance, he grows on you."

"I'm not interested in dating moss," Lizzie balks.

The manager brings over a final round: two skinny margaritas, a pear martini, and two glasses of pinot grigio. The women grow louder.

"Oh, my god, we are going to need a nap," Maddy says.

"TGIF!"

. . .

When Lizzie leaves lunch, she wonders why the ladies are always trying to set her up—and with losers. Maybe they pity her. Maybe she should take a closer look at herself. Is she delusional? An emptiness washes over her. She never feels this way after leaving a lunch with Maeve and Hadley. No matter how much of a hot mess she is, Lizzie knows they see her worth.

Chapter 22

HADLEY

Hadley pulls the packing tape off the box titled "bedroom" and tosses it onto the floor. "Ooh, I wonder what kinky things I'll find in here." She smirks. She's helping Macy unpack Wade's boxes in her Beacon Hill apartment—the apartment that was once *hers* is now *theirs*. The sound of cars honking and construction drilling permeates.

Macy raises an eyebrow. "Wade may enjoy a toy or two—and maybe some handcuffs!" She giggles, then hovers over the box. "Actually, wait, let me see that first..."

"You must be so excited. This is the start of your next chapter together!" Hadley coos. "I remember when Jack and I got our first apartment together. We went to Crate and Barrel for kitchenware and argued over whether to get an electric juicer or a toaster oven!"

"Who won?"

"Jack, of course," Hadley says. "Margaritas with fresh lime juice trumped a toaster roasted chicken. So, would you like a toaster oven for a housewarming gift?"

"You don't need to get me a gift," Macy says. She is meticulously folding Wade's silk underwear into thirds and stacking them in his top dresser drawer.

"Stop. A toaster oven it is!"

As Hadley walks around the apartment, she can't help but think of Lizzie. It seems like just yesterday that she helped Lizzie unpack her and Wade's apartment in Brookline. She always loved those green sponge-painted walls of theirs. Hadley wonders how she can break the news to Lizzie that Wade and Macy have moved in together, and if she should tell her about it before they get together at Friendsgiving. She doesn't want to ruin her party, but she can't shock Lizzie with another Wade surprise.

"You guys are coming to Friendsgiving, right?" Hadley asks. She grabs a box of Wade's shirts and arranges them by color. "Do you have a label maker?"

Macy grimaces. "For what?"

"Oh, just thinking it would be nice if you could label his shirts in the closet for him, like 'weekend shirts,' 'work shirts,' 'golf shirts?'"

"Have you lost your mind?! I think Wade can figure out on his own which is a weekend shirt without me having to label it. That's psycho!"

Hadley laughs. "Wait, is it? I do that for Jack!"

"That's next level. And yes, we are coming to Friendsgiving." She hesitates for a moment. "Will Lizzie and Pope be there?"

Hadley considers her response. "Yes. They will both be there... but not together." Her skin starts to itch.

"They broke up?"

"Yep. Lizzie can't seem to get out of her own way." She shrugs. "It's too bad because Pope is a great guy." Hadley starts in on another box marked "bathroom."

"Well, I can't say I'm surprised. I know she's been texting Wade." Macy rolls her eyes.

"Really?"

"Yeah, I guess she was in town for some conference, and they met up? Wade, *of course*, told me about it."

Hadley carries the toiletries to the bathroom and begins to line the medicine cabinet: Pepto Bismol, Advil, deodorant, face cream, Neosporin. "I'm sure it was nothing," she says, sticking her head out the bathroom door, holding a bottle of lubricant up to Macy. "More importantly, do you want this lube in the medicine cabinet or next to the bed?" She tosses it.

"Oh, my god!" Macy shrieks, tucking the lube in her nightstand. "And I know it was *nothing* for Wade," she continues. "I'm just not so sure about Lizzie." Macy's emphatic reply suggests that she's over-compensating, so Hadley changes the subject.

. . .

An hour later, Hadley drives home to Hingham to surprise Jack in the shipyard when he gets off the commuter boat. He is often a little buzzed when he takes the boat home, especially on Fridays, as the younger crowd gets rowdy drinking beers. Hadley's been abstaining from alcohol, so she can ready her body for the pregnancy. She hasn't officially started trying again, but she is never *not* trying. Every time she and Jack have sex, she lays in bed after with her legs up in bicycle position for a solid twenty minutes to help the sperm swim upstream faster. She also meditates. It seems like everywhere she looks there are babies: the library, Nona's, the Barrel. Hadley won't be able to take it much longer before she has a complete meltdown.

"Hey!" Hadley shouts, as Jack walks down the dock. "I came to surprise you!"

Jack spots her and smiles. "Well, this is a nice surprise." They kiss. "To what do I owe this honor?"

"No reason, I just missed you."

"Aw, I missed you too, baby."

"I kind of feel like going out," Hadley says. "Or we can just join your ferry mates at Ocean Kai." She sneers, rolling her eyes.

"How do you know about that?"

"The Ocean Kai trick? Where y'all pretend you got a later boat to hide from your wives and tie one on before going home?"

Jack chuckles.

"Yeah, we know all about it. You guys think you're being so smooth."

"Man, I thought we had one over on you girls."

Hadley never minds when Jack refers to her and her friends as "girls," being from the South, but Maeve and Lizzie think otherwise. "*We're not girls, we're women,*" they balk. But Hadley thinks it's endearing to be called a "girl." It's more romantic, like he still sees her as a young, blooming flower.

Jack and Hadley agree to get wine and oysters at Alma Nove and sit at the bar. There is a middle-aged couple seated to their left. They are both scrolling on their phones and not talking, except to engage in conversation about their kids' sports schedules: soccer Saturday, lacrosse and field hockey Sunday, flag football Monday, and volleyball Tuesday.

"Remind me when we have kids to talk about something other than their sports," Hadley whispers.

"Seriously," Jack says. "So, what's the plan for Friendsgiving? Do you think Pope and Lizzie can be in the same room without it being awkward?"

"I think so. I mean, we can't worry about the mix. We're just going to invite whomever we want, and people can put on their big-girl panties and suck it up."

Jack pours some mignonette sauce on his oyster with a tiny spoon, lifts the shell to his lips, and slides the oyster down his throat like a sled. "These are amazing," he says. "I love the tiny ones from Duxbury. They're firm, and you can taste the brine."

"Yeah, the huge ones are gross. I can't look at them," she says, scrunching up her nose. "They look like snot."

"Just swallow and don't look. You're good at that!"

Hadley squeals. "Shut up! Oh, my god, you're terrible," she says. But she secretly loves being "a lady in the streets, and a freak in the sheets." *Don't all men want that*, she thinks?

The bartender pours Hadley a second glass of rosé. She reaches for the blushing pink wine by the glass's stem, between her thumb and two fingers, to take a sip. Hadley is about to make a toast when she feels a tap on her shoulder.

"Hadley!" Amanda shrieks, coming in for a hug. "So good to see you! I was just asking about you the other day at Blackbird Wellness. I haven't seen you in forever."

"Hi," Hadley says. "Amanda, this is my husband, Jack. Have you two met?"

Amanda beams. "I am sure we've seen each other somewhere along the way. My husband is BJ, but people like to call him Bogey?"

Jack nods. "Ah, maybe we've met?"

"So, what's new?" Hadley asks. "You look radiant! New skincare routine?"

Amanda looks down and places her hand on her belly. "Well, I have been waiting to announce it, but... I'm pregnant! Fourteen weeks today!"

Hadley is suddenly on the peak of a roller coaster, racing downhill. Her stomach drops to the floor.

"Oh, my gosh! Congratulations!" Her face turns the shade of pink wine.

Jack looks nervous. "Great news, congrats!"

"Thanks." Amanda grins. "I mean, we weren't *planning* on having a third. We weren't even trying! But sometimes, God has another plan for us in His mind."

"That's wonderful," Hadley says. "I'm happy for you and Bogey. Great to see you." *Now can you leave*, she thinks?

"You, too," Amanda says. "I'll let you get back to your fun. This pregnant bus has to go home! I'm exhausted!"

Hadley nods uncomfortably.

"But we must have lunch soon. I'll text Lizzie about it."

"Sounds good," Hadley says. She turns around quickly, facing the bar, and gulps her rosé. It's difficult to swallow with the lump in her throat. Her eyes begin to pool. She wants to leave immediately. *Why does this always happen? Everyone else can get pregnant so seamlessly, and by accident, even. What the hell? This is so unfair.*

Jack puts his hand on the small of her back and rubs it in circles. "Are you okay?"

Hadley wants to scream and cry that, no, she's not okay, but she doesn't want to put a damper on the night. She will suck it up for Jack's sake, and for her own. She will survive this, and it will be okay. She must have hope. It will happen for her, too. *It has to.*

Chapter 23

MAEVE

Maeve has kept to herself at work since losing the Royal Lobster account. Between Lizzie dumping Pope, and Rick yelling at them for screwing up, she knows Pops is struggling. Lizzie, of course, texts Maeve umpteen times today to check in on Pope since the breakup, but Maeve always gives the same answer: *He seems fine; we haven't really talked.* To be honest, Maeve misses her conversations with Pope, and even his loud yapping on the phone. He's been quiet and reserved. She desperately wants to engage with him, but she doesn't want to pry.

Pope sneezes.

"God bless you!" Maeve shouts. This is the first thing she's said to him all day.

"Thank you."

Thirty minutes go by without another word.

Maeve pokes her head into his office. "Do you want to talk through the Citizen's account before we have our call?"

Pope stares at his computer. "I'm good."

Maeve returns to her desk. She waits a few minutes and can't stand it any longer. She sits in front of him. "Listen, I know you're 'good,' and 'fine,' and all that. But it doesn't seem like it. And I'm kind of worried about you. So can we talk candidly for a minute here?"

Pope stares at her blankly with his cornflower-blue eyes. He doesn't say anything.

Maeve continues. "Well, um, I know about you and Lizzie..."

"No," Pope says, holding up his hand, as in *stop*. "This has nothing to do with Lizzie."

"Huh?"

"I am fine about Lizzie. It's not like we were ever that serious. I just have some other stuff going on, and it really doesn't have much to do with you either, so I wouldn't worry about it."

She fidgets in her chair. "Well, I mean, I wasn't worried it was about *me*, per se. I am just worried about *you*."

"Well, don't be, okay? I said it's fine." He closes his eyes for a moment and rubs his temples. "Listen, I really have a lot to do here with the marketing plan to get back the Royal Lobster account. I have like six calls to make, a few unanswered emails, and Rick is up my ass about next steps." He leans into his work.

"Fine," Maeve huffs, getting up. "Sorry I cared!" She storms out of his office, her hands trembling, and heads for the bathroom.

Pope gets up to follow her. "Maeve," he calls out, but she keeps walking. "Maeve!" he says louder.

She turns around. "What is it?"

"What's going on with you? Why are you so upset?"

Maeve wonders this, too. Why is she so upset? Since when did she start caring about Pope's feelings?

She straightens out her skirt. "I don't know," Mave says, her voice cracking. "I guess... I just care if you're mad at me."

Pope relaxes his stance and softens. "Does this mean you kind of like me?"

"No," she says, narrowing her eyes.

He laughs. "As a friend, I mean! You've acted as though you've hated me since the day I started working here. And Lizzie told me you feel like I stole your job."

Maeve's stomach flutters. "What? She told you that?" *Fucking Lizzie. Why does she do this? So aggravating.*

Pope approaches her. "It's not a big deal," he says. "I get it."

"Well, I don't hate you," Maeve says, folding her arms across her chest. "I guess I feel like we are friends now, is all, so I was worried about you." She meets Pope's eyes, which have a slight twinkle.

"That's actually nice," he says. "I like that."

Is this weird, Maeve wonders. *I feel weird. But I am going to try to appear normal... We are at work, I don't understand what I am feeling, and I think I'll compartmentalize this.*

. . .

Later that day, as Maeve rides the train home, she thinks about when she met Sam and how she also hated him at first. They were in graduate school at Emerson. Sam was getting a master's in broadcast journalism, and she was studying for her master's in print. In J-school, there was a distinct divide between these two areas of study, because the print folks insisted that the broadcast reporters were merely talking heads and not real journalists. They were the pretty people, who just wanted to be on television. They weren't gritty, dark, news junkies, like the print folk. Maeve suspected Sam was just another bobble head, because he was very attractive, at 6'3", with blond hair, and a beaming grin.

Each weekday morning, the J-school students gathered in the auditorium for a current events quiz. With that in mind, Maeve had the *Boston Globe, Herald,* and *The Wall Street Journal* delivered to her dorm room. Before class, she scoured the headlines, local and national, memorizing them, aware that questions about both would appear on the quiz. The Metro section, which included things like house fires, murders, and policy, couldn't be ignored. These stories were their local beats as reporters. Sam often arrived late to the quiz, harried, like he'd just rolled out of bed. Maeve, on the other hand, was showered, primped, and early for class. On one particular morning, Sam heaved himself into the desk next to Maeve right before the quiz. This is the first time they spoke.

"Did they hand the quiz out yet?" Sam whispered.

Maeve turned her head and shushed him, her index finger resting on her lips. She shook her head.

"'Kay. Sorry," Sam whispered.

The quiz arrived, and Maeve set to task, scribbling answers at a rapid pace. She noticed Sam looming over her paper for answers, so she built a wall with her forearm to shut him out. *Typical*, she thought. *He is just here to be on TV and isn't going to put in the work.* When the class was over, Maeve gathered her things and walked toward the elevator when Sam stopped her.

"Hey," he said, tapping her on the shoulder.

"What?" Maeve asked, shirking him off.

He grinned, a forgiving and bright smile. "You forgot this."

It was her pencil bag. "Oh, thanks."

"You thought I was going to bother you, didn't you?"

"Well, you kind of did, looking at my paper."

He chuckled. "What? I did not look at your paper!"

She rolled her eyes.

"Okay, maybe I looked at your paper for a few seconds. I had no clue about the oil spill question."

"It was in the Metro section today," she said. "But you probably don't read the paper, seeing as you're in broadcast."

"Ouch! Someone has an acerbic tongue!"

Maeve started down the stairs to escape the conversation.

"But I like it…And I will have you know, we both got into this program on merit, not on looks. It's not like we submitted a photo. I'm as much of a news nerd as you!"

She stopped short in the stairwell and turned to face him. "Who says I'm a nerd?"

"I do."

She blinked. She wanted to reply with a pithy response, but she had nothing—nothing but laughter. She started cracking up. *He has some nerve, this guy.* Soon enough, they were both laughing in the stairwell.

"So, Nerd, you want to hang out later?" Sam asked.

"Sure," she said. "Just don't be late!"

Chapter 24

LIZZIE

On the day of Hadley's Friendsgiving, Lizzie arrives on time with a bottle of Veuve. A catering staff member greets her at the door, wearing a black vest with a starched white shirt and black pants.

"May I take your coat?" she asks.

"Yes, thank you," Lizzie says. She walks down the hallway that is scented with gardenia candles. An enormous crystal chandelier hangs from the ceiling on dim. Hadley is at the kitchen island, dressed in a ruby-red wrap dress, with lipstick to match, and an apron. She's arranging a tray of scallops wrapped in bacon.

"You're here," she squeals, piercing the scallop with a toothpick.

Lizzie hands her the champagne. "Looks and *smells* amazing."

"Can I get you a drink? Would you like the Veuve? Or, we have a signature cocktail: The Friendsgiving Crush. It's crushed ice, bourbon, basil, lime, and soda."

"Sounds delish. I'll try one." Lizzie heads to the living room where Jack is bent over, butt crack showing, as he huffs and puffs to get the fire started. Snickers glares from the ottoman.

"Hi, Snickers," she mutters, leaning in to pet him.

Snickers leaps down and circles around her calves, purring.

"Hey, Jack," Lizzie says, fanning the smoke away.

Jack juts his head around, crack still apparent. "Oh, hey, Lizzie! I didn't see you there. This fire is a stubborn one, even with my Boy Scouts background." He rolls up balls of newspaper and places them strategically around the logs. "How's things with you?"

"As well as you can imagine. You know, broke up with one guy, lusting after an ex, the usual." She forces a guffaw and plops down on the couch.

"I heard," Jack says. "Sorry about that."

She wrinkles her nose. "Does Pope hate me?"

"Not at all. In fact, he'll be here tonight," Jack says. He gives up and grabs a Duraflame.

Maeve joins them in the living room. "Hey, hey," she says. "You just get here?"

Lizzie hugs her hello and then grabs a cracker with brie from the silver tray on the marble coffee table. A staff member rushes over to her and hands her a cocktail napkin that reads: *I drink to take the edge off other people.*

"Thanks," Lizzie says, cleaning the brie smudged across her red gel manicure.

Maeve sips at her martini. "What's up?"

"I'm okay. Feeling sort of bad about Pope. Does he seem okay?"

"You mean about his mom?"

Lizzie shakes her head, confused. "His mom? No, I mean, because of us. Wait, did something happen to his mother?" Lizzie never met Pope's mom, but she spoke to her on the car phone once when they were on their way to dinner in Southie.

"She has pneumonia," Maeve says. "And they kept her in the hospital for a few days."

"Oh, my gosh, that's terrible! Is she going to be okay?"

"I think so? He was in Cleveland visiting her last week."

"Is he coming tonight?"

"Yeah, he said he'd be here when I saw him at work."

As if on cue, Pope strolls into the living room.

Lizzie stands and moves toward him, kissing him hello on the cheek. "I heard about your mom," she says. "I'm so sorry. Is everything okay?"

"Thanks," he says. "I think it will be. But it's just stressful. She's older, ya know?" He reaches for a bread stick and bites the crunchy top off. "How are things with you?"

Lizzie takes a deep breath. "Good, fine. I don't know. The usual."

"How are the kids?"

"They're doing awesome," she says, pulling on her earlobe. "Busy with sports and school."

"Good, that's good to hear." He eats his way down the bread stick, one bite at a time, then sits on the other side of Maeve.

Lizzie's mind races. "I'll be right back."

She goes to the kitchen to see if she can help Hadley and escape her discomfort. Hadley removes the turkey from the oven to cool, and the chef is stirring a giant pot of mashed potatoes. He is sweating in his black-and-white checkered chef pants.

"Need any help?" Lizzie asks.

Hadley smiles widely as Macy and Wade stroll into the kitchen, carrying a bottle of Silver Oak cabernet sauvignon.

"We're here!" Macy sings, handing the bottle to Hadley. "From us."

Us. Lizzie turns white as her heart sinks. Even though Hadley warned her they'd be there, she is not prepared. She thought, surely, they might break up by now. Was she imagining her and Wade's intimate connection at 75 Chestnut? *Why are he and Macy an "us?"*

"Hi, Lizzie," Macy says, her mouth set in a hard line.

Wade gives Lizzie a puppy dog look. "What's shaking?"

She glares at him. "Not much. Interesting to see you both here."

"Yeah," Wade says. "I wasn't sure I'd make it, but Hadley was so helpful with the move that I couldn't miss it."

The move. Wade said he wasn't ready for that, that it was a conversation for another day! Maybe Macy gave him an ultimatum, forced him into it. Yes, that must be it. Surely, he can't be that serious with her.

Macy excuses herself to use the ladies' room, and Hadley follows, leaving Wade and Lizzie alone.

"I guess congratulations are in order?" Lizzie says.

"Thanks." Wade nods. The air between them is thick, like a dense fog.

"Yeah, I wasn't sure it was going to happen so soon, but—"

Lizzie interjects, "Just stop, Wade." A muscle in her jaw twitches.

"Well... I mean, I don't owe you an explanation, Lizzie."

"Oh, I didn't say that you do, *Wade*."

"Why do I sense this hostility from you then?"

"Just forget it," Lizzie tuts. "Honestly, forget everything. I hope you and Macy are happy in your perfect little apartment with your perfect little life."

Wade laughs. "How is it little?"

"Maybe you two can have a paint fight while sponge-painting her living room, just like we did. Hope history doesn't repeat itself. Goodbye and good luck."

Lizzie storms out of the kitchen, holding back tears. She passes Macy on the way to the powder room and doesn't acknowledge her. She closes the door behind her, leans her back against the door, and silently cries. *Why does this always happen to me? I'm a good person. I just can't get a break.* After she washes the mascara from her face, she hears footsteps and a faint knock on the door.

"Lizzie, it's Wade."

"Go away."

"Can we talk for a second? Please?"

Lizzie smooths down her hair and takes a deep breath before opening the door a smidge. She peeks her head out. "Fine, come in."

Wade enters, and she backs up near the toilet, making room. "What?"

He stares at her. Her face is red and splotchy.

She picks at her cuticles. "Whaaat?" She starts to laugh. "Stop staring at me. I know I look gross." She sniffles.

"You don't look gross," Wade says.

"What do you want?"

Wade inhales, as if he's going to give a speech. "I guess I just want to say I'm sorry if I misled you in some way." He puts his hand in his pockets.

Lizzie softens. "No, you didn't."

"Well, you're obviously mad at me about something. You just indicated as much."

Lizzie puts the toilet seat cover down and sits. "Honestly, I'm just mad at myself."

"Why?"

She gazes up at Wade, her voice cracking, her mouth turning downward. "Because I fucked things up with you so many times, and... I still love you."

Wade blinks, sadness clouding his features. "Lizzie..."

"No. You need to hear this," she says. "I have always loved you, Wade. I know this now. From the very beginning. But I always fucked it up. I *know*. And I hate myself for it. I should have married you. You are the love of my life. *You*. I was young and stupid and thought, like, the grass was greener, or whatever. But I don't think that now. I know the grass is burnt and brown and smells bad. Like, rotten."

Wade laughs. "I can't take you seriously sitting on the toilet seat."

Lizzie stands. "I'm serious, Wade! You have to believe me. I want you back. I need you. I know we are good together! You must have felt it, too, the other day!"

Wade places his hands together, forming a temple, and covers his nose. He breathes deeply. "I can't do this, Lizzie. I appreciate everything you're saying, but it's just... I can't."

"Why not? You can!"

He shakes his head. "No, I actually can't."

"What do you mean?"

"I mean, I won't let myself be hurt by you again. Like I said, I can't trust you."

"But you can," Lizzie says, reaching for him.

"No, I can't trust you... with my heart," Wade says, his eyes welling up.

They stare at one another in the bright lights of the powder room, neither saying another word. There is just the din of the ceiling fan.

Lizzie inches forward. "Well, I... think you can. I wish you would."

Wade looms closer, his shoulder sagging. She can feel his breath on her face. She's dying to kiss him. For a moment, it seems it could happen.

But then, there's a knock on the door. It's Macy. "Wade?"

Wade's eyes widen. "Coming!"

Lizzie grabs his hand. "Stay," she whispers.

"I can't," Wade says. He drops her hand and turns to leave.

. . .

When Lizzie pulls herself together and returns to the party, the guests are seated at the dining room table with place cards in front of them.

Clearly, Hadley placed Lizzie far from Wade and Macy—and several seats down from Pope. She might as well be seated in Uganda.

She pours some cabernet into her chalice and places the cloth napkin, wrapped in a gold ring with a turkey on it, on her lap. Her face begins to cool from the tears and emotion just minutes before. The catering staff brings the dinner out and places the turkey down in the center. There are fingerling potatoes, black-eyed peas, butternut squash, stuffing, rolls, and cranberry sauce.

"This looks amazing," Mave says. "Thank you, Had."

Hadley smiles, grasping Jack's hand, and puts her head down to say grace. "Thank you, Lord, for this bounty and these blessings. And for our health, happiness, families, and friends. Amen."

"Amen," Lizzie whispers. And just as she is about to dig in, Hadley makes a request.

"I think we should go around the room, and everyone say one thing they are grateful for. And it can't be generic, like, I am grateful for my family," Hadley says.

"I'll start," Jack says. "I'm grateful for my friends at this table. They are my *chosen* family."

Well, that's nice, Lizzie thinks. *But this exercise is painful.*

"Aw," Macy coos, squeezing Wade's hand.

Lizzie balls her fists under the table. "I thought you said we can't say a lame thing about being grateful for our families."

Maeve's eyes bulge as she shoots a glare at Lizzie. The others force a weak chuckle.

"I think she meant like your *nuclear* families," Jack clarifies, shifting in his seat.

Everyone goes around the table saying their blessings, and it's Lizzie's turn. She has a mouthful of fingerling potatoes when she feels the weight of their eyes on her. She raises her hand to indicate a "pass."

"Oh, come on," Hadley pleads.

Lizzie stifles her tears. Besides her children—who are with her ex—she can't think of anything to be grateful for. Her mind goes blank. Suddenly, she feels a potato wedged in her throat, and she chokes. Coughing uncontrollably, tears stream down her face, as she puts her head in her lap. Pope stands and races to her aid.

"I'm okay," Lizzie wheezes, waving off Pope. "Thank you."

"I think it's safe to say she will pass," Jack announces, lightening the mood.

Embarrassment grips Lizzie with the heavy stares, and she excuses herself from the table.

Maeve follows her upstairs. They sit on the edge of the bed in the guest room, and Snickers leaps up like he's going to chime in.

"Don't do this to yourself, Lizzie," Maeve says. "It's not helpful. You can't live in the rearview mirror, and you made those choices for a reason. Trust yourself."

This all makes sense, Lizzie thinks, but she can't help but feel remorse.

"I'm going to go," she says, straightening out her dress.

"No, you can't. Hadley will be so upset. Just take a beat."

"No, I need more than a beat. I feel so stupid and embarrassed. Tell Hadley I'll text her later. I'm going to dip out."

"Are you sure?" Maeve asks. "I can sit with you for a bit. I love you."

Lizzie nods, hugging Maeve. "I know. I love you, too, thanks. I just don't love myself right now."

. . .

When Lizzie leaves, she desperately wants to go get her kids, to feel their love, but they're with Hank and Heather. She attempts to Facetime them, but they don't answer. She's suddenly gripped by fear. *I can't be alone*, she thinks. *What in the hell am I going to do?* The realization that she will end up solitary in the dirt, a notion that occasionally plagues her, creeps into her mind. Her heart thuds, her hands grow sweaty on the wheel. *I need to turn around*, she thinks. *I can't be alone at the house.* Instead, Lizzie drives to the country club. For sure, she can find *someone* to hang with. Any company is better than her own.

DECEMBER

Chapter 25
LIZZIE

"Thank you so much for coming," Lizzie says. "Make sure you take a card and please reach out with any questions!" The open house on Hersey Street was a success. Seventeen potential buyers passed through, and Lizzie swears she overhead one of them talking about an offer in the driveway when she pretended to look for her keys.

Brandon packs up the folders and takes a bite of a chocolate chip cookie they baked to warm up the homey vibe. "Don't let me finish this," he says. "I can't be bloated for tonight."

Tonight is the find-a-man-for-Brandon-night. Lizzie heard from a reliable source that closeted married men go to the bar near Nantasket Beach for clandestine meetups. They meet, and then they have sex at the hotel down the street. When Brandon got word of this, he had to see for himself.

"I just hope we don't run into anyone we know," Lizzie says, driving to Hull. "I mean, like, someone's husband on the prowl."

"Well, we have to have a plan," Brandon says, combing his hair in the passenger seat. "Like, we need to figure out how to tell if someone is just there to have a drink, or if they are there to pick up a guy."

"Duh," Lizzie says. "You're the bait!"

Brandon covers his mouth with hands. "Yes! I love it! This is so *Magnum P.I.*"

. . .

One martini later, Brandon pokes Lizzie under the bar. ""I think I spot one," he whispers. "There, in the pinstriped shirt."

Lizzie tries not to look, but she stares directly at him. "I don't know," she says. "He has a straight vibe to me."

"No, I'm telling you. I can smell it from here. He wants some dick."

"Okay, that is just gross."

"Is it though? You love a good hog! Thick and juicy," Brandon says, biting into a blue cheese stuffed olive.

They giggle, and Brandon makes eye contact with Mr. Pinstripes.

"He just eyeballed me. I'm on it."

Brandon sashays over to the stool next to the man in question while still holding the stem of his martini. Lizzie checks the time and reapplies her lip gloss when she spies her friend Anna across the bar. She waves and motions for her to come over.

"You alone?" Anna asks.

Lizzie shakes her head. "No. Brandon is here, well...over there." She points at him with her toothpick.

"Oooh, did he meet someone?"

"We don't know," Lizzie says. "Maybe? Maybe not. We're not sure if that guy's straight, or gay, or married, or unmarried."

Anna peers across at the man's ring finger. "Well, he doesn't have a ring on."

"That doesn't mean anything."

Anna grimaces. "I hate that—when men don't wear rings if they're married. Like, don't waste our time."

"Some women—not me—find men with wedding rings more attractive. Like, it's reassuring that someone wants them, and they've been trained," Lizzie says. "Speaking of, have you been dating anyone?"

Anna raises an eyebrow. "Dating? No. Fucking? Yes."

Lizzie laughs. "Tell me everything! Do I know him?"

"Definitely not."

"How do you know?"

"Because he is younger and lives in the city."

"Wait, how old is he?" Lizzie says.

"Well, it's not *one*, as I said..."

Lizzie gasps. "Shut up. How many?"

"I dunno. I mean, it's just like a *thing* now. We go into Boston, grab a young hottie, take him back to the suburbs, and pay to Uber him home." Anna sips at her martini as a punctuation point.

"Wait, it's a *thing*?" Lizzie's intrigued.

"Yeah," Anna says. "All of us single moms are doing it. It's like these guys want to try out a M.I.L.F., and we don't want another marriage, and they have no money, so it's mutually beneficial."

"Sounds kinda hot," Lizzie says. "Is it? Hot?"

"Sex with a strapping young man who is thirsty for you? Yeah. Not going to lie. You're missing out."

Lizzie shakes her head and closes her eyes. "I don't think I can do it."

Brandon strolls back over. "Hey, gurl," he says, grabbing Anna by the wrist. "Love the Hermès cuff!"

"So??" Lizzie says. "What's the verdict?"

"Gay," Brandon says, sitting down. "But in the closet. So, I gave him my number and told him to call me if he ever gets lonely."

"Oh, my god. You're hilarious," Anna says. "Think he will?"

"Oh, I bet I get a dick pic tonight. Stay tuned."

But Lizzie tunes out. She stares at the fire, imagining Wade Ubering to her house from Boston late-night. He surprises her when she's sleeping. She thinks it's an intruder. She screams. But he reassures her with the familiarity of his smell and his kiss...

Then she wakes from her trance. She considers texting Wade to apologize for how she acted at Friendsgiving. She wasn't fair to put him on the spot like that. She only proved that she hasn't changed. She was selfish. But she can't forget how he looked at her, inching closer to her in the bathroom. If Macy hadn't knocked, who knows if they would have kissed! The sexual tension was crazy! She will just give it time. *Yes*, Lizzie thinks. She will wait to see if he comes around. Maybe Wade just needs to absorb what she told him. Maybe she needs to show him, not tell him, that she is a new woman who can be trusted.

Chapter 26

MAEVE

Maeve stands in the center of North Beach, squinting in the sun. Blue, yellow, and green overturned paddle boats rest in the sand for the winter. A boy and his mother hold hands, bending down to pick up seashells. Lady slippers and oyster shells are everywhere. Maeve walks to the edge of the water and dips her hand in. It's freezing. Sam always loved this spot. He would rush down to the beach after work to get a swim in during the warmer months. And in the colder ones, he'd still bring a chair down with a couple beers in his Yeti backpack and call it his office. The beach is where Sam's soul lives now, Maeve believes. Well, aside from in her heart.

The sand is covered with pebbles, tiny clam shells, and crunchy brown seaweed. They make a crackling noise as she steps on them. Maeve discovers a piece of green sea glass: lucky. She places it in her pocket and continues down the beach. She feels lost, like something must give. Her life is incomplete, at a standstill. How can she give Lizzie advice about not living in the past when that's all she's been doing? She hasn't been able to get over Sam's death, and it wasn't until she started to feel something for Pope that she realized it.

But she's afraid, and she's sad. She worries that if she lets herself fall for Pope, she will forget Sam, the memory of him, and she will lose him all over again. His memory is what keeps her company. It's like he never died—he's always with her. She fears that new love will push his memory away, or that she will disappoint him. What if there is an afterlife, and he is, indeed, watching her every move? What if he's up there somewhere in the sky, looking down on her now, upset? She can't bear disappointing him.

She peers up at the sky. "I'm so sorry, Sam," she whispers. "I'm confused, scared, and lost."

She kicks at tiny rocks with her sneakers. "Sam," she mutters. "Give me a sign that you hear me."

Maeve is quiet, hopeful. She waits for a gust of wind, a loud noise, or a seagull to fly overhead. Nothing. She asks again, "Sam, honey, please. I need to know you see me, and that you are okay with me." There is still no sign.

"Well, *damn you*, then!" she shouts, tears streaming down her face. "Damn you for dying on me! For leaving me here! I miss you, goddamn it, and I can't do this alone!"

The boy and his mother stare at her from down the beach.

Maeve drops her shoulders in defeat and starts to leave when she suddenly spots a harbor seal surfacing in the water. Seals were Sam's favorite. He worked as a harbor seal trainer and feeder at the aquarium one summer when he was younger, and ever since, he has loved seals.

"Is that you, Sam?" Maeve calls out, quietly. She looks behind her to make sure the boy and his mother aren't watching. She feels ridiculous talking to a seal. "Sam?"

The seal stares at her, his head bobbing on the surface of the ocean. He blinks with his large brown eyes, like saucers.

"Oh, Sam," she cries. "I miss you!"

She walks to the edge. The seal goes under.

"Sam! Come back!" Maeve searches for the seal.

His head pops up again, closer to her now. She can see the brown spots on his gray body.

"There you are," she says. "I need to know everything is going to be okay. I need to know you're okay." There is silence. "And that I have your permission..." Her voice cracks. "To move on."

The seal blinks, staring through her.

"Sam, honey, I'm so sorry. I love you with all my heart. But I'm not living here. I need to close this chapter and know you'll be okay with me living my life." Her nose is running, and she can barely make out the seal's face through the tears that have filled her eyes.

The seal swims closer to her, almost at shore. She reaches for him. He gives her a look, a look she interprets as validation.

"Thank you, Sam," she whispers. "I'll never forget you."

The seal swims off. Maeve stands at the shore, waiting for him to surface.

But he is gone, just like Sam is gone. Maeve presses a hand to her chest. *It's time I swim, too*, she thinks. *I have permission.*

Chapter 27

HADLEY

Hadley paces the room, waiting for the phone call from her OBGYN at Boston Medical Center. There is nothing left to organize or clean, but she needs a distraction. She must stay busy to keep her mind from unraveling. She can practically feel the cortisol coursing through her veins, like soda through a crazy straw, begging for solace.

She checks the *New York Times* cooking app on her phone to see if there's a new recipe that she can cook Jack for dinner. She searches "Soups," "Steak," and "Sides," and then decides to scrap the whole idea altogether. Maybe she will just get takeout from The Square.

She turns the television to QVC and is mesmerized by Lisa Rinna and her new skin care line. *How does she get her lips so plump and amazing? How does her hair style never change? Why is she so thin? I want to look like that!* Hadley pulls out her credit card and orders the Rinna Lip Plumper. Two hours, and a facial scrub, toner, mascara, night serum, and bronzer purchase later, the phone call arrives. Her doctor tells her to come in for an appointment. He has some results.

. . .

The doctor's office smells like Clorox disinfectant and disappointment. Hadley shifts in her gown on the crinkly white paper. Her mind races with thoughts of doom.

"I know this isn't what you wanted to hear," the doctor says. "But your hormone levels are low. Very low."

"So, like, what does that mean? Just give it to me straight," Hadley says.

"Well, it indicates diminished ovarian reserve."

Hadley's eyes widen. "Can I still get pregnant?"

"Yes, but we need to take measures to increase the chances. We are going to have to take a more aggressive approach. There's a good chance conception won't happen naturally."

Flustered, Hadley clarifies. "But I'm only thirty-five."

"I understand. It can happen early."

"But I've been doing everything right. Taking vitamins, not drinking, checking my ovulation?"

"*It's not your fault,*" the doctor says. "What's really promising is that we now have information. And there are options."

Hadley only hears *not your fault.* The remainder of what the doctor says, something about AMH levels, follicle counts, IUI, IVF is all a blur. She nods, grabs some pamphlets, and walks out, disappointment in check. When she gets to reception, she searches for Jack. He isn't there—only a young woman with a large baby bump and a toddler drawing with crayons by her feet. She wishes she started this journey earlier, like that woman. She's kicking herself now. Were all those parties in her twenties worth it? What an utter waste of time and hormones! Now it's too late, and she likely can't conceive. Where the hell is Jack?

HADLEY: *Where are you?*

JACK: *Sorry. Meeting ran long. I thought we agreed you could handle this one solo?*

Her stomach turns. *No, we didn't agree*, she thinks. She just gave him an out, because that's what she assumed he wanted. Looks like she was correct.

Later that night, Jack strolls into the kitchen around seven forty-five. She's doomscrolling on her phone. He removes his tie and kisses her on the cheek. "Hey, baby."

She doesn't answer. *I'm not a baby, and I can't have one*, she thinks.

"So what did the doctor have to say? You didn't text me back." His tone is atypically cheery, which is all the more infuriating. He reaches for a beer in the fridge and tosses the cap in the sink.

"Diminished ovarian reserve." She continues to scroll, unfazed.

"I don't even know what that means. Translation?"

"It means my eggs are rotting. It means I probably need IVF. It means we don't have time to just 'see what happens.' We have a lot to consider. And you weren't there."

He blinks. "I told you the meeting ran late."

"It wasn't just any appointment, Jack," she says, her jaw clenching. "It was about our future."

"Jeez," Jack says, taking a swig of beer. "I didn't think it was that serious."

"Are you joking? Tell me you are... because I've been trying since the honeymoon! I've tracked every ovulation, peed on countless sticks, measured basal temperatures, wolfed prenatal vitamins, and suffered and smiled through every baby shower while secretly dying inside. How is it not serious?"

Jack sits next to her and pauses. "Hadley, maybe we need to talk about why you want this so badly."

She freezes. "Excuse me?"

"You've been obsessed. It's like... like having a baby has become your entire identity. And I'm not even sure if you want me in this, or just someone who checks the right boxes."

She shoots a death stare his way. "That's cruel." She can't believe he can even be so callous right now. *How can he pile onto me at this time? My eggs are depleted! I am depleted!*

"I'm not trying to be cruel," he says. "I'm being realistic. You created this plan, and I've been along for the ride. But I'm not sure I've arrived yet. I thought I would be, but I don't know if now is the right time. We just got married. Do we have to jump into things so quickly? Can't we just enjoy each other first?"

Her heart pounds. *Thump. Thump. Thump.* "You said you wanted kids."

"I do," Jack says. "Eventually. But it seems like it's all we talk about. It's, like, not romantic. It feels forced."

She stands, her eyes bugging out. "The relationship is forced? Or the sex?"

Jack stutters. "Neither. I don't know what I'm trying to say. Basically—"

"No, I think I know what you're trying to say. I've bulldozed you into this plan, and you've been mailing it in for months. You're all talk, no action. I could have really used your support today, and you were nowhere to be found."

Jack folds his arms across his chest. "That's not fair, honey. You told me not to."

"Because I didn't want to have to beg!" she screams. "Jesus! I thought we were on the same page!"

. . .

Later that evening, Hadley sits on the floor of the guest room—the one that was supposed to be a nursery. Snickers lies on a folded baby blanket on the rocking chair. She stares blankly at the yellow walls, freshly painted. She lays back on the plush carpet, closes her eyes, and cries. Not the polite kind of cry. Not the Southern Belle, small kind... but the snotty, heinous, loud kind that only comes with crushed disappointment and loss.

. . .

The following week, Hadley doesn't leave the house. The fridge is bare, and the laundry is toppling over. She spends the majority of her day in her bed, eating ice cream and watching QVC. She purchases more than $65,000 in "luxury goods;" perfumes, luggage, hats, and caftans. *The more I have, the better I will feel*, she thinks. *I mean, if I can't have children, I may as well have a lot of stuff.*

When Jack checks the Amex bill, he calls Constance and asks her to come visit.

"Hadley, honey, Mommy is here," Constance whispers, clutching her clammy hand. Hadley is in the dark, with the glow of the television screen on her face. "Let go of the remote control now. We're going to turn this thing off."

Hadley clenches the clicker tightly, hiding it under her armpit. Her eyes are dilated like a cat's in a carrier on the way to the vet. "No, I want it on. Isaac Mizrahi is going live in a few minutes." She rolls onto her side, facing away. The room is stifling hot, and Hadley doesn't appear fazed that she's in all sweats with her hood up in bed.

Constance motions for Jack to leave the room. She leans in close and whispers, "Sweetheart, I know this is hard for you, but you must get out of this funk. It's not becoming, and Jack is very worried about you. We all are." She pets Hadley's once silky hair that is now greasy and unkempt. "Let's get you in the shower."

"But I've almost completed my Christmas shopping," Hadley argues. "There's a Zwilling steak knife set of six I want to buy for Jack. It's on at three, during *In the Kitchen with David*."

"Hadley? Listen to your mother," Constance begs. "I'm very worried that you might need to see a psychiatrist. Your father got in touch with Dr. Hoffman. Remember him? He helped your dad get through that rough patch he had a few years back."

"I don't want to see Dr. Hoffman," Hadley whines. "I just want this knife set."

"Well, after that, honey. You can get the knife set, and then maybe we can get you out of this house."

"I am not leaving the house, Mother," Hadley replies. "I have a lot of shopping to do, and Jack is here. He can take care of me."

"Honey, that is not fair to do to your husband. Haven't I taught you better? Now, get up and get out of this bed at once before I drag you out. Don't make an old Southern gal get all rough and tumble. That's not a pretty sight."

Hadley closes her eyes tightly and begins to hum. *Hmmm, hmmm.*

"What in God's name are you doing?" Constance says.

Hadley doesn't reply, but her hum gets increasingly louder, until she sounds like a swarming bee's nest.

"HMMMMMMMMMMMMM, HMMMMMMMMMM!" Hadley shouts. She wraps her fingers around the remote tightly, eyes shut. "HMMMMMM! HMMMMM!!!!" The shrill sound is deafening.

Constance runs downstairs to fetch Jack. "Jack! We need help!"

Chapter 28

MAEVE

On the eve of the office holiday party, Maeve and the HR team unpack a box of decorations. There's the fake tree with colored lights, a menorah, a Santa statue, and a wreath with red and gold bows. Trish, who is dressed in a Christmas sweater and a jingle bell hanging on a string around her neck, is a big fan of tinsel. She strews it about the room recklessly.

Trish giggles. "The cleaning crew is going to murder me!" She refills Maeve's glass with eggnog.

"Ooh, that's probably good for now," Maeve says, covering the top of her glass. "This stuff goes to your head fast, especially when you're exhausted. Pope and I basically pulled an all-nighter two days in a row, making sure to get at least forty press mentions for Royal Lobster."

Trish's eyes widen. "Forty? That seems excessive."

"Well, that's what it will take," Maeve says, crossing her fingers.

As if on cue, Pope turns the corner and ducks his head into the conference room. "Great news," he says.

"What?" Maeve asks.

"We got Royal Lobster back!"

"Oh, my god!" Maeve shouts. Without thinking, she rushes over to Pope, grabs his cheeks with two hands, and lays a big kiss on his lips.

Trish shrieks with joy, and Pope stiffens before kissing her back.

"I am so sorry," Maeve says, pulling away. "I don't know what came over me!"

Trish throws a few pieces of tinsel on them, like a priest. "I know what came over you." She winks.

Pope laughs. "No worries. I enjoyed it."

Joy bubbles up in Maeve. Her spirits soar as the eggnog and dopamine swirl through her body. *I kissed Pope! What the...?! Well, I mean, it's not like I haven't wanted to. And it wasn't a real kiss, per se, but it was... nice. No, it was more than nice. It was... hot.*

"Me, too." She smiles. "So, wait, how did this happen?"

"You jumped me!" Pope says.

"Shut up!" She laughs. "No, the Royal Lobster account! Did we get forty mentions?"

"Forty-five," he says, raising the roof with his hands. "You owe me five."

"Well, I'll make it up to you at the party later. I'll give you my Yankee Swap number."

"Aw, shucks," Pope says. "And here I was thinking we could swap more than your number."

Maeve turns a shade of red. "Maybe that, too," she says, catching herself, then walking out of the room quickly. She doesn't know what's come over her, but whatever it is, she likes it.

. . .

A few moments later, Trish dims the lights and announces it's time to party. The office has been transformed with strings of white lights on the cubicle walls, the smell of pine, and the conference room doors propped open to reveal a makeshift dance floor. There's a DJ setting up in the corner, playing a mix of Mariah Carey and Nat King Cole, and the staff congregates in the lobby, grabbing drinks and snacking. Rick makes his lame, annual, holiday party speech, thanking the staff and informing them that bonuses will be in envelopes on their desks. He ends it with a congratulatory acknowledgement of Pope and Maeve.

"To Pope and Maeve! For getting Royal Lobster back on board."

"Thank you, Rick," Maeve says, chagrined.

"Just don't fuck it up again." He winks.

She smirks, refraining from saying what she really wants to say.

When Trish passes around the numbers bag for the Yankee Swap. Maeve pulls a fifteen, and Pope grabs a three.

"Here you go," she says. "As promised." She hands Pope her ticket. "The higher numbers are better, because you can pull last and get the best gift."

"I know how to play, silly," he says. "Want to go grab a drink?"

Pope and Maeve walk to the copy room, where the bar is located next to the printer and fax machine. He pours them each a glass of cheap chardonnay. The whir of the copier is in the background, and it's heated the room to tropical temperatures.

"I feel kind of dizzy," Maeve says. "I think I need to sit down."

Pope puts his arm out for her to lean on. "Are you okay?"

She grasps his forearm, feeling woozy, as he escorts her out of the copy room and down the hall.

"Yeah, I think I just got really hot in there, and maybe too much eggnog and wine? I don't know." Her heart thuds with both nerves and a dangerous awareness of the situation. *What should I do? I want this. I want him*, she thinks.

As she steadies herself, still clutching him, she feels Pope's warmth emanating from beneath his shirt. He smells fresh, like soap and sandalwood. The hallway is empty and dark, but "Jingle Bell Rock" plays loudly over the speakers. Pope peers into Maeve's eyes and, without caution, leans in for a kiss. It is passionate and fervent, with the urgency of delayed gratification exploding into motion. She surrenders to him. Their tongues swirl, lips opening and closing. They pant, wince. Pope slides his hand up the front of her shirt and cups her lace bra.

"You're so hot," he whispers.

Maeve reaches around his back and moves her hands up his spine. His flesh is smooth, silky.

"So are you."

Her knees wobble as he presses her against the wall. She didn't think she could ever feel this again, if her body would remember how. But it did. It was electrifying.

"Can we do this?" she asks.

"Yes," Pope says, consuming her. Then he pauses, pulling back. "But only if you want to."

Of course I want to, she thinks. *Please don't stop.*

"You know this is a terrible idea, right?" She gasps as he lifts her atop a table, papers scattering to the floor. He kisses down the curve of her neck. For a moment, the world outside and the office party ceases to exist—just two people, tangled in temptation, chasing temptation. For the first time in so long, she lets go.

"Are you okay with this?" he whispers.

"Yes..." she says. "Yes."

. . .

At work the next day, Maeve adjusts the collar of her blouse for the third time, her reflection in the elevator's polished steel walls taunting her. The digital numbers tick upward—eleven, twelve, thirteen—each one hammering her chest. She clutches her phone, perhaps a lifeline. Hadley and Lizzie are just a dial away.

She didn't mean for that to happen with Pope. The holiday party. Drinks. The copy room. *Ugh, what did I do?* Pope made her feel a way she hadn't since Sam, and in that moment, she had let her guard down. Just a little. And then again. And again. It felt so amazing, so *different*. She and Sam had a rhythm, something honed and practiced. But with Pope, this was all new—his touch, his kiss, his smell. It felt forbidden, thrilling, like a secret just between them.

When the elevator doors open to Watts, Maeve braces herself. She steps out, her heart in her chest, her kitten heels grazing the carpet without a sound. Every step closer to Pope's office is unnerving. When she finally sees him, he glances up from his computer. She's terrified how he will react. But his eyes warm—just enough to reassure her. She smiles, a knowing smile. They have a secret.

She takes a deep breath and heads to her office. Their company town hall is in ten minutes. They'll sit far apart and pretend nothing happened.

A text message pops up.

POPE: *You okay?*

Maeve hesitates.

MAEVE: *Yeah. Just nerves.*

A moment passes.

POPE: *I hate pretending. You know that, right?*

She agrees. She hates it, too. But what choice do they have? No one at work can know. Not after how hard she's worked to get here. Years of ingratiating herself to Rick and putting in eighty-hour workweeks could not go down the drain. And yet, she wonders: *What's the point of all this?*

. . .

Maeve stands, smoothing her skirt, steadying her breath. She can do this. She's done harder things. But as she walks toward the conference room, Rick's voice rings out from behind her.

"Maeve, can I speak with you for a moment?"

She freezes. Turns. Nods.

"We need to talk. Privately."

Maeve's stomach sinks. Her world is tilting. Has he found out? And if he has—is this the beginning of the end?

Rick closes the door behind Maeve as she takes a seat, her heart in her throat. Maybe someone saw them, and she's violated some kind of interoffice romance rules? She can't remember any at the time, but what does he want to meet about privately?

Rick smiles at her from behind his desk. She can't help but laugh, an anxious chuckle to relieve some of the fear bubbling over.

"Is everything okay?" she asks. "This feels ominous."

Rick rests his hands on the table. "Well, Maeve, you did it."

She gulps. "Did what?" Her stomach drops between her legs.

"You managed to prove to me that you deserve that promotion."

She trembles with disbelief. "Wait, what?"

"You're getting promoted to chief publicist of the restaurant division."

Is this really happening, she thinks? "I am?"

"I thought you'd be thrilled. You've been giving me the stink eye since the day Pope walked in here."

Maeve blinks. "I mean, yes! No, I am thrilled!" She pauses. "But what about Pope?"

"He's getting promoted, too. But I'm moving him into Finance. You two won't be working together anymore."

Maeve's shoulders release as she unhooks her ankles from the chair legs. "Wow, okay, then. Wow."

Rick laughs. "Speechless?"

"Kinda."

"Well, I'll give you a moment to take it all in. We can talk contracts later this week. For now, just know you did a great job with the Royal Lobster account. You both did."

"Thank you," Maeve says.

. . .

Moments later, she's at the company meeting in the conference room, and she gets a text from Pope, who's seated across the table.

POPE: ?

MAEVE: *You're never going to believe this (mind exploding emoji)!*

Chapter 29

LIZZIE

Lizzie can't remember the last time she was completely and utterly single. Typically, she's at least got one man in her back pocket, someone to have dinner or drinks with. But not now. Now she's alone, and she feels naked, like a shorn sheep in the winter cold.

Lizzie recognizes that a lot of her codependency stems from her tumultuous upbringing with her mother. Her parents were divorced, and she spent a lot of time moving in and out of different men's homes, based on whomever her mother was dating. She had a hard time keeping track of all their names. But she never forgot Pete. "Pete the Perv," as she used to call him, who told inappropriate sex jokes and leered at her. Pete had yellow teeth, like corn on the cob, because he didn't believe in going to the dentist. He wore dirty jeans and a flannel, and he reeked of hand-rolled tobacco and beer. Lizzie can still smell his hot, rancid breath close to her face. This was right before she ran from the trailer to her friend's house, scared he might touch her. Lizzie told her mother about it, and that night, they moved all of their stuff out of Pete's trailer and didn't look back.

Lizzie married Hank when she was living in the North End. She met him at The Improv Asylum. She was seated next to him, and when the improvisors asked for a food suggestion, Hank called out something very obscure but meaningful to Lizzie: *Spam*. That pink and slimy canned meat had been a staple for Lizzie growing up, when her mother was out of work, and they'd lived on food stamps. She'd nudged Hank and muttered, "A man after my own heart!"

He smiled, and the rest was history... until Lizzie decided to sabotage it. Hank couldn't please her, no matter how hard he tried. The grass was greener...

. . .

Lizzie invites Maeve and Hadley to dinner. She hasn't seen them in person since the Friendsgiving meltdown last month. They meet at Salt Society in Scituate. The room is dimly lit with orange lightbulbs hanging from the ceiling, and the smell of sushi and seaweed salad permeates. Lizzie orders a Diet Coke with a lemon to start. No booze. She wants to be on her best behavior around Hadley after making a scene at her dinner. She's seated in the front room at a high-top table.

"Hey, hey," Maeve chirps, taking off her coat and placing it on the back of the chair. "How goes it?"

Maeve seems lighter, fresher, Lizzie thinks.

"Hi! So good to see you." Lizzie stands for an embrace.

Maeve strategically places both of her hands on Lizzie's shoulders and makes a concerned face with a downturned smile. "How are you *doing*?"

"I'm *great*," Lizzie says emphatically.

"Seriously?"

Lizzie frowns. "Why do I always have to be sad? Can't I be *great* for once?" Lizzie hates that this is her narrative, the sad one.

"Sheesh! Okay, I am glad you're great. Sorry," Maeve mutters. She

---

sits and reads the menu.

Lizzie fiddles with her earring and motions for the waiter. "We may just go ahead and order," Lizzie says.

"What's the rush?"

Then Hadley arrives, dressed in pajamas and rain boots. Her hair is unkempt in a top knot, and she's not wearing any makeup. "Sorry. Am I late?" Hadley asks, short of breath.

"No, we just got here," Maeve says.

"Okay, cool." Hadley sits down and swivels her head around the room, like she's in witness protection. "I haven't been here in forever. I've been so busy with my projects, and organizing, and the holidays. It's been *insane!* I finished all my Christmas shopping!"

"Already? Impressive," Lizzie says.

Hadley grins. "Yep! Did it all on QVC!" She wags her eyebrows like Groucho Marx.

Lizzie shoots an alarmed look at Maeve. *WTF?*

"I didn't even know QVC was still a thing," Lizzie says. "Isn't that where, like, D-list celebrities go to sell weird clothes and skincare lines?"

"It's not D-list celebrities!" Lizzie chides. "In fact, there are some real A-listers on there!"

She stands, motioning for the server. "Do they have bread?"

"I don't know," Maeve says. "But we can ask?"

"Good. I'm *starving!*"

Lizzie wonders what is going on with Hadley. Not only does she appear crazy, but she's acting crazy, like she's experiencing some sort of mania. Her speech is pressured and rapid, and she can't stop fidgeting.

"Hadley, before we say anything else, I want to apologize," Lizzie says.

Hadley laughs. "Oh no! No need to be sorry. It happens... We all have our moments." She folds and refolds her cloth napkin in her lap.

197

"Well, I hope I didn't ruin your Friendsgiving. I was just so out of sorts after running into Wade and Macy. And then, seeing you and Pope, Maeve, I just got triggered."

"I'm sorry," Maeve says.

Lizzie reaches across the table, touching Maeve's hand. "No, it's fine," she says, shaking her head. "It's me, not you. I just… I don't know. The holidays are hard when the kids go to Hank's house. All the back and forth. I just feel like I got robbed of the opportunity to have a normal family. Like, I will never have an entire Christmas and New Year's school vacation with my kids."

I just want to be normal, she thinks. *I want what everyone else has. What I have isn't enough. I'm not enough.*

"I know that feeling," Maeve says. "Holidays without Sam are especially painful, and just the idea that I never got to have a full life with him. I was robbed of that."

Lizzie shakes her head. "Oh, my god. I am so *selfish*. Here I am complaining about my divorce when your husband is no longer even here."

Hadley nods and tears at her bread like a bird of prey. "Can we order a bottle of wine?"

Lizzie and Maeve exchange glances. "I'll have some. Sure," Lizzie says.

"Me, too," Maeve says. "Why don't you choose?"

Hadley orders a bottle of expensive cabernet sauvignon.

"Well, on the topic of Pope…" Maeve says, grabbing her water, taking a sip. "I have some news."

Hadley's eyes grow wide. "What?"

"Well, really two things… First, I got promoted!"

"Oh, my god! Yay!" Hadley claps.

"And second, Pope and I hooked up after the office holiday party."

"Whhhaaat?!" Lizzie shrieks. "Holy shit! That's huge!" *Why don't good things happen for me?*

"Well, to start, I'm sorry if this is upsetting to you, Lizzie."

Lizzie sighs and takes a sip of wine. "No, it's okay. I mean, we never even did it."

They erupt in laughter.

"Wait, so did you guys do it? At the holiday party?"

Mave giggles. "No… not at the holiday party?"

Lizzie and Hadley's mouths drop open. "O.M.G. Tell us everything," Hadley says.

Maeve holds her napkin over her face and closes her eyes. "We had sex."

Both Maeve and Hadley shriek, then quiet themselves to avoid a scene.

"Stop. It," Lizzie whispers emphatically. "What?!" She wonders why Pope chose to have sex with Maeve and not with her. Is something wrong with her? Should she take this personally?

"It was good. Like, really good," Maeve says.

Hadley clasps her hands together. "Well, this is something to celebrate! Maeve, your card is up. This is your year!"

Lizzie senses something very off with Hadley. "Hey, Had, you okay?"

Hadley's eyes narrow on her. "Yeah, why?"

"I don't know. You seem sort of jumpy and stuff." *She seems insane.* "Really?"

Maeve nods. "Yeah, is all okay? Are things good with Jack?"

Hadley pauses. She opens her mouth but then stops herself. "I can't do this," she says, getting up from her chair.

The conversation halts.

Lizzie blinks. "What?" *What is going on here? I'm scared.*

Hadley sits back down, her shoulders sagging. "I can't keep sitting here pretending I'm fine while everyone else—" Her voice cracks. "Everyone else is living their best lives." She starts to cry.

Lizzie reaches for her. "Honey, what's going on? And for the record, I am not living my best life." *That's for sure.*

"I'm not talking about *you*," Hadley says.

Maeve shoots Lizzie a look, like *shut up.*

"Just, like, everyone else in Hingham," Hadley continues. "Do you even know what it's like to hear about baby showers, sports, and dance recitals when your body has failed you over and over? When every doctor's appointment ends in some version of *not this time?*"

Maeve extends her hand across the table, but Hadley recoils.

"No. Let me finish," she says. "For the past six months, I've been on a relentless rollercoaster of hope and despair. Every month, I let myself believe that maybe, just maybe, this time I'll see those two pink lines or—even more crushing—hear a heartbeat. And every month, I'm crushed. I've peed on countless ovulation sticks, pestered Jack to have sex on my fertile days, and avoided personal questions from my mother. Every phone call. Every single negative test. And through all of it, I have smiled. I have shown up! I have hosted parties, I've bought baby gifts, I've congratulated women on their bumps of joy. I haven't cried—well, not until I was home or with Jack. But I'm tired of pretending I'm okay. Because I'm not…And I don't know if I ever will be."

"We didn't realize," Maeve says, reaching for her. "Had we known—"

"No, it's fine. I'm not upset with you guys. I'm just, like, *over it.*"

"I'm so glad you're coming to us now and telling us all of this," Lizzie says. *God, I feel so selfish and terrible,* she thinks. *How did I miss this?*

"We are here for you, Hads. Whatever you need. Just let us know what we can do," Maeve says.

Hadley exhales and softens. "I'm not asking you to fix it. I'm just asking you to see me. I'm inviting you in, because I can't do it without you guys."

"How's Jack in all of this? Does he know how you feel? Is he supportive?"

"I mean, he's suffering, too. Sometimes he will be super quiet, and other times, he will lash out at me."

Maeve nods. "Do you think you guys should talk to someone? Like a therapist?"

"Maybe," she says. "I just keep hoping it will right itself, that I'll get pregnant, and it will all be fine."

"Did it ever occur to you, though, that maybe this isn't about the pregnancy? Like, how will everything just be "fine" when you get pregnant or have a baby?"

"What do you mean?" Hadley says.

"I mean, maybe your tunnel vision about this—and excuse me if I'm going out of bounds here—"

"No, say it," Hadley says.

"Well, I just think you've always put so much pressure on yourself. First, to be the perfect Southern Belle; then the perfect student; then the perfect wife, and now it's the perfect mother. Like, at some point, you need to think about why you have to be *perfect*. For who? Is it for you? For your parents? For Jack? What does perfect look like to you?"

God, I wish I could take my own advice, Lizzie thinks.

"I guess." Hadley sniffles. "I don't know what it's about, really."

"You don't have to figure this all out tonight," Maeve says.

"Yeah, no, I didn't mean that," Lizzie affirms.

"No, I know," Hadley says. "I feel better just that I said it, you know? I felt alone."

"You are never alone," Maeve reassures her. "*You have us.*"

Lizzie nods. "Yes, you always have us."

Hadley wipes the tears from under her eyes with her napkin.

"Now, I'm not sure that's such a great thing to have?" Lizzie jokes, trying to elevate the mood. They erupt in laughter. "But it's the truth. We're always by your side."

"Thank you," Hadley says, a tear trickling down her face. "I don't know what I'd do without you guys."

. . .

A week later, Lizzie, Track, and Colby drive home from Weston Nurseries with a Christmas tree. It's become their annual tradition, now in its third year. She wants to decorate for the holidays, add the much-needed cheer to her life that embroidered stockings hanging from the fireplace bring.

"Okay, guys. I need you to grab me some scissors to cut the string off the car, and then I want you to help me bring the tree in," Lizzie says.

The boys grumble, and Colby begrudgingly hands her a pair of scissors from inside. Lizzie cuts the pieces of twine, one by one, freeing the netted tree. They went with the seven-foot Frasier fir, a bit more expensive than the other kinds, but more sturdy for the heavier ornaments. She heaves the tree onto the driveway, careful not to scratch the car, and directs the boys to lift the top while she carries the trunk. They shuffle inside backward, and she snips the white netting before imploring the boys to help her guide the tree into the stand. *Why did I not hire someone to do this?* she wonders. This is no easy task for little ones. They fall over the tree, hold it at a sixty-degree angle, and make it impossible to position. Lizzie is underneath, panting and sweating, her face mashed against the wood floor as she turns the screws into the sappy tree. Her fingers are sticky with syrupy goo.

"Get Mommy some sugar water, baby." She coughs, still on the floor. "We need to feed the tree while we let it fall overnight."

"But I want to decorate it tonight," Track complains.

"Just get me the sugar water."

As Lizzie pours the water into the stand, the tree topples over. The water spills out, gradually sopping the carpet and the hardwood floors.

"Fuck!" Lizzie yells. She wishes she had a man around to help. Between the Christmas tree, home repairs, garbage, and the lawn, it's overwhelming being a single mom. She's tired of it.

"Mommy, you cursed!" Colby laughs.

"Sorry. I'm just irritable and hungry, honey. Let's do this later. I'll call you down for a redo."

The boys head upstairs to play video games while Lizzie pours a glass of Faust cabernet sauvignon and makes a plate of Manchego cheese, Greek olives, and crackers. She then flips the switch on the gas fireplace, and it ignites with a *poof*.

"At least I don't need to a man to help me make a fire," she mumbles.

Lizzie lights the fir-scented candle and sips her wine, tasting black cherry, vanilla, and spice with a long, smooth finish. It slides down her throat, relaxing her, as she leans back into the plush couch. The box of Christmas ornaments sits in the corner. Every ornament has significance: There is the plastic ball with the photo of Track in it, playing in snow, which he made in preschool; a pinecone with blue paint that Colby crafted, with his name faded in marker on masking tape attached to yarn; a Christopher Radko dachshund ornament for their wiener dog Bart, who passed; and a blue and gold mermaid that Hank bought Lizzie when he went to Martha's Vineyard, because he called her "his mermaid." Lizzie doesn't want to put the mermaid up. It upsets her.

Lizzie recalls the first Christmas she had with Wade. They were in Boston and attended the five o'clock service at Trinity Church on Christmas Eve. This was followed by a prix fixe dinner for two at The Four Seasons, where they dined on fois gras, lamb chops, seared scallops, bok choy, and pear parfait. Then, just as they were about to pay the tab, Wade handed Lizzie a small box. She gulped, thinking, *Is this what I think it is?* But then, to her dismay, it was not an engagement ring, but rather a promise ring: an emerald cut sapphire in a white gold setting with two small diamonds on either side.

. . .

Sitting before the fire now, Lizzie reaches for her glass of wine, wearing that same sapphire and diamond ring Wade gave her that Christmas. She even wore it when she was married to Hank. She didn't tell Hank it was her promise ring from Wade, of course, but she would gaze at it occasionally, wondering *what if*. Hank was her safe choice, but Wade was her true love. *If only I hadn't broken his trust*, she thinks. *I messed it all up. Now he's promising Macy a future instead.*

But maybe he won't propose, she thinks. *I am not giving up. It's not too late. Until she has a ring on her finger, there may be a chance.*

Chapter 30

HADLEY

The phone rings. "Hi, Lizzie," Hadley says, putting in her air buds. She's busy in the kitchen making a pot roast.

"Hey, hey. Just doing a wellness check."

Hadley chuckles. She actually, for the first time in a while, feels a bit better. "Thanks, I'm okay. Just keeping busy, one foot in front of the other." She puts the wooden spoon down on the counter. Snickers licks it.

"Oh, good. Dinner was fun, no?"

"Yes, thank you. I needed that." Hadley dices carrots and celery. She grabs a new wooden spoon and throws the Snickers one in the sink.

"So, when are we going to do our annual present exchange? Should we get a date on the books?"

"I haven't heard from Maeve in a couple days, but yes, we should find a date," Hadley says. She wonders why Lizzie is really calling. Something is up, and this whole wellness check vibe rings false. She knows Lizzie better than that.

"So what's up?" She unties her apron and walks into the living room toward her snowman-themed Christmas tree and straightens out the homemade string of cranberries.

"Not much, really." She pauses. "What is Macy up to for the holidays?"

I knew it! Hadley thinks. "I was just waiting for you to ask. Is this why you're calling?"

"No, I mean... yes. I'm sorry. I'm a psycho."

Hadley laughs. "I think they're staying in their apartment, and their parents are coming in to meet each other. But it shouldn't matter to you!" She really wishes Lizzie would get over this already. Wade has moved on. So should she.

Lizzie sighs heavily into the phone. "That sounds serious."

"I'm sorry. I don't want to depress you."

"I'm already depressed; you just made it worse."

Hadley sits. "Oh, Lizzie, you *have to* move on. You didn't want Wade when you had him. Remember that." She starts to recount the myriad of reasons why Lizzie and Wade didn't work out in the past: he's more like a roommate, he's lacking edge, he doesn't have ambition.

"I know, I know," Lizzie mumbles. "I just hate this time of year."

"Want to come over?"

"No, that's okay, thanks. I have the boys. We're going to Christmas in the Square tonight."

"Oh, I love Christmas in the Square! Have some hot cocoa for me."

Lizzie is quiet. "Thanks. Love you, friend. Talk to you later."

. . .

Later that day, Hadley considers adoption. At first, she was against it, insisting it be her egg and Jack's sperm. Or she could go with a surrogate. But there are so many children who need homes, she thinks. She searches online for adoption agencies and learns what's required to match with a child. First things first, she will need something called a *portfolio*.

Easy enough, she thinks. She will include photos of her and Jack, Snickers, Constance, her father, Maeve, and Hadley. Just the feeling of starting this, of starting anew, makes her tingle with excitement. She prints out a few adoption agencies and writes a note to Jack on them: "Thoughts? Xo." Will he be on board? Is this the answer?

Chapter 31

LIZZIE

Lizzie takes Track and Colby to downtown Hingham to meet their friends at Christmas on the Square. She parks by Nona's ice cream shop and puts on her pom-pom hat, gloves, and down jacket to keep warm. It's a frosty thirty-two degrees, and no amount of alcohol will keep her blood warm.

The boys leap out of the car and rush to view the ice sculpture, shaved and aglow with blue lights. A man with a chain saw is carving a dolphin out of a block of ice. Lizzie searches for her friends, who are standing across the street at Zona's barber shop, holding Yetis filled with booze.

"Where's your road soda?" Preston asks.

"I totally forgot," Lizzie says. "I was rushing from an open house."

"I have more in my cooler," he says, pointing to a large Yeti bag filled with ice and hard seltzers. "It's legit the hair of the dog. I'm so hungover from the school social last night. I had one bite of that psychedelic mushroom chocolate bar, and I swear, it made me insane."

"Tell me about it," Meg says. "I had Denise come over and give me an IV this afternoon."

"Oh, my god. She is a *savior*. I legit got an IV last weekend and pumped it up with Vitamin C because we were heading to Stowe for the week. I *cannot* get sick."

"That's smart," Meg says. "Have you tried the home IV's, Lizzie?"

Lizzie shakes her head. "I hate needles."

"You're missing out," Preston says. "It's like a rebirth if you've overdone it. I wish I could have one every day. And Denise is a nurse, so I trust her."

. . .

Carolers sing "Silent Night" in front of Talbot's while children wait in line for hot cocoa with marshmallows. The crowd gets more intense as it nears 7:00 p.m., when Santa arrives on the fire truck, beeping, to rounds of applause and cheer. Lizzie spots Cassidy riding the fire truck, holding up her real estate sign while wearing an elf suit. *Barf. That's so Cassidy*, she thinks. And why does it say she's the #1 realtor in Hingham, again? She shamelessly plugs that, and it's false! Lizzie shakes her head, confident that everyone who's anyone knows she's at the top. She's the go-to for the more discrete, affluent buyers.

"She has no shame. Tacky A.F.," Brandon whispers.

Lizzie raises a shoulder. "It reads desperate."

"And desperation is a stinky cologne," Brandon says, tightening his scarf.

"Amen. Speaking of which, what happened with you and Pinstripe, the closeted married man?"

"Oh, I was right. He sent me a dick pic later that night."

Lizzie cups her hands over her mouth. "Shut up! And?"

"I may or may not have met him last week," Brandon says, chuckling.

"You didn't!"

"But I did." He grins like the cat who ate the canary.

. . .

Brandon and Lizzie stroll down Central Street, gossiping about Pinstripe in search of Colby and Track, who are standing in front of CVS eating licorice and drinking Pump. The snow begins to fall, and it looks like a scene straight out of *It's a Wonderful Life*. Lizzie sticks her tongue out, catching a snowflake. She peers up at the falling sky and senses a moment of gratitude. *My life is good*, she thinks. *I have so many blessings. Remember that.*

Feeling the Christmas spirit—and some liquid courage—she gets the nerve to finally text Wade the apology she's been meaning to write. *I'm such an idiot*, she thinks. *But I feel like we were on the same page. There was definitely a moment there, right? I know he still loves me. He just needs encouragement, she thinks. Honestly? I don't have much to lose at this point. I'm just going to tell him the truth. Is that bad?* she wonders. *I mean, who even cares at this point? It's Christmas, I'm alone, I want him back, that's it. I'm going to throw caution to the wind. What the hell?* She takes her phone out of her purse and sits on a nearby bench. She removes her gloves, as snowflakes cool her knuckles.

"What are we doing?" Brandon asks. "This looks suspect."

LIZZIE: *Hey. I've been meaning to text since I was a freak at Friends-giving. Just wanted to say sorry and hope you're well. Merry Xmas. xo*

Later that evening, Lizzie fumbles for her ringing phone in the dark. It's 2:43 a.m. *Who could even be calling?* The kids are at their father's, but maybe there's an emergency. She picks up.

"Lizzie, it's Wade."

"*Wade?*" She clears her throat and shoots up in bed. "What's going on? Are you okay? Is someone dying? Are you mad I texted?" She can't believe it's Wade. Is she dreaming?

Wade laughs. "No. Sorry, I didn't mean to alarm you. I just was calling to...I don't know...this is hard." He breathes heavily into the phone. He sounds drunk.

"What's hard?" Lizzie's heart drums.

"I still love you."

She cups her mouth then gasps. "What?"

"You heard me."

She stands, pacing. *This has to be a joke*, she thinks. *Or was I right?* "Is this a joke? Because I'm finally feeling grateful, and I don't need cruelty right now."

"Why would I joke about that?" Wade asks. "I got your text, and—"

Lizzie places her hand over her eyes. "What about Macy? You're practically *engaged*."

"That's just the thing, Lizzie. We're not engaged. She was expecting a ring for Christmas, but I told her I just can't do it. I feel terrible, but I...I don't know. I'm lost."

Lizzie's eyes widen. She begins to sweat. "Wait, are you serious?" She runs to the mirror, watching herself in disbelief. *This is insane. Am I dreaming?*

"Deadly," he says. "I didn't want to admit it to myself, or to you, when I saw you last, but I'm still not over you, or us. I'm beside myself! I'm going crazy over here, Lizzie. I can't sleep."

"Well, I must say, this is kind of—shocking...but..." She pauses. "I mean, kinda great?" She giggles. "I'm happy!"

"Are you? Are you really? Because you know I can't trust you."

Lizzie considers this for a moment before responding. She wonders: *Am I ready now? I can't fuck this up again.* "You can trust me this time, Wade. I mean it," Lizzie says.

"I want to see you. Can I come over?"

"Now?"

"No, tomorrow... Yes, now!"

Lizzie grins. "Um, sure? Uber here! I'll see you in a bit."

Lizzie hangs up and jumps up and down with joy. She dashes to the shower to make sure she is fresh, clean, and shaven. She applies two coats of deodorant, just to be sure, and greases herself up with body cream. She then puts on her La Perla, lavender, lace thong and bra to match and a transparent white tank top, allowing her cleavage to spill over the top. She affixes Crest whitening strips, sprays frizz serum on her hair, and rubs highlighter onto her cheekbones.

When the Uber's headlights illuminate the dark dining room wall, Lizzie double checks herself in the mirror and inhales deeply. She's going to have to do things differently this time. She has to show Wade that she's changed, that she can be trusted with his heart. But how? What kind of gesture would reveal something so intangible.

I've got it, she thinks, rushing down the stairs. She dashes to the front door, her heart beating fast, turns off the security alarm, unlocks the deadbolt, and leaves the door wide open. When she hears his footsteps approaching, she runs upstairs.

"Hello?" he calls out. "Lizzie?"

"Up here," she says.

He moves toward her. She can hear his breathing. "You leave your door wide open?"

"It's a symbolic gesture," she says, her hands clammy with anticipation.

He reaches the top of the stairs. "A symbolic gesture?"

She smiles. Wade grabs her by the hips, pulls her toward him, and kisses her passionately, like it's the last kiss they'll ever have. *Please don't leave*, she thinks.

She pulls back and whispers in his ear, "I left it unlocked because I'm done with locks, with keeping a part of myself from you, shutting you out."

He smiles, eyes glassy. "Come onnnnn," he says. He chuckles.

"What's so funny? I'm serious!" She doubles down. "If you walk away tonight, I'm leaving it open anyway, because that's the choice I've made. I will love you without defenses and locks, or I will lose you forever."

Wade tilts his head, his eyes narrowing. Lizzie doesn't break.

He pauses. "Well, I appreciate that."

"I mean it," Lizzie says, swallowing hard. "It's where we begin again. Baby steps. No locks. Not here," she says, pressing her hand against her chest.

She kisses Wade long and hard, removing his coat, pressing her body against his. He grabs her ass and reaches his hand up the back of her shirt, undoing her bra. It's so familiar: his touch, his smell. She's transported back to their apartment in Brookline when they made love on their black and white tiled kitchen floor.

They fumble their way down the hall to her bedroom. She falls backward on the bed, taking off her thong.

Wade pauses, standing above her in the dark. "I've missed you," he says, rubbing his hands gently along her legs, up her calves, then her thighs.

"Same," Lizzie says. She pulls him on top of her.

This is the moment I've dreamed of, she thinks. *It's finally here.*

Chapter 32

MAEVE

The Christmas holiday has never been one of Maeve's favorites, and this year is no different. There are reminders of Sam, like his red knit stocking with the green-striped candy cane and jingle bells sewn onto it, and an abyss of loneliness because she doesn't have children or a family of her own. There's no counting down the days on the advent calendar, no wish lists hanging on the fridge, no elf on the shelf, and no hiding toys and leaving out cookies and milk for Santa. She decorates the house for herself and Brutus, but there are no tiny hands to shake the snow globe or turn on the toy train.

Maeve never considered children before now, mainly because she has been razor-focused on her career. But now she experiences little tugs inside, moving the needle in the direction of motherhood, like when she gushes over small baby shoes and onesies or longingly stares at the infants in Bjorn's when she's walking around town.

Today, Maeve decides she will decorate her Christmas tree. She pulls the string to the attic in her bedroom ceiling, and the wobbly wooden ladder with metal steps unfolds with a gust of cold air. Uneasy, she climbs up the squeaky ladder to the platform at the top and drops to her knees so as not to hit her head on the roof's beams. There is pink insulation strewn about, ratty with sawdust, perhaps the home of a racoon or squirrel for the winter. She gropes in the dark for the ceiling light, and feels the short, beaded, string to pull. A solo light bulb is aglow.

There are boxes, rugs, sleeping bags, roller blades, skis, and snow-shoes. She and Sam used to hike in Warren, Vermont, near Sugarbush and stay at the Pitcher Inn, a cozy, boutique hotel with an awesome basement tavern that has pinball machines and air hockey. She spies the box marked "Albums" and shudders to think of all the memories inside that she's repressed, unable to process, in fear of having a mental breakdown. She knows if she starts going down memory lane it's like opening a dam, and a tsunami of tears will ensue.

But something compels her to dive in. She reaches for the box and pulls it toward her. It's heavy as she drags it across the floor and down the attic ladder. Maeve places the box on the floor next to her bed and grabs the navy-blue leather album on top. It has a rectangular, gold, metal square on the cover with *Friends* in italics. She smiles, recalling that this is the college album with Lizzie and Hadley, some of the best years of her life.

She turns to the first page, and it's a photo of the three of them, younger and more cherubic, smiling wide with their arms around each other's shoulders in front of the student center. Maeve's wearing Doc Martens combat boots, ripped jeans, and an Abercrombie and Fitch T-shirt; Hadley is dressed in a Lilly Pulitzer romper with pointy-toed flats; and Lizzie is in a tight, short, pink skirt with a tank top. *Those were the days.*

Maeve flips through the album's glossy pages, turning them over the large, metal, three-ring binder clips until she gets to page that has "Sophomore Spring Break" written in ball point ink at the top. They are photos from their trip to Jamaica, where she kissed this guy Andrew

Cooke. They were at Señor Frogs, a favorite among the underage, party crowd looking for cheap shots and hookups. There's a photo of Andrew resting his head on her shoulder while she has a huge grin, like she just reeled in the prize-winning fish. She remembers that Hadley took this photo with one of those disposable cameras, where at least one third of the photos taken are terrible and you'd have to wait a week to develop the film at CVS. It was right after she and Andrew had their first kiss, and Hadley joked that she wanted to document it "to laugh about it later."

Maeve puts the album in the box and heads back up to the attic to grab the empty tubs that hold her Christmas decorations. A wave of seclusion, like she's never felt before, washes over her, and she shudders. She rushes down the ladder, closes the attic door, and heads downstairs to make a cup of tea. When she gets to the kitchen, she checks her phone, and there is a text from Pope.

POPE: *Thinking of you...*

MAEVE: *(heart emoji) Same.*

Maeve places the phone down, and the eerie sense of isolation evolves into panic. *What the hell am I doing? This is not going to work! Pope is my coworker, and now I'm having sex with him? What in the world am I thinking?*

No, Maeve, stop. He's more than that, and you're just self-sabotaging because you can't be happy. It makes you too uncomfortable to feel joy. You should be suffering, just as Sam did. It's not fair that you got to live and he had to die.

Maeve grabs her phone and hits "unsend" on her last text.

It's too risky. She's not ready.

Not... yet.

JANUARY

Chapter 33

MAEVE

Maeve's hunched at her desk, tackling a press release for a new bar on Stuart Street called Slope. Its Aspen vibe is accentuated with wooden beams, fireplaces, dim lighting, and bearskin rugs. She picks at her corn muffin from Stephanie's on Newbury, but she isn't hungry. She's been nauseous since New Year's Eve, which she initially thought was because of the numerous cosmos she imbibed at The Range with Pope, Hadley, and Jack. But now she realizes it's something more—maybe the flu. This is the time of year everyone gets it. She continues to tap away on her keyboard, while Pope yaps away on the phone to the Food & Wine editor at *Boston Magazine*. She suddenly feels like she's going to throw up and rushes to the bathroom.

"I'm going home," Maeve mouths to Pope. "I think I have a stomach bug."

Pope frowns and cups his hand over the phone. "Boo," he says. "I'll call you in a bit and bring you some soup." He winks.

Maeve smiles and nods. She grabs her tote bag and heads for the elevator. She decides to Uber home, because navigating the crowd at South Station and waiting for the commuter rail is too much to handle like this.

. . .

A few days later, Maeve's symptoms have quelled, but it occurs to her: she missed her period. She examines her Google calendar to see when she last had it last. There was the night at the Christmas Pops downtown, and no, she didn't have it then. She and Pope definitely got down and dirty that night. And then, a couple weeks back, there was the cookie swap. No tampon then. And before that, there was... *Wait a minute. Noooo*, she thinks. There was the night she and Pope had sex without a condom—when they were on the couch after watching *The Heiress* at the American Repertory Theatre. It was just so romantic, and they threw caution to the wind in the heat of passion because they were so exhilarated.

Maeve rushes to the corner Walgreen's to buy a pregnancy test.

"Would you like a bag for this?" the clerk asks.

"Um, definitely," Maeve says, her hands trembling. She checks behind her to make sure no one she knows noticed.

When she gets home, Maeve tears open the EPT and goes to the bathroom to pee on the stick. Five seconds later, she places the stick on the back of her toilet, and she waits.

And waits.

It's a long five minutes.

As the faint blue lines begin to appear, she sees them. It's not one line; it's two. It's a cross.

"Jesus," she mutters. "I'm pregnant."

Chapter 34

HADLEY

Hadley uncorks the champagne and tilts the bottle into the Simon Pearce glass flute. She tops it off with fresh squeezed orange juice.

"A toast to the new year!"

Maeve smiles. "Yes! But sadly, I think I'll just have a club soda."

"That's so *not* cheery." Hadley frowns, opening the refrigerator and handing her a raspberry and lime seltzer. "This year was hideous. We need to celebrate its end."

"If I start drinking alcohol now, I'll be a puddle by five, and I need to get some work done later. I'm seriously behind in emails. And besides, this year wasn't entirely bad. You got married!"

"Boo; that's lame," Hadley says, sipping her champagne.

"I know. I suck..."

Hadley raises her brows. "Speaking of sucking." She laughs. "How are things going with Pope? Are you totes in love?"

Maeve's face turns a shade of crimson. "I wouldn't say that, but we are enjoying each other's company."

"Sex?"

"It's good," Maeve says, shifting uncomfortably in her chair. "I don't know. I have no one to compare it to but Sam. I think it's good?

I mean, it's *great*. What am I saying? I don't know." Maeve shakes her head, gets up, and starts to pace around the room. She appears frazzled.

Hadley approaches her, placing a hand on her shoulder. "Hey," she says. "Are you okay?"

"Yeah. Well, no. Sort of. I don't know."

"What's going on? You can tell me."

"Well," Maeve says, wringing her hands, "I don't know how to say it, and I'm afraid if I do then I will hurt your feelings, and you won't want to see me."

Hadley's stomach drops. She wonders what sort of news Maeve could possibly deliver that would make her not want to see her. *Is Jack cheating? Did Lizzie say something terrible behind her back?*

"Just say it. You can't leave me in suspense now," Hadley pleads.

Maeve gulps. "I'm pregnant."

Boom. A grenade explodes. Hadley feels like she's drowning. She can see Maeve's mouth moving, but she can't hear anything other than the incessant ringing in her ears.

"I'm so sorry," Maeve says. "I can't imagine how this must feel for you."

"Don't be silly," Hadley says, even though she is crushed by this news. Her hands start to tremble, so she clasps them together, as if in prayer. "This is amazing!"

Hadley hugs Maeve, and it takes everything in her not to start bawling. What was the name of that self-help book she read, she wonders? *Time Heals Everything?* She's trying to channel that now. If only time would pass.

But it won't pass, she realizes, because she will have to watch Maeve grow bigger and have a protruding belly. She will have to see sonogram photos and discuss baby names. There will be a baby shower with oohing and ahhing over tiny clothes, or worse yet, a gender reveal party. Hadley doesn't think she can handle it. She wants to be there for her best friend, she desperately does, but this is a tall order. How could Maeve have done this to her, especially now, when she is so weak? Her feelings of blue sadness begin to turn a shade of red.

"Well, Jack is coming back from paddle tennis soon, so I probably should get showered," she says abruptly. She can't think. The only word coming to mind is *exit*.

"But I thought we were having brunch," Maeve whines.

Hadley pours the remainder of her mimosa down the sink. "I think maybe we should take a rain check."

"I can tell you're upset, Hadley. I am so sorry. I didn't know how to tell you. And truthfully, I don't even know how I feel about it."

With her back to Maeve, Hadley throws the champagne flute in the sink so hard that the glass shatters. She spins around. "Are you fucking kidding me? How can you say that? And to me of all people?"

"Say what?" Maeve asks, bewildered.

Hadley's eyes turn onyx, like she's in the dark. "That you don't know how you feel about it."

"Well, I mean, I don't." Maeve shrugs.

Hadley laughs. "That's rich, Maeve. Really! After all I've done for you, the years I have been there for you. You have some *nerve* to say this to me when you know I would *kill* to have a child."

Maeve moves toward Hadley, recognizing her flaw. "I am so sorry. I didn't mean it that way." She reaches for her.

"Don't," Hadley says, pushing her hand away. "I need a moment." She walks toward the kitchen windows and watches the falling snow. She can hear Maeve breathing heavily behind her. "A moment *to myself*," she affirms. "If you'll excuse me. You can let yourself out."

Hadley scurries up the stairs and heaves herself onto the bed. Snickers, who was peacefully sleeping on his pillow, screeches and leaps to the floor. She reaches over to her nightstand for an Ativan to quell her anxiety. All she wants is a good sleep and to be left alone.

Chapter 35

LIZZIE

Lizzie wakes to the sound of bacon sizzling and the smell of coffee. Wade is cooking breakfast in the kitchen. She can't believe this is not a dream! The last few weeks with him have been utterly blissful, even though he had to break Macy's heart (something Hadley was not happy with Lizzie about). Wade and Lizzie spent Christmas alone together, when Hank had the boys, and, on New Year's, the four of them went into the city for a trip to the aquarium and dinner. Colby regaled Wade with shark facts, and Track showed him how to walk like a penguin. Since then, Wade and Lizzie have spent nearly every free night together. And last night... well... last night was something else. Lizzie's bedroom is evidence to prove it: an empty bottle of Whispering Angel rosé, her thong and bra at the edge of the bed, his pants rumpled into a ball in the corner, wet bath towels, Mr. Bubble, Gatorade, and a vibrator. *Good god*, she thinks. *My room is like a brothel!*

"Well, good morning," Wade says, holding up tongs.

Lizzie shuffles into the kitchen in her furry slippers. She has that post-sex, new-love glow about her, and she's not sure if she's overtired, hungover, oversexed, or all three, but she feels light-headed.

"Hi," she says, giggling like a schoolgirl. "Aw, you made b-WEK-fast," she says in a baby voice.

"Yes, baby," he says. "And I was thinking we could go for a walk or something, or just back to bed, unless you have work to do today."

She shakes her head. "No, I don't have to work. And the kids are with Hank." She moves toward him and wraps her hands around his waist, pressing her head against his chest. He is muscular and smells like Tide detergent. He folds his arms around her.

"I am happy you're here," Lizzie whispers.

"Me, too," he says, kissing the top of her head gently.

"Is this for real?"

"Lizzie, I always told you: I love you most."

Lizzie melts into him, closing her eyes. *I never want this moment to end.*

. . .

Two days later, Lizzie poses in downward dog at Krigsman yoga. Sweat trickles down her pink face as the blood rushes to her head. The 9:35 a.m. is Lizzie's go-to class following her school drop off. Plus, it's around the corner from her office at Coldwell Banker. As it's the beginning of a new year, the class is full, more so than usual. All the "JV" newbies are there with New Year's resolutions to lose weight and get fit. But Lizzie knows it's nearly impossible to compete on fitness in Hingham, as it seems all the women are a size 0-4. Most of the retail stores only carry these sizes. "But we do go all the way up to a 30-waist in jeans!" one said.

When class ends, Lizzie grabs a towel and refills her Stanley cup with water from the bubbler. She grabs her coat, heads outside, and stops for a coffee at Brewed Awakenings. When she gets to the office, Brandon is there.

"Hi, Lizard," he says, using her pet name. "Cute high ponytail! Barbie-esque."

"Hiiiii," Lizzie sings. She's in a particularly good mood this morning, post-workout, and post orgasm with Wade. She has kept him a secret from Brandon, and it's eating her up inside. She typically tells him everything right as it happens, usually because he's by her side, but she wants to keep this little treasure to herself.

"Someone is all shits and giggles this morning," Brandon says. "What did I miss?"

"What is that supposed to mean? Am I usually a troll?"

Brandon shrugs affirmatively then laughs. "No. So, what's up?"

"Nothing much. I got a new listing in Liberty Pole," she says.

"Boring... I was hoping for some piping hot tea!"

"Nope, no tea," she says, walking into her office.

Lizzie feels a bit guilty for not disclosing the news about Wade, but truthfully, she needs to keep it on the downlow. Only Maeve and Hadley are in the loop, and Hadley begged her to keep it that way for the sake of Macy. On the one hand, Lizzie feels bad for Macy. But on the other, she believes that Wade was hers in the first place. She did, in fact, have a relationship with him first. It just took a few rounds and a couple of exes before they circled back together.

. . .

Later that day, Lizzie lets herself into Hadley's house. She discovers Hadley on the couch, curled up with a bag of potato chips and French onion dip, watching Bravo. She doesn't acknowledge her.

"Hellooooo?" Lizzie snaps, moving her head in front of the TV screen. "Anyone home? Earth to Hadley, come in, Hadley!"

Hadley makes eye contact. "I'm watching *Southern Charm*," she says flatly. "Shep's waxing poetic. It's adorable."

"I don't watch it. But sounds intriguing? Can I join?"

"Sure," Hadley says, moving over to make room for Lizzie on the couch. "Everything okay?"

"I was going to ask you the same thing," Lizzie says. "And from the looks of it, it seems maybe not. Are you depressed? How are you feeling? Are you still seeing your therapist and that outpatient group?"

"Yep." Hadley smirks. "I'm fine. Ya know, doing the best I can—given that Maeve is now having an unplanned baby, and I am barren."

Lizzie turns to her. "What did you just say? Maeve is having a *baby*? Shut the hell up. You're joking!"

Hadley reaches for a chip and bites down on it for effect. "Not joking."

"You can't be serious. With Pope?"

Her face doesn't move. "Yep."

"Wait, this is *in-sane*. She hasn't even mentioned it to me!" *How could she not tell me first*, she thinks?

"Well, it's new. I just found out."

"Well, maybe it won't stick. Maybe she will misc—" Lizzie stops short before using the *M-word*, but it's too late.

Hadley glares at her.

"Sorry, I didn't mean..."

"It's fine."

Lizzie reaches for Hadley's hand and squeezes it. "I'm so sorry, honey. I know this is hard on you."

"Thanks," Hadley says flatly. "You should call Maeve and congratulate her."

"You don't sound sincere."

"Well, I basically threw her out of my house when she said she wasn't sure she was going to keep it."

Lizzie's mouth drops open. "Did she say that?"

"Not in so many words."

"Well, I'm sure she didn't mean it. She's probably just confused is all."

"Probably." Hadley sighs. "Can we go back to watching *Southern Charm* now?"

Lizzie nods and sits in the chair next to Hadley. She peers out the window as she tries to digest the news that Maeve is pregnant! *Why didn't she tell me*, she wonders? And how could she have been so insensitive to Hadley? She's going to have to address this. In the meantime, she will stay with Hadley as long as she needs. She's got her back.

Chapter 36

MAEVE

Maeve exits South Shore Health's main entrance, gripping the results of the positive blood test in her hands. She's six weeks pregnant, the gynecologist affirmed, and she can come back to hear the heartbeat "with the father" at her next appointment.

With the father! I have to tell the father first, she thinks.

Maeve drives over the Quincy Bridge to Trader Joe's to get the ingredients to cook turkey chili for Monday Night Football. The Patriots are playing the Cowboys, but Maeve doesn't really care now that Tom Brady is no longer on the team. It was more fun to watch when they were kicking ass. Now, they are getting their asses kicked.

She puts onions, garlic, black beans, ground turkey, parsley, red peppers, and diced tomatoes in her cart. She purposefully omits the jalapeno peppers, as eating anything spicy hasn't agreed with her and this baby. The idea that a *baby* is growing inside her is crazy! How did this even happen? But she has gotten used to the idea—and rather attached to it, truth be told. She just needed some time to sit with it. She wants to see this through, to be the best mother she can be. It doesn't mean she will have to quit her job. No, many of her friends have nannies. She will get a nanny and work part time in the office and part time at home. Watts Communications has a great maternity leave package. She already checked. But what will they do if both she and Pope are on leave? Will he take paternity leave? *Oh, right,* she thinks. *Pope has to know about the baby first.*

. . .

When the Patriots score a final touchdown to win the game, Pope clears the dishes and joins Maeve in the kitchen.

"Awesome chili," he says, kissing her lightly on the lips.

"I have something special for dessert," she whispers.

"Oh yeah? Is it wearing jeans and a sweatshirt and smells like roses?"

Maeve laughs and hands him a small box with a bow on it. "No, that's the second part. This is the first."

"A box?" He places it against his ear and shakes it. "Is it chocolate?"

"You'll see," she says. "Just open it." Her heart is beating rapidly, and she feels both faint and exhilarated.

Pope unties the bow and opens the top of the box. He furrows his brow. "What is this? Candy?" he asks, picking up the tiny rattle inside of the box.

"No, silly," Maeve says. "You can't eat it."

"So I can't eat it, but it's dessert?"

"Well, no. It's a message, a clue." Maeve shuts her eyes. "Oh, forget it. This is silly."

"What's silly?" Pope asks.

"I'm pregnant."

Pope places the rattle on the table as his eyes grow wide. "You're—"

Maeve's throat starts to close. Maybe this was a terrible idea. A rattle. *What a freak,* she thinks. *This is like a low-key gender reveal party. He should just walk out and leave me right now.*

But he doesn't. Pope stands and grabs Maeve by the shoulders, pulls her in close. "You're pregnant! *We* are pregnant?" he shouts.

Maeve weeps tears of joy and relief. "Yes! Is that okay?"

"Yes! It's more than okay! It's wonderful!" He kisses her hard on the mouth, then pulls back. "I mean... it's mine, right?"

"Shut up! Of course, it's yours!"

"Honestly, baby, I am truly happy with you, *with us,* and now our *baby.* I mean, I can't even believe it! Can you?"

"I can't," she says. "It seems too good to be true."

. . .

Later that evening, Maeve walks Brutus to North Beach. The brisk January wind chaps her face as her eyes water. It's only 4:05 p.m., but sunset is at four-fifteen. She hates the New England winters. It gets dark so early. Maeve's bundled up in a down jacket, a red knit cap with "Hingham" stitched on it in white letters, and duck boots. Brutus wears his dog fleece and carries an unwieldy branch in his mouth.

As she nears the yacht club, she smells the salty ocean air, and the wind picks up as the flags flap. Boats are lined up on trailers and covered in white shrink wrap for the winter. She can see Boston across the ocean, a view which she is forever grateful for: proximity to the city. This is why she loves it here. It's the best of both worlds: close to the city but also on the water. She considers how it will work with Pope living in the city while they raise the baby. Will he move in or stay the night? Or will she stay in the city? They will have to buy a crib for the baby there, and then they will need a stroller as well. Shit, she will need doubles of everything! *This is already getting expensive,* she thinks.

North Beach is cold and desolate when she and Brutus arrive. The construction trucks have gone home for the day, and no one is parked at the stone wall taking a smoke break. Brutus drops his stick and runs in circles, doing crazy eights, kicking sand behind him. Maeve buttons up as the wind whips, and she throws Brutus the tennis ball from her pocket.

She gazes across the ocean, recalling the time she saw the harbor seal. *Was it Sam*, she wonders? *Sam. What would Sam think about the pregnancy?* Maeve supposes Sam would be happy, but maybe he'd be sad that it wasn't his. He often opined about wanting a big family when they were ready, but Maeve never seemed ready. It was always "someday," and "I have to focus on my career." Well, someday is *now*, and it's a lot sooner than she could have predicted.

Then again, she couldn't have predicted she'd be widowed by now, or that she and Sam wouldn't age side by side, drinking lemonades in rocking chairs until the day they died. That had been the plan. But as she's grown older, Maeve's learned you can't plan. Man plans and God laughs. Isn't that the old Yiddish proverb? *God's most likely hysterically laughing at me.*

. . .

Maeve's phone rings. It's Lizzie. Should she answer it? She doesn't feel like talking, and she hasn't told Lizzie about the baby yet.

"Hello?"

"What up?" Lizzie says.

"Not much. Just walking Brutus on North Beach."

"Oh, I'm right by there! I had a showing on Merrill Street. I can swing by?"

Maeve pauses. "Okay? But I won't be here too long. Pope's at the house."

"Ooooh, *Pope!* I am so glad he takes precedence now!"

"Shut up," Maeve says.

"See you in a few."

. . .

As Lizzie stumbles onto the beach in her skirt and stiletto pumps, Maeve can't help but laugh. She looks like a tightrope walker, balancing with arms outstretched, as she weaves her way through rocks and sand.

"You're going to break an ankle," Maeve shouts.

"What in the actual fuck!" Lizzie screams, circumventing a massive pile of black seaweed. "I was not prepared for this."

"Well, that's what happens when you come to the beach in heels."

"What? Am I supposed to carry around a pair of flats, like subway shoes? No, thanks." Lizzie approaches Maeve with a death stare. "I have a bone to pick with you."

"Oh, Jesus. What is it?"

Lizzie's long, blond hair blows in the wind, covering half of her face. She pushes it to the side. "Do you have some news to tell me?"

Maeve shrugs. "Maybe?"

"I just left Hadley's."

"Oh, *that.*"

"Yes, *that! My god,* Maeve! This is major! Give me a hug!" They embrace. Lizzie's warm body is soothing, like a heated blanked.

"Does Hadley hate me?"

"No! And will you not worry about her? You need to focus on yourself right now, and that baby. Hadley will get over it."

"Not sure about that."

"She is *fine,* Maeve. I just saw her. She told me to reach out to you."

"She did?"

"Yes! Sort of…" Lizzie replies.

Maeve frowns.

"Listen, no matter how she felt or feels, Hadley is still our best friend. She was just upset. You know. The whole thing—"

"Yes, of course," says Maeve. "I was afraid to tell her about it for that reason."

"Well, you had to tell her, and now it's done. BUT! *But!* You didn't tell me, you bitch!" Lizzie exclaims, punching her hard on the forearm.

"Ow! I'm pregnant!" Maeve screeches.

"How often are you going to use that as an excuse now?"

"As much as I damn well, please!" Maeve says.

Chapter 37

HADLEY

Hadley kneads dough in an apron with miniature dachshunds on it when she's startled by the sight of Macy in her kitchen.

She shrieks. "Oh, my god! You scared me!"

"Sorry," Macy says. "The front door was unlocked so I let myself in."

Hadley reaches for her. "Aw, come here. I'm sorry about Wade. You look so sad."

The women embrace, and Macy begins to shudder and cry. Hadley swiftly guides her away from Jack, into the living room, where they sit on the couch and talk privately.

"Sweetie," Hadley says. "Talk to me."

"I just don't understand how Wade could have done this to me. I was blindsided."

Hadley nods. She's torn between her allegiance to Macy and to Hadley. Macy is blood, but Lizzie has been her chosen family for over a decade. She's supported her at every turn; Macy only recently became close to her since the wedding.

Hadley rubs Macy's back in circles, soothing her. "I am so sorry. Have you spoken to him? What did he say before he left?"

"He told me he can't do it."

"Can't do what?"

"Get engaged! Buy the ring! Anything!" Macy weeps. "I gave him an ultimatum," she says, trying to catch her breath.

Hadley grimaces. "Oh..." *Guys never respond well to ultimatums*, she thinks. Constance had told her those are a desperate no-no.

"What? Was that bad? Do you think that's why he dumped me?" Macy asks, wiping runny black mascara from under her eyes with the back of her hand.

Hadley reaches for a crumpled-up paper towel in her apron pocket. "Here." Hadley hands it to her. "No, that's not why. If anything, it was just an excuse, or a catalyst to a breakup that was already in the works."

"I feel duped, bamboozled." Macy heaves. She begins to hiccup.

"Let me get you some water." Hadley excuses herself to the kitchen to fetch Macy a glass of water. She glances at Jack sitting at the kitchen table, drinking orange juice and scrolling through Instagram reels. She whispers in his ear about the breakup, and Jack sets down his phone. "Maybe you can join us in a few? Give a man's perspective?" she whispers.

Jack nods, but Hadley knows it's the last thing he wants to do. *Men hate this kind of thing*, she thinks. *He'd probably rather stick a fork in his eye.* But this why Hadley loves him. "Thanks! Love you!"

"Love you, too," he mutters.

When Hadley returns to the living room, Macy is holding her breath with her cheeks puffed out like a Cabbage Patch Kid. *Hiccup*, she squeaks. *Hiccup*.

"Here, drink this," Hadley says, handing her the glass. "I hope you don't mind, but I told Jack. I figured he might have some good advice, you know, from a man's perspective."

"That's fine," Macy says. *Hiccup!* She gulps down the water and begins to choke and cry simultaneously. "I am a hot mess!" she wails.

"You are not, and don't talk about yourself that way. You must be kind to yourself. *This too shall pass.* That's the mantra I always say. My therapist suggested it."

Jack enters the living room and sits on the rocking chair next to the fireplace. He lifts Snickers up onto his lap and rubs behind his ears. "So, tell me what's going on."

. . .

When Macy leaves, Hadley joins Jack by the fire. She's holding an adoption letter she drafted for the agencies. "You're so good with talking my friends off the ledge," she says. She remembers the many times that he consoled Lizzie after her numerous breakups with Wade, or when he pepped up Maeve after she didn't get the promotion. She sits next to Jack, placing the letter in his lap. "So, I know we talked about this, and you said you are good with it, but I just want to make sure."

Jack pauses, almost as if he's trying to find the right words. "Is that what you want, honey? Are *you* sure?"

"I can't tell if you're serious," Hadley says.

"Of course I'm serious. You're not the only one going through this," Jack says.

Hadley stands. "What's that supposed to mean?"

Jack reaches for her hand. "No, I'm just saying we have both struggled with this baby journey... I mean, you more than me."

"Oh, right," Hadley says. "Sorry. My nerves are frayed. I just feel so bad for Macy, and then Maeve telling me she's pregnant. It's just so much all at once."

Jack nods. "Why don't we put a pin the adoption for right now, until things calm down. We need to go into this with clear heads. It's a huge decision."

Hadley's shoulders slump, deflated. "Maybe you're right."

"Honey, this will happen," Jack says. He kisses her on the cheek. "I promise. We just can't force it."

Hadley nods. "I know. I just don't get it. Why does it all seem so unfair?"

"Life isn't fair."

. . .

Hadley retreats to her bedroom and flops down on the bed. She closes her eyes and presses her palms together upright on her abdomen. She says the serenity prayer:

"God, grant me the serenity to accept the things I cannot change.
Courage to change the things I can.
And wisdom to know the difference."

Chapter 38

LIZZIE

Lizzie sits in the Starbucks on Lincoln Street, scrolling through the Hingham Yard Sale on Facebook. Lizzie jokes about spending so much time looking at it when she can afford new things, but it's just so fun to land on a gem, like an $180 sweatshirt for only $20. Plus, everyone knows: the Hingham Yard Sale is bougie, to say the least. It's like the dump in Nantucket at the end of the summer. Thrifty residents flock to it like seagulls waiting for the discarding of perfectly nice beach chairs, coffee makers, coolers, and appliances that tourists dump at the end of their vacations.

Lizzie stumbles upon a $45 Aviator Nation large, hooded sweatshirt and types "Next" in the comments. Her phone dings with a private message from the seller and a photo of her Venmo. When she opens the Venmo app, she catches a glimpse of Wade's recent payment to his friend Justin marked "golf." Then it occurs to her to look at his other charges. What's he been up to, she wonders?

She scrolls down and notices Maeve's payment to someone named Kelly with a sushi emoji, and Hadley Venmo'd someone named Margaret for "House." Maybe this is a new housekeeper? She doesn't know a Margaret.

She continues to scroll, curious, and finally lands on another payment from Wade. *Here we go*, she thinks. One to his friend Mike for dinner at Tosca, and then... one to someone named Samantha? It doesn't have a note. Samatha? *Who is Samantha?* Lizzie sips her coffee hoping to jolt her brain to remember any reference Wade has made to a Samantha. She can't think of one. Feeling frazzled, she starts to do a deep dive into Wade's contacts on social media when she's interrupted by Jenny Pratt and Julie Walters. Lizzie met them at the Hingham Yacht Club a few summers back when Track and Colby had sailing camp with their boys. Jenny and Julie are nearly indistinguishable, with matching weighted vests, running shoes, leggings, and platinum highlighted hair.

"Hey, Lizzie!" Jenny says, standing over her. "Can we join you? It's so crowded here!"

At ten a.m. on a Wednesday, the Starbucks is jam packed with people.

"Of course," Lizzie says, surveying the room. "Isn't it a workday? Why is it so crowded?" She thinks of Chris Rock's joke that you can always tell an affluent town by the number of women out to lunch having cocktails. "Did you guys just work out?"

"We're going for a walk. I'll probably hit Orange Theory later. Do you work out there?" Jenny says.

Lizzie doesn't work out. "No," she said. "I tried it once, but I was paralyzed for three days after that. Why does everyone push that place so hard?"

"I love it," Julie interjects. "But more importantly... are you still dating Pope?" She grins and raises and eyebrow. "He's adorable, I heard."

God this town is small, she thinks. How do they know about Pope? Lizzie shakes her head. "No. I'm just focusing on work." *And stalking Wade.*

"How's real estate going? I see you have a new listing in Crow Point," Jenny says, sipping her coffee.

"Yes, just got that one," Lizzie says. "Know anyone interested?"

"How much are they selling it for?"

"Two point five million."

"Seriously? I feel like they bought it only a few years back for one point eight," Julie balks.

"Well, they have done a lot of work inside: new kitchen, master bath, and carpeting. Plus, they added a pool house and hockey rink."

"I still think it sounds pricey!" Julie says.

I have sold houses for years, Lizzie thinks. *And there is a reason I'm the number one realtor in this town and you are not. Please refrain from passing judgments about my pricing when you simply follow Zillow.*

"No, it's accurate," Lizzie says. "You need to not go by Z-estimates so much; they're not always correct. A lot of other things factor in."

Julie folds her arms across her chest and shrugs. "Well, I hope it sells soon."

Lizzie forces a flat smile. "It will." Her blood pressure is peaking. Not only is she completely annoyed that everyone seems to think they are a realtor simply because they sold or bought a house, but she can't figure out who this Samantha person is!

Lizzie gets back to her online sleuthing when the two J's leave. Samantha… She's not on his Facebook, and there is one Samantha on Instagram, but it looks like she's one of his mom's friends or an auntie. *This is going to drive me nuts.*

Lizzie walks to her car and checks her phone, hoping for a text from Wade. *Maybe he's with Samantha,* she thinks. She decides to call Hadley.

"What's up?" Hadley asks.

"Do you know someone named Samantha, like who Wade might know?"

"Um... Samantha Fitzpatrick, maybe?"

Lizzie eyes bulge. "Who is that?"

"She works in the registrar at Town Hall."

"Hmmm."

"Okay, what is this about?" Hadley sighs. "I know there is more to this. It seems very Lizzy-ish."

Why is my name used as a verb, adjective, and noun, Lizzie wonders. "I found her name in the subject of Wade's Venmo."

"Why on Earth are you scrutinizing his Venmo?"

"Because I can't trust him!"

"You can't trust him, or you can't trust yourself?"

And it dawns on Lizzie. *I can't trust myself. Yes, that's it.* Just as Wade said he couldn't trust her with his feelings, she can't trust herself either. *How can I prove to him that I won't screw things up this time around? I have to do something,* she thinks, *to show him that this time is different. This time, I won't freak out. This time, it will be forever.*

She just doesn't know how.

Part Two

MAY

Chapter 39

LIZZIE

Lizzie and Wade return home from an amazing weekend together on Cape Cod and are shopping online for a new bed at One King's Lane. Lizzie has always dreamed of a canopy, but Wade thinks it's too girly. He's vying for the more austere, Beverly bed with the black iron frame, and she's advocating for the Allaire Oak canopy in white. Since Wade has essentially moved in with Lizzie, they have decided to redecorate and make room for his tastes and belongings.

"Let's ask the boys what they think." Wade laughs, knowing full well that the boys will not vote for the canopy. Wade has spent a lot of time with Colby and Track over the last few months, taking them to lacrosse games, playing Fortnite on their Xbox, and helping them with homework. He's a natural father, which makes Lizzie wonder if maybe she should have another child. *No way*, she thinks. *Over and done with that.* But she's enjoyed watching Maeve embrace motherhood now that she's nearly seven months' pregnant with her baby boy. *Will she name him P.J., for Pope Junior*, she wonders? Or perhaps Sam, as a tribute to Sam? *No, that would be too creepy*, she thinks, but Maeve won't share their name choices.

Wade begins to unpack the grocery bags and makes a Mediterranean plate of food: hummus, grape leaves, and tabouleh. He warms up some pita bread in the toaster oven and cuts them into eighths. He presents the dish to Lizzie, who is now shopping for duvet covers.

"Thank you, sweetie," she says, grabbing a pita and double dipping it into hummus. "What did I do to deserve you?"

"I ask myself that every day!"

"Shut up. Take that back!"

Lizzie stands, ready to punch him, and he scurries into the living room. She chases him. When she gets hold of his of his arm, he tosses her onto the couch. Wade then leaps on top, tickling Lizzie as she erupts in laughter.

"Stop! I'm ticklish," she screeches, writhing back and forth.

"I know that, silly! Why do you think I'm torturing you?"

"Because you love me?" she squeaks through the laughter.

"That's right. I love you," he says. Wade stops tickling and leans down to kiss her. He kisses her on the forehead first, then then the nose, then gently on the lips.

"Mmmm," she says. "More, please."

Wade lowers himself onto her with the weight of his body. He moans. They kiss more fervently, and he grasps either side of her face. She wraps her arms around his back, embracing him. Then she moves her hands down the back of his pants. She's intoxicated by the electricity between them.

"You have the cutest butt," she whispers.

"It's tiny!" he says. "I can barely keep my pants up!"

"I love it," she utters.

They continue kissing, and he unbuttons her jeans, one by one. She guides his hands in her underpants, breathing heavily.

"Should we go upstairs?" he says softly. "Will the boys be home soon?"

"No," she says. "Just do me right here."

She gasps as their bodies yield to desire, in sync, like a well-oiled machine. She melts.

"I love you," she whispers.

"Love you most," he says.

Chapter 40

MAEVE

Hingham Harbor is still after two days of high heat. The morning air is thick and drowsy with the stench of dead fish from a seagull's banquet. Maeve stands at the edge, her bare feet in the briny low tide. She pokes a finger into the side of her now protruding belly, tight like she's hiding a basketball. *Poke.* She waits. No kick. She stirs it again, hoping for a reaction. Again, no response. Anxiety creeps over her. *I just wish I could grow it a bowl, so I can stop worrying every time it doesn't move,* she thinks.

Maeve reaches into her tote and takes a swig of now-tepid orange juice. She keeps it on-hand in case of low blood sugar. Her doctor says O.J. and ice cream can stir the baby. *She waits.* A minute or two pass and then BOOM! *Swish.* She feels a teeny motion in her tummy, like a kernel popped. She sighs with relief.

But not for long.

Rick is blowing up Maeve's inbox with crisis emails. Each one is marked with a red exclamation point: urgent! *So much for bare feet and low tide,* she thinks. Back to work. On Tuesdays, Maeve works remotely. So does Pope. While this arrangement is often nice—having lunch together and intermittent brief shoulder rubs—sometimes, it can be *a lot.* Like, *a real lot.* Maeve has her own shit to worry about, and she can't worry about Pope's, too. And his voice. *Oy.* The decibel of it, the timbre, when he's on the phone—speaker phone, of course! It reminds her of the days when they first met and he irritated the crap out of her.

Maybe it's just hormones, she thinks. *But he's driving me nuts today.*

. . .

When Maeve returns home to work at her desk, she squirms, shifting, trying to get comfortable. *Maybe if I stand it will be better,* she thinks. *But then my ankles will swell.* She concentrates, reading through four more "urgent" emails from Rick. Her annoyance flares.

Pope strolls in, whistling, with a mug of tea. He sets it down beside her and plops into the wingtip chair.

"Thanks," Maeve mumbles, furrowing her brow.

"What's wrong?"

Maeve shakes her head, typing. "Nothing. What's up?"

"Just saying hi is all. Is Rick up your ass? I've gotten like ten emails from him in the last hour."

Maeve nods, her jaw clenched. "I just have a lot of work to do."

"Okie dokie," Pope says, rising from the chair. "Just trying to be nice."

A flush creeps up in Maeve's face. "Got it. I'm sorry. I'm just really overwhelmed and... tired... *okay?*"

Pope holds up his hands, as if he's surrendering. "That's allowed. You're carrying our whole future in there." He gestures toward her stomach with a happy-go-lucky ease that causes her chest to tighten. "Can you believe that this time next year we will have a little one crawling around our feet—probably walking?"

Maeve snaps and turns to him. "Stop," she says with precision. "You're talking like it's somehow guaranteed. Like we ordered a baby on Amazon and it's going to arrive on schedule in a box." Her voice grows pressured. "Don't you get that nothing is guaranteed in this life? People die. Futures blow up in flames. I know this, Pope. I *know*."

Pope reaches for her. "Honey—"

"No." She pushes him away and begins to pace around the room. "You didn't wake up one day and find your entire life gone. You didn't have to watch the person you love gasp for air and die. You didn't have to bury this person before you even had a chance to live the life you planned together. The one you thought was guaranteed. How silly I was," Maeve says, shaking her head. "I was so naïve."

"No, you just were young and in love," Pope says softly.

"What if it happens again? What if the umbilical cord strangles the baby during delivery? That happens, you know. What if I don't make it? People die in childbirth all the time!" Terror flashes in her eyes.

Pope titters, shaking his head. "That's not going to happen."

"Is this *funny* to you?"

"Of course not. Honey, I just think you're really overtired and anxious."

Maeve's clenches her fists. "This is real for me. Real scary. What if it happens again? What if I let myself believe in this—believe in you—and it gets torn away?" Her voice cracks.

Pope stares at her, silence ensuing, his expression sober.

What are you thinking? Maeve wonders. *You've got nothing? No response?*

Finally, he speaks, pointedly. "You think I don't get it? I don't know what loss feels like? I know this is scary. But this isn't Sam. It's not him. This isn't the past. This baby is *us*. This baby is *ours*."

"You don't get it. Why are you making this about you? It's not."

Pope huffs, shaking his head. "Oh, right. It's not. How dumb of me.

It's about you and Sam, right? I mean, why wouldn't it be? It's always about you and Sam."

"What's that supposed to mean?" Maeve says.

A vein pops out of Pope's neck, his voice taking on a sharp edge. "I can't fight with the ghost of Sam forever, Maeve. At some point, you're going to have to let *me* in! *Me.* Not Sam!"

His words strike her like bricks, landing heavy. Her expression hardens, and she is suddenly overcome with a feeling of rage. "Don't. Say. His. Name," Maeve snarls.

Pope's eyes widen. "Excuse me?"

"Just leave me alone. I need some space."

"Not a problem," Pope says. "Take all the space you need. I'm leaving." He storms out of the room and slams the front door shut.

Maeve's frayed nerves course through her. Her stomach drops. She wants to chase after him. But she stops herself. *No,* she thinks. *Maybe this is what needs to happen. Maybe we should be apart. It's better to lose him now than later,* she thinks.

Chapter 41

HADLEY

"Well, hello there." Hadley smiles, placing her yoga mat on the kitchen island next to Pope and Jack. "Funny seeing you here this afternoon. Day off?" She goes in for a hug, and he stiffens. "Are you okay? Sorry, I'm sweaty."

Pope doesn't respond. She turns to Jack. *What gives?*

"He's hit a road bump with Maeve," Jack says, taking a swig of beer.

"What kind of road bump?"

"Sam," Pope says. "I'd say it's more like a detour than a road bump."

Oh no, she thinks. *This is not good.* "I'm sorry, Pope. I'm sure she didn't mean it, whatever she said."

"No, she meant it," Pope says firmly.

Jack interjects. "She told him to never say his name." Snickers leaps up onto the kitchen island. "Snickers, down!"

"It's okay; I don't mind," Pope says, sliding his hands up Snickers's tail, smoothing out his coat. "At this point, any affection is good affection."

"Aw, Pope," Hadley says, rubbing his back. "It's going to be okay. It's just a little blip. You are having a baby together!"

"She will come around, man. You just have to be patient. She can be... what's the word I'm searching for... *Prickly*? *Stubborn*?"

Hadley nods. "Yes, she can. It's really just a defense mechanism. She pushes people away before they can reject her."

"But I've done nothing to suggest I'll reject her."

"It doesn't matter. She has PTSD and abandonment issues."

Pope drops his head, closing his eyes. "I just can't be in Sam's shadow anymore. It's exhausting. I will never measure up."

"That's not true," Hadley reassures him. "Listen, Sam was amazing. He was. But he certainly wasn't perfect," Hadley says. "She had her issues with him, too."

"Yeah, buddy. Don't take it to heart. She's probably just really emotional and needs some time."

Hadley nods. "I'll talk to her."

"No, don't," Pope says. "I need to take a beat myself."

Hadley doesn't like the direction this is going. She has to call Maeve and talk her down from this ledge. She can't self-sabotage. She has *the baby* to protect! *God, why can't she just be happy? She has a baby! What I wouldn't do for that!*

"Let us know how we can help," Jack says.

Pope stands, combing his fingers through his hair. "I'm not sure you can," he says.

But Hadley has a plan. She will make sure Maeve doesn't ruin this. They have a *family* to protect.

Chapter 42

MAEVE

The next day, Maeve stares blankly out her Boston office window. She can't concentrate. All she can think about is Pope. He didn't come home last night, and he hasn't answered her calls or texts. He's also not in his office. She tossed and turned all night, fearful that she pushed him away for good. *Why do I do this?* she wonders. *How could I have fucked this up so badly? I don't want to be alone. I want to be with Pope. I need him.*

She scrolls through her text messages, re-reading:

M: *I am sorry. Please come back.*

M: *Pope? Can you please pick up the phone?*

M: *I am not sure what's happening here. Are you okay? Are we not okay?*

M: *Please reply. I am starting to worry. Just send a thumbs up.*

M: *Fine, whatever. Apparently, you don't care anymore. I don't know what else to say, but I'm sorry.*

M: *Seriously?*

M: *I hate fighting with you. (broken heart emoji). I'm really sorry.*

She tosses her phone back in her purse. *I am not going to check anymore*, she thinks. But then she does. *I mean, where could he be? Why didn't he show up for work?* Maeve starts to blame herself for something terrible befalling him before she has an idea: she will send a work email to Rick and copy Pope to test the waters. If he responds to Rick, then he's choosing to ignore her, specifically, and she will know he's okay.

She crafts the email, a fake question about the Citizen's account, and hits send. *Whoosh.* She waits anxiously.

Ding. Rick responds.

Ding. Pope responds.

Shit. He hates me, she thinks. *I've lost him.* Maeve's face flushes, and she feels like she might faint. She reaches for her orange juice.

This can't be good for the baby, she thinks. Worry gnaws at her. She bites her cuticles. Not only is her blood pressure rising, but now the baby won't have a father in the picture! She worries she will be a single mom, working full-time, and she won't be able to afford childcare. Maybe she will have to change jobs and work for a company that provides in-house babysitting. Maybe she will have to quit, raise the baby alone, and try to make money as a freelance writer.

These thoughts race through her mind before she gets up to refill her water bottle. The back of her neck, underneath her hair, is sweaty. As she rises from her chair, her ears start ringing, and she sees spots. She braces herself on her desk. *I'm going to die*, she thinks. She reaches for her phone and texts Lizzie and Hadley:

You need to come get me.

Chapter 43

LIZZIE

The first time Lizzie, Maeve, and Hadley met, they were freshman in college, waiting in line at the bookstore for textbooks. Maeve had grabbed the last Plato's *Republic*, and Lizzie needed a copy for her Literature Humanities 101 class. She'd poked Maeve on the shoulder and propositioned her, saying she'd pay her twenty bucks if she could have it. Maeve happily complied, and it was the first of many bets they'd make over the course of their lives together: there was the time Lizzie bet Maeve fifty bucks to walk across the bar at Beacon Hill Pub and kiss Sean Phillips, the senior basketball star. And the time Maeve earned twenty bucks for licking the dirty handrail on the T. Now, Lizzie is betting all her chips that Maeve and Pope will get engaged.

But then she gets her text.

Holy shit. I'm coming to get you.

She races to the city. When she arrives, Maeve's slouched next to Hadley on a park bench outside of the Park Street T-stop. It smells of cigarette smoke. Pigeons scurry around their feet like rats with wings.

"I got here as fast as possible," Lizzie says, breathing heavily. She's sweating profusely. "Are you okay?"

Hadley purses her lips. "Maeve scared off Pope."

"Stop," Maeve says, swigging Gatorade. "I didn't scare him off. He *chose to* leave."

"Wait. Slow down. What happened?" Lizzie shoos a pigeon away.

"I freaked out. I panicked and took it out on him. I spewed a bunch of existential crap about death and no guarantees, and then I told him to never mention Sam's name."

"Oh, boy," Lizzie says.

"And she growled at him," Hadley adds.

Maeve blinked. "I didn't growl at him."

"That's not what he said," Hadley mumbles.

Lizzie grabs Maeve's hand. "Are you okay?"

"Well, thank you for asking, Lizzie. I'm glad one of us here is concerned about the pregnant woman who just lost her boyfriend and father of her unborn child. Who almost died at work." Maeve's face flushes and her eyes well up.

Hadley reaches for her. "I'm sorry, sweetie. I didn't mean to upset you. I just really care about you, and I want this for you. Pope is a great guy."

Lizzie sniffs her armpits and applies a travel stick of deodorant from her purse.

Hadley shoots her a look.

She shrugs. "So where did you leave it?"

"She hasn't heard from him," Hadley says. "Since yesterday."

"Have you and Jack spoken to him?" Lizzie asks.

"We did right after their fight, but not since then, no. He hasn't returned our calls or texts." Hadley reaches for her phone and checks it.

"What about you, Maeve? Have you reached out?"

"Yes." Maeve sniffles. "He won't answer."

Okay, that's it, Lizzie thinks, shifting into gear. *I am going to right this situation. Maeve will see I am the person to come to when the shit hits the fan. I'm a fixer, the go-to girl.*

"Don't worry," Lizzie says, standing. "We are going to fix this."

"What do you mean? Where are you going?"

"To find Pope."

Maeve wipes the tears from her face and chuckles.

"I'm going to get his ass back here, where you will—sorry, if you don't like this—*apologize* and tell him you made the biggest mistake in your life."

"I already apologized like fifty times. He hates me."

"He doesn't hate you," Lizzie says. "Now buck up and let's go."

. . .

Moments later, Maeve, Lizzie, and Hadley Uber over the Summer Street bridge. They turn right and drive past construction along the canal. Maeve is breathing in and out, her lips in the shape of an O, like she's in delivery.

"Are you good?" Lizzie asks. *Please don't have this baby early,* she thinks. She remembers when she went into labor with Track three weeks early and was put on bed rest in Mass General. The food was terrible, and she'd had to share a room with a woman who ate ranch Doritos all day and stunk up the room.

"Yeah," Maeve says. "I'm just a little nauseous, is all."

Lizzie chuckles. "This reminds me of the time we ambushed Wade's apartment that night after I broke up with him."

"Which time?"

"Oh my gosh, stop!" Lizzie shouts. *They can't let that go,* she thinks. *It's annoying.*

"How are things with you guys?" Maeve asks, rolling down her window.

Lizzie shrugs. "Good. I don't want to jinx it."

The Uber drops them off at Pope's apartment on A Street, across from the popular restaurant, My Diner. A young, twenty-something guy, carrying a six pack of microbrews, holds the door open for them, allowing them to enter without the passcode or buzzer. They take the elevator up to the fifth floor, turn right, and Pope's apartment is dead ahead at the end of a long hallway.

"Pretty nice," Lizzie says. "What did he pay for this?"

"You're the realtor, not me."

"Probably a chunk of change, if he has a corner apartment with views."

A strip of white light appears under the doorway, indicating Pope might be home. Lizzie looks at Maeve and gives her the nod to ring the doorbell.

"Is this kind of stalker-ish?" Maeve whispers.

"Have you seen yourself?" Lizzie asks. "Pretty sure his baby mama has the right to stalk."

Lizzie hears footsteps approaching the door, and Pope opens it.

"Surprise!" Lizzie sings.

"Sorry," Maeve says, scrunching up her nose. "This wasn't my idea."

Pope smirks and invites them inside.

He looks like shit, Lizzie thinks.

The apartment is a generous two-bedroom, two-and-a-half bath, with large floor-to-ceiling glass windows. Lizzie imagines she could get a hefty commission selling it once Pope and Maeve move in together for good. She makes herself at home, walking to the kitchen and grabs a seltzer from the fridge.

"Okay to have this?"

Pope nods. "Help yourself."

Lizzie gulps down the seltzer water. The bubbles tickle the inside of her nose, causing her to sneeze.

Pope laughs, and Maeve takes a seat, heavily. "Can I get you anything to drink?" he asks.

"Um, I'll just have a glass of water, thanks."

Pope passes Lizzie in the kitchen, and she gives him an "I got You" nod of the chin. He then returns with a glass of water and sits across from Maeve. "So, what's up?" he says.

Lizzie crashes next to Maeve, ribbing her in the side. She recoils.

"I'm sorry," Maeve says. "I owe you an apology, but you know that."

Pope makes a steeple with his hands, raising his eyebrows. "I don't know that."

"Well, I left you countless messages, and you didn't return any of them!"

This is not going well.

Lizzie interjects. "What she means to say, Pope, is that she is really sorry that she made you feel invalidated, hurt, and like you did something wrong." She looks at Maeve. "Am I correct?"

Maeve nods solemnly in agreement.

"I'm listening," Pope says.

"No, she's right." Maeve shakes her head. "I just..." Her voice trembles. "I get triggered sometimes when people bring up Sam, and I just... I don't know. I lost it, and that's not fair to you. It was really wrong of me, and I regret it, deeply." She begins to cry, her shoulders slumped.

Lizzie places and arm around her.

Pope cups his hands over his mouth and nose, like an oxygen mask. "I appreciate that," he says. "But I can't always come second, Maeve. If we are going to continue this journey together, and raise our child, I need to know that *our* family is your priority."

Maeve rises and walks toward him, placing her hands on his shoulders. She looks him in the eye, intently. "You are my priority," she says. "And I shouldn't have made you feel any less."

They embrace, though he barely can get his arms around her. Lizzie wells up with tears and claps as all three of them let out a sigh of relief.

"Let's go home," Lizzie says.

"Thank you," Maeve mouths.

"No need to thank me," Lizzie whispers. "I got you."

JUNE

Chapter 44

MAEVE

Hingham is vibrant and abuzz just before the official start of summer. Maeve is awoken by the sound of landscapers and the trucks carrying deliveries to summer homes that will soon reopen. The snowbirds will soon flock back, and Crow Point's population will double.

I wish I had a second home, Maeve thinks. Growing up in an affluent town without financial security has always been a challenge. Maeve remembers how the girls in middle school all carried designer handbags while she had a hand-me-down from her cousin Rachel.

While Hadley is headed to the Cape for the weekend, and Lizzie to Kennebunkport, Maeve is home working. PR jobs don't stop for the weekend, especially with events. But this doesn't bother Maeve because she thrives on her routine. Routine is safe and reassuring. She's like a dog with a crate; the confines encourage calm. Ever since Sam's death, Maeve has developed a desperate fear of the unknown, and she anticipates the worst. She knows this isn't an admirable personality trait, but she can't help it. She needs to protect herself from further harm. And if she can see it coming, she will be more equipped to shield herself when the shit hits the fan.

Riding the commuter rail home together from work, Pope watches out the moving train as they pass UMass Boston. Maeve can't help but stare at him: his chiseled jaw, wavy blond hair, and cornflower-blue eyes. She remembers the first time she saw him all tanned and in a seersucker suit, how much she despised and (mis)judged him. Now, as he flips through *Ad Week* across from her, she can't help but smile as she absorbs his long, curly eyelashes. He has become her everything in such a short amount of time, something she would never have thought possible with any man aside from Sam—let alone Pope.

He glances up from his magazine. "What?" He smiles.

"Nothing," Maeve says. "Just happy to be here with you."

He leans forward over the train table and gives her a kiss. "Hey, want to walk to the beach when we get home? Have a little picnic and drink?"

Maeve nods. She's been searching for a reason to use her wicker picnic backpack ever since she got it at the Yankee Swap party. She packs beer, sparkling water, lemon, crackers, sharp cheddar cheese, red grapes, and strawberries. Pope grabs a beach blanket from the closet and puts the harness on Brutus. The air is humid and the sky still bright as they walk to the beach. Maeve is dressed in cutoff jeans shorts and a lavender, spaghetti strap, tank top.

"You look really pretty," Pope says, gently caressing her arm.

Maeve blushes and reaches for his hand. "Thanks."

Bright blue hydrangeas and orange tiger lilies burst, lining the road, and the smell of honeysuckle permeates the air. When they reach the yacht club, the boat launch is packed and busy, and two very pale and scrawny boys jump off the dock into the frigid water. A mother sporting a hot pink dress with white bows holds her daughter's tiny hand, who is wearing the smaller version of her mom's dress.

"I'm sorry, but that is just weird when mothers dress like their daughters," Pope whispers. "It's super neutered."

Maeve giggles. "Well, rest assured I don't plan on matching this baby." The mother waves at them. Maeve waves back.

"Do you know her?" Pope asks.

"I don't know. Maybe? She looks like every other pretty mom."

Maeve leans down to pick up a shell from the pavement. "And then there's me—large and in charge." She throws the shell over the bushes into the harbor as they hang a left up the street toward the beach.

"Oh, stop. You're beautiful, and you know it. If you weren't, I'd be able to resist you, which clearly, I can't."

It's hard for Maeve to take a compliment or just say "thank you," so she just walks in silence instead. She veers off slightly and dips her foot off the curb.

"Careful," Pope pleads, pulling her in close. "Let me take the outside."

. . .

When they get to North Beach, it's low tide. Maeve spots two other couples down on the end. She scans the sand around her feet, looking for sea glass, before deciding on the best spot to sit. She spies a dried-out horseshoe crab whose carcass is fully intact and grabs it with two fingers.

"Aw, this is sad," she frowns, holding it up.

Pope doesn't react. His mind seems to be elsewhere, and he looks super fidgety.

What is with him, she wonders? *Come to think of it, he's been fidgety all day at work, too,* Maeve thinks. "Are you okay?"

He emerges from his stupor. "Oh, huh? Yeah, sorry," Pope says, shaking his head. "Should we sit here?" He places the beach blanket down and drops four large rocks on the corners to keep it from blowing away.

Maeve takes off her picnic backpack and sits down on the blanket.

When she gets the crackers out, noisy seagulls start to hover, and two piping plovers hop nearby, eager for an afternoon snack. Brutus took a swim and is chewing a stick, covered in sand, with his mouth open.

As Maeve watches the ocean waves roll in and out, it occurs to her that this is the same spot she asked Sam for permission to have feelings for Pope months back, when she saw the harbor seal in the water.

"Did you find any good luck, green sea glass?" Pope asks.

"Not today, but I already have a ton of green. I think the boaters around here drink a lot of Heineken." She reaches for the two wine glasses in the backpack, which are secured by leather straps. "How cute is this backpack?"

"I like it," he says. Pope gets up from the blanket and walks toward the water. Brutus follows him.

"Where are you going?"

He doesn't answer, so she pours herself a glass of alcohol-free rosé and brings a beer to him by the water's edge.

"Look!" Pope says, pointing to the left, a little bit farther down the beach.

"What?"

"I see a piece of red sea glass. That's super rare, right?"

"Yeah, you never find red. Where is it?"

Pope squints and points. "Down there a bit."

She squints. "You can see that far?"

Maeve walks toward the spot, Pope following behind. She keeps her head down, circling the area. "Where? Are you lying?" She laughs.

"Here," Pope says, kneeling in the sand.

"Where?"

Pope reaches into his pocket and pulls out a small, square, black box. *Shut up*, Maeve thinks. *Is this what I think this is?*

He gazes into her eyes, slowly opening the box, and inside is a stunning, four-prong, diamond engagement ring in a platinum setting. Her mouth drops open.

"Maeve Marie," he says, from one knee, "You have surprised me with how amazing you are since the moment I met you and took your job."

Maeve laughs, and tears trickle down her face.

"You continue to inspire me and make me the happiest man on Earth every day. Even when you hated me and tried to push me away, I always gravitated back to you, and I always will. So with that, I ask you, here in front of Sam and Brutus and the people having happy hour down the beach, will you marry me?"

Maeve wipes the tears from her eyes. "Yes," she says, as he places the ring on her left hand. "It's beautiful."

"You're beautiful," Pope says. "And now you're my fiancée!"

She wraps her hands around his neck and kisses him as the couples down the beach cheer them on. Maeve and Pope chuckle, waving back, as they lift their glasses.

"You mentioned Sam," she says. "Do you think he's here?"

"I do," Pope says. "Sam and I are good now."

Maeve smiles. "You think he approves?" She peers out to sea, searching for a sign. *Maybe that harbor seal will reappear*, she thinks. But it doesn't.

"I do," Pope says.

Pope and Maeve return to the blanket. "Did you tell the girls?" she asks. "I feel like we should call them."

"As a matter of fact, Lizzie and Hadley are back at the house now, setting up for a little surprise celebration."

"Shut up! That's so sweet."

"I think of everything."

She kisses him again on the lips. "Let's go! I'm too amped to sit here! I want to celebrate and tell everyone we know!"

"Really? That's so unlike you."

"I know! What is happening to me?" She giggles, grabbing the backpack.

As they walk off the beach, it begins to drizzle, and then the sun comes out, bright and hot.

"Look!" Maeve says. "Look up! A double rainbow!"

Two huge rainbows hover over them in the sky, a symbol of hope, good luck, and prosperity. As Maeve reaches for her phone to take a photo, a gust of wind blows her backward. She thinks it's Sam giving his approval. The storm has passed; she has weathered the storm.

Chapter 45

HADLEY

Hadley grips Jack's hand in the waiting room and runs her fingers over his wedding band. She remembers the day they went to Tiffany's to buy it. It was on a spring trip to Manhattan. Hadley stopped at Kleinfeld's first, to pick up her wedding gown with adjustments. She had the seamstress add on a Carolina Herrera lace and pearl belt around the waist as an accent piece. When she met Jack at Tiffany's, they rode the escalator up to the second-floor ring gallery, passing by the giant statute of the signature blue jewelry box with a white satin bow. A salesperson greeted them with a glass of champagne before they sat down to try on different bands. Jack initially thought he wanted a gold band, but Hadley convinced him to go with platinum, as it was more "classic, like him."

As Hadley anxiously manipulates Jack's platinum ring now, she starts to fear for the worst. It's their eight-week obstetrician appointment, to check for the baby's heartbeat. She and Jack have been worried sick since they found out they were pregnant, but they're hoping, praying, that this time will be different. For the last few weeks, Hadley put herself on bed rest, meditated, and practiced deep breathing to relieve stress.

She turned down invitations to lunch, cocktails, and even shopping trips. This is now her job: bake the baby.

Hadley looks around the room at the other expectant mothers. Across from her sits a woman in her twenties, with a nose ring and tattoos, who appears far along in her pregnancy, watching reels on her phone. To her left is a woman who appears to be in her early forties, based on the gray hairs around her temples, who is furiously typing on her laptop. Hadley envies their big bellies. *If I can just have this one baby, God, I will be forever grateful*, she prays. She makes the sign of the cross on her chest, and then side-eyes Jack, who is laughing at her.

"What?" she asks. "Are you making fun of me for being religious?"

"No, of course not! I just think it's funny when you do that."

"What? Make the sign of the cross?"

"Yeah. I don't know. It's fine! I'm just laughing because I wouldn't say you're exactly a devout Christian who goes to church every Sunday."

"Bite your tongue! I am, too. I say grace to myself every night, and I pray before bed. You just don't realize it. I do it silently."

"Honey, relax. It's all going to be okay."

Hadley lays her head on Jack's shoulder before a nurse in blue scrubs and white clogs enters the waiting room.

"Hadley?" she calls out, reading her clipboard.

"Yes." Hadley stands. "Should he come, too, or?"

"Whatever you wish," the nurse says.

Jack and Hadley follow her down the sterile corridor with cream tiles and gray walls. They pass a nurse's station on their right, comprised of three young NP's giggling and talking about childcare issues during the summer when their kids aren't in school. Hadley hopes that she can also have those conversations one day, but she has to get through this appointment first.

Hadley and Jack enter the exam room, and Jack takes a seat in the tan chair in the corner. The nurse tells Hadley to undress from the waist down and that a technician will be in shortly. She pulls a shower curtain across the room and exits. Hadley begins to undress, the hair on her arms standing up with the cold chill of the air conditioning.

"Are you freezing?"

"It's a little chilly in here."

Hadley ties the hospital gown around her neck, leaving the back open. She sits on the exam table and places the white, parchment-like paper over her bottom half.

"You could probably bake cookies on this stuff," she jokes before lying down to notice the posters on the ceiling. There is one of a red and blue hot air balloon flying through the sky and another of cows and horses standing behind a wooden fence in a field.

The door opens, and a nurse wheels in a sonogram machine. Dr. Adams, her obstetrician, follows, holding her chart.

"So are we ready?"

"Kind of?" Hadley winces.

"Just try to relax," the doctor says.

How can I relax, Hadley wonders. She clenches up, her mouth dry like she ate a bale of hay.

"This will be a little cold," he says, inserting the wand inside her.

The sonograph machine whirs and hums as Hadley stares intently at the black and white images on the screen. She's trying not to panic. *Please, God. Please...* she prays, her eyes closed tightly.

Bu-boom, bu-boom, bu-boom, bu-boom.

"This is your heartbeat, folks. You hear it?" Dr. Adams says, pointing at the screen. "And there's your baby." He points to a tiny, white circle with what looks like a flashing white light, moving quickly.

Hadley's eyes fill with tears, and she gasps. She can't believe it! Her baby has a heartbeat! She is having a baby! A real, live baby!

Jack scoots over in this chair, smiling wide, and reaches for Hadley's hand. He's crying.

This is the best day of my life, Hadley thinks. *Thank you, God!*

. . .

As Hadley and Jack drive home, she keeps her hand placed over her abdomen. She imagines feeling something, even if it's just the pain from the sonogram.

"Hey," she says, turning to Jack.

"What's up?"

She reaches over. "I'm really sorry for being such a psycho all these months."

"You weren't a psycho," he says.

"I was." She chuckles. "But seriously, I'm sorry. Thank you for... just everything."

"You don't have to thank me. I'm your husband. But you're welcome." A few beats pass. "And I'm sorry, too... ya know... for just, like, getting frustrated and leaving you alone."

"It's okay," she says. "I would have left me alone, too."

Chapter 46

LIZZIE

"I think we should move in together," Wade says, biting into a fish taco. A drop of mayonnaise and slaw oozes down his chin and lodges cozily into the crevice of his cleft.

"Nice chin slinky." Lizzie laughs, rubbing the slaw off with her finger.

"I'm serious," he says, doubling down. "We've already done it once. It's like it's grandfathered in."

Lizzie sips her margarita. "Yeah? You think we should try again? What if this time it doesn't work?" Her stomach drops.

Wade glares at her, wiping his fingers, one by one, with his napkin. "And why wouldn't it work? Are you having doubts?" An engorged vain appears in his neck.

"No," Lizzie says, leaning back in her chair. *His stare is intense.* She wonders how she could have uttered such a thing out loud. *I mean, she cannot be doing this again, can she?* "I'm just saying I am petrified I'm going to ruin this." *Seriously petrified.*

"But why are you saying that? Do you think you'll ruin it?" he presses.

Lizzie isn't great when she's painted into a corner, but Wade has just the right amount of prosecutor in his DNA to box her in.

"No," she insists, flustered. "Wade, stop." Lizzie feels herself sinking deep into quicksand. She's having trouble breathing. "Just forget it."

"Lizzie, if you have something to say, just say it, because—"

"No! *I'm fine!*" she pleads. She leans across the table to kiss him. He freezes.

"Okay, I mean, if you want out, you need to let me know, like now." *This feels a little threatening*, she thinks.

Lizzie shifts. "Wade, seriously? No. And what's all this urgency? Are you pregnant?" She will do anything to lighten the vibe and ease the tension. She tosses her napkin at him, and he catches it with one hand.

"Ha-ha. No." He smirks.

"Okay, well then let's just be happy and stop talking about this. I'm happy! Are you?" *I can't believe I just lied, straight-up*, she thinks.

"Of course I am," Wade says. "I'm just making sure you are, too."

. . .

As Lizzie lays awake at three a.m., her internal dark passenger arrives to pick away at her security and sense of well-being. She starts to wonder if she made a mistake by asking for Wade to come back. She should have trusted herself the first few times, just like Maeve and Hadley told her. *Why did I do this again?*

Unable to fall back asleep, she takes two Unisom and crashes hard. When the clock strikes 11:30 a.m., she shoots up, removes her gel face mask, and surveys the room. She's alone.

"Wade?" she calls downstairs. "You here?"

Lizzie gets out of bed and walks to the bathroom to brush her teeth. As she closes the door, she notices that Wade's robe is conspicuously missing from the hanging rack. *Perhaps he's wearing it and cooking me breakfast*, she thinks.

"Wade?" Lizzie calls out again with a mouthful of toothpaste. "You here?"

She spits into the sink and heads downstairs to the kitchen. She peers out the window and notices Wade's car is missing. Her mind starts racing. *Where is Wade? Why is he not here?*

Lizzie turns back and leaps up the stairs, two at a time. She hurries to her bedroom closet, where she finds six empty hangers dangling, the same hangers that held Wade's dress shirts. Lizzie moves to the dresser and pulls open the drawer designated for Wade's socks and underwear: empty. She paces back and forth, and then something strange happens: Lizzie's emotions morph from stress and panic to an overwhelming sense of calm and strength—relief. *I can do this*, she thinks. *I am okay being alone. I don't need a man to feel better about myself. This is what I wanted all along. I needed to see that Wade isn't for me, and now I do.*

She puts on her cozy, pink robe and heads back downstairs to the kitchen to make some coffee. After she pours the hot liquid into her favorite monogrammed cup, she fills it to the rim with oatmeal creamer. She then walks to dining room table and sits, wondering when she should call Wade to have the dreaded break up talk.

But she doesn't have to wonder long, because Wade pulls into the driveway and enters the front door.

"Hey, hon," he pants, out of breath. "Sorry I scooted out early, but I have a surprise for you..." He's smiling ear to ear, giddy, like a child on Christmas morning.

Lizzie's face melts, turning a shade of white. She swallows, shoving the dread down her throat and stands.

"Wait, what?" Lizzie asks, realizing that Wade is in fact not *gone*. He is right here in her living room with "a surprise."

Wade approaches, his arms outstretched. "What's the matter, baby?

Did you sleep poorly? You were flip flopping around all night then crashed." He wraps his arms around her waist and nuzzles her neck.

She disengages. "Yeah, I took a sleeping pill," she mutters.

"*Sooooo*, don't you want to know what the surprise is?" Wade asks.

"I mean, of course. What is it?" She's nervous, the opposite of how she should feel.

Wade reaches into his front pant pocket and pulls out a set of keys. "For you," he says, handing them to her.

"What are these?" she asks, gripping the set in her sweaty palms.

He stands back as if to make a presentation with jazz hands. "The keys to our new apartment!"

Lizzie doesn't react.

"I was going to tell you last night," Wade continues, "but then we had that sort of yucky talk, so I just waited 'till today to surprise you. I already moved my stuff over. We can work on packing you and the boys up slowly, too!"

Lizzie's ears feel muffled and start to ring. It's as if she's underwater, drowning. She's not sure how to reply, so she just blurts it out.

"*You did what?*" Lizzie screams.

Wade's eyes grow like saucers. "I got us an apartment. To live. All of you. You said—"

"I never said I wanted to move into the *city!* The boys go to school in Hingham! My work is here! Where would you ever get the idea that this would be okay?"

Wade shakes his head, struggling to follow. "I don't get it," he says. "I mean, I thought we were on the same page about this..."

"No, Wade. We are not on the same page! *You*, not *we*, made this rash and impetuous decision that affects *my children* without even asking me! We are not twenty-four anymore. Is that what this is about?

Recreating our past? We're not in Brookline, sponge-painting our walls, Wade. We are grown adults with jobs and families to consider, but I guess consideration was not part of this surprise."

As Lizzie fires off, she affirms more and more that she and Wade are no longer suited for one another. They are not only on separate pages, but they are in different books. She hands Wade the sweaty set of keys. "Here. You should go."

Stunned, Wade takes the keys and places them back in his pocket. His brow furrows, and Lizzie watches as his face contorts, shifting from sadness to rage.

"*I knew it!*" Wade says. "I *knew* you would do this again. I said you can't be trusted, and once again, you proved you can't!"

"Oh, stop it," Lizzie chides. "Don't turn the tables on me. Nice deflection. This is a you issue, not a me issue." Lizzie starts up the stairs. "I'm done with this conversation."

As she reaches the top of the stairs, Lizzie glances back. Wade is gone. Her nerves frayed, she decides to rest in bed. But her eye catches something on the nightstand, something she didn't see before: a box and a card. The box is black velvet, a ring box. Hands trembling, she opens it. It's a diamond engagement ring with *Samantha's* written in gold cursive on the satin underside. *Samantha's!* This was the Samantha she wracked her brain about in Wade's Venmo months back! He'd been planning this all along! How could she not have seen this coming?

She places the box down and opens the card.

Dearest Elizabeth,
I will always love you most.
Forever Yours,
    Wade

Lizzie goes numb, almost dead inside. She places her hand on her chest, her heart beating fast. Then she drops the card by her side and lays back on the bed. It's quiet. Very quiet.

I am by myself, she thinks. *Alone.*

And, for the first time in a very long time—maybe forever—alone feels okay.

It feels right.

JULY

Chapter 47

MAEVE

Maeve never anticipated a second marriage, let alone a second wedding. The first time around, she and Sam had a medium-sized wedding with 120 invited guests. It was at his parents' house on Moosehead Lake, the same house they were traveling to when Sam died of a heart attack. They hosted a beautiful rehearsal dinner on a sunset booze cruise around the lake, followed by dinner at the Twin Peaks Inn. Hadley and Lizzie were bridesmaids, and they performed a memorable roast of Sam and Maeve's shenanigans.

As Maeve sits in front of the mirror, blending her foundation with a sponge, she thinks of Sam and wonders how he would react if he saw her now, readying to marry Pope, pregnant. She moves her face to the light, plucking a few stray eyebrow hairs and stops. She sets the tweezers down, pausing to examine her reflection. It appears foreign with her hair swept back into a low bun, pearls in her ears, the white dress glowing like it belongs to someone without shadows trailing behind her. She gazes past her own eyes and sees another day, another dress. This version is younger, pink-stained cheeks, and the naïve certainty that forever meant what it promised. She stands and smooths the dress over her protruding belly.

This is my present and future, she thinks. In this tummy—with Pope, today's groom. He is patient with her mercurial moods, a life preserver in rough tides, and a piece of red sea glass: rare. He's willing to take a chance on her and their unborn child, not afraid of living in Sam's shadow and embracing him as part of their lives. He isn't trying to change her or deny her grief. Maeve realizes she can love him and marry him without betraying the memory of Sam.

She grabs a tube of lipstick, rolls it over her lips, and places her shoulders back. Her face is revitalized with color. She, too, feels more alive. Today isn't about erasing her love with Sam. It's about having the courage to love again. It's about pulling the curtain aside, not deflecting, and embracing the unknown.

When Lizzie and Hadley arrive with their bridesmaid dresses in hand, Maeve turns to them.

Hadley cups her hands over her mouth and nose, shaking her head. "You look stunning."

"Wow," Lizzie says. She drops her bag, and a curling iron, makeup bag, and hair dryer spill out. "I brought all my stuff to be your glam squad, but you don't need to change a thing."

Maeve smiles. "Thanks."

Hadley's strawberry hair is pinned up in hot rollers like she's a Dallas Cowboy's Cheerleader in the locker room. Lizzie's hair is in a tight bun at the nape of her neck—more *Vogue* than Dallas.

"Do you want me to put one of the peonies from my bouquet in your hair?" Lizzie asks, staring at her reflection next to Maeve in the mirror. She grabs a bobby pin and begins to pick at her bouquet.

"That might look nice, sure," Maeve says. "Whatever you want."

"So, also, I have some news," Lizzie mutters, turning to face them. "You might want to take a seat for this one."

"Please don't vampire Maeve's wedding day with 'news,'" Hadley pleads.

"Stop, it's fine," Maeve says. "But it better be good news."

"Well, it is... kind of," Lizzie hesitates. "Wade and I broke up."

Maeve and Hadley look at each other, rolling their eyes.

"I'm having déjà vu," Hadley says. "We have been here so many times before. What in the hell?"

"Yeah, I can't say this is shocking," Maeve says. "But sorry? Are you okay?"

Lizzie smiles, taking her hair down out of the bun, the flower falling to the floor. "I am," she says. "Honestly, I'm better than I've been in a long time. I feel, I don't know... free. Like I actually want to be single."

"Hm... this seems very *un-you*," Hadley says.

"Well maybe it's the new me!"

"I mean, you never cease to amaze me, girl, but I am happy for you. Truly," Hadley says, walking toward Lizzie to give her a hug.

"Really? I thought you'd yell at me because I ruined things between Wade and Macy."

"Well, I do hate you for that." Hadley laughs, wiping away a tear. "Sorry, I'm very emotional these days."

Maeve rubs Hadley's back. "Gosh, I'm supposed to be the one crying today!"

"Naw, I'm good. Now let's get on with this wedding!" She sniffles and stands, grabbing her bouquet.

. . .

The car service waits outside at the end of the walkway. Maeve gives herself one final look, grabs her bouquet, slides on her white flip flops, and calls for Brutus. "Come on, boy. We're ready to roll," she says.

Brutus pants, following her out the door.

The chauffeur gets out of the car. "Big day for you," he says. "Where should we put the dog?"

"I think in front," Hadley says. "Is that okay?"

The chauffer nods. "No problem. They gave me a heads up he was coming."

Lizzie and Hadley shuffle in their flip flops to the car, holding their bouquets and plastic champagne flutes.

"You forgot yours," Lizzie says, handing a glass to Maeve that has the word *Bride* written on it in pink cursive. "I'll give this one to Pope when I see him." She sets the *Groom* glass next to her.

Hadley claps her hands together when she sits. "This is so exciting!"

Maeve grins, trying to quell the butterflies in her stomach. "I'm nervous."

"What for? You got this!" Lizzie says.

"I don't know. I just... it's all so surreal."

. . .

Maeve peers out the window as they drive toward the beach on Downer Avenue. Lizzie and Maeve sit across from her.

"I can't believe how much has happened this year," Maeve says.

"A fuck ton," Lizzie says, shaking her head.

"It's been one messy year," Hadley says.

The car pulls up to North Beach and parks on the side of the road, next to the railing. Maeve reaches across and grabs the hands of her best friends, her family. "I really couldn't have done this without you guys," she says.

"Me either," Lizzie says.

"Same." Hadley smiles.

As Maeve emerges from the limo, she holds down her hair that's blowing in the wind. Lizzie grabs the back of her dress so it doesn't drag, and Hadley steadies her over the rocks and sand.

Squinting in the sun, Maeve sees Pope standing, waiting for her, down the beach. He's wearing his douchey seersucker suit.

"I always hated that suit." She laughs. "But I sure love the man in it."

THE END

ABOUT THE AUTHOR

 *Alexandra Slater* is the author of three novels, *Honor Girl, Friends with Boats,* and *The Messy Years.* She is also an award-winning journalist who received the Edward R. Murrow Award for Writing when she worked as a reporter for NPR. Alex graduated from Columbia University with a degree in English Literature and attended Northwestern University's Medill Graduate School of Journalism. She spends winters in Boston and summers in Cleveland. (#saidnooneever)

www.ingramcontent.com/pod-product-compliance
Lightning Source LLC
Chambersburg PA
CBHW050027120726
47903CB00006B/1946